Praise for *Thursdays in the Park*

'A tender and intriguing love story . . . Boyd is as canny as Joanna Trollope at observing family life and better than Trollope at jokes' *Daily Mail*

'A warm and well-written case for love affairs in later life' *Daily Telegraph*

'A beautiful and insightful first novel written by an author who has the perfect experience to write it' chicklitreviews.com.

'A sweet story of romance . . . Hilary Boyd has a way with words' Top Romance Novels website

'One of my favourite summer reads' Eleanor Mills, *Sunday Times*

Hilary Boyd is a former health journalist. She has published six non-fiction books on health-related subjects such as step-parenting, depression and pregnancy. Now she turns her hand to fiction with this wise and witty first novel. She lives in London.

Hilary Boyd

THURSDAYS
IN THE PARK

Quercus

First published in Great Britain in 2011 by Quercus
The paperback edition published in 2012 by

Quercus
55 Baker Street
7th Floor, South Block
London W1U 8EW

A CIP catalogue record for this book is available
from the British Library

ISBN 978 0 85738 517 8

10 9 8

Printed and bound in Great Britain by Clays Ltd, St Ives plc

Typeset by Ellipsis Digital Limited, Glasgow

*To Tilda with love – my inspiration and the reason
I was in the park on Thursdays.*

I

'You shouldn't drink so much.' George's whisper hissed into the heat of the summer night as they walked home along the silent pavement.

'I didn't have more than three glasses,' Jeanie protested. 'I'm certainly not drunk.'

She unlocked the door and made her way through to the kitchen. It was hot, so hot, even at ten-thirty at night. She threw the keys and her bag on the table and went to open the French windows on to the terrace.

'It's bloody embarrassing, you get so strident and loud,' George went on as if she hadn't spoken. 'As if anyone's interested in vitamin trials. If you hadn't been so drunk you would've seen the man was bored out of his brain.'

Jeanie looked at her husband, stung by the venom in his voice. He'd been uncharacteristically tense all evening, snappish even before they'd left for Maria and Tony's. Then, when they'd hardly finished coffee, George had jumped up and said they had to go, some feeble excuse of an early meeting she knew he didn't have.

'I wasn't drunk, George. I'm *not* drunk. He was the one who kept asking questions,' she told him quietly.

George picked up the keys she'd flung on the table and went to hang them on the rack of hooks by the doorway. Above each hook was a label in George's careful, even script: George–H, Jeanie–H, George–C, Jeanie–C, Spare H, Spare C, to denote house and car keys for them both.

'Let's have a nightcap outside. It's too hot to sleep.' She checked her husband's face to see if she were yet forgiven, but his eyes were tense behind the heavy tortoiseshell glasses.

'I'm sure he thought you were flirting,' George persisted, staring pointedly at his wife.

'Oh, for heaven's sake.' Jeanie felt the breath short in her chest and looked away from him, a blush flooding her cheeks. Not a blush of guilt – the man had been weedy and dried up with discoloured teeth: nice

2

enough, but hardly a sex object – but of anxiety. She hated confrontation. Brought up in a dank Norfolk vicarage, she had watched her mother swallow the brusque, domineering dictats issued by her father, never questioning his right to abuse her in this way. Jeanie had lived in fear of him, but she remembered willing her mother on, hoping that just for once she would finally explode, make a stand against his bullying, and vowing that she would never let herself be treated in that way. Mild-mannered George, she believed, was nothing like her father.

George raised his eyebrows. 'You're blushing.'

She took a deep breath. 'Come on, pour us an Armagnac and let's sit outside and cool off.' She heard the wheedling tone in her voice and hated herself for it. 'You saw him,' she added weakly, and moved towards the terrace. She felt the adrenaline twitching in her body, and was suddenly just tired.

'I think I'll go up,' he said, but he made no move to go; just stood, his tall, gangly frame sagging and rooted, in the middle of the kitchen. He seemed miles away, the stupid tension about the dinner party obviously forgotten.

'George . . . what is it . . . what's wrong?' She went over to him and looked up into his face. Shocked, she

3

saw a heavy, blank desperation in his brown eyes that she'd never seen before. 'George?'

For a second he held her gaze, frozen. He seemed about to speak, but instead turned abruptly away.

'Did something happen today?'

'I'm fine . . . fine.' He cut across her question. 'Nothing happened. What could happen?' She watched his face twitch and pull distractedly, as if he were trying to change his expression, then he headed for the stairs. 'Are you coming?' he muttered as he left.

The bedroom was airless and stuffy from the day's heat, despite the sash window thrown wide. George turned to her as she sank into bed, and drew his long finger across her cheek, her mouth, then brought his hand down slowly over her body in a determined gesture of desire. She didn't want him, but there was something single-minded about his caress that was hard to refuse. This was not lovemaking, however, nor did it seem to be anything to do with her; she could have been anyone. In fact she had the odd feeling that neither of them was there, naked on that hot, damp sheet. It felt like a remote access engagement, mechanical, an anonymous exercise in sex.

Then without warning George suddenly pulled

away, throwing himself up and back against the wooden headboard, for all the world as if a scorpion had just crawled across the sheet.

Jeanie blinked up at him in the darkness. 'What's the matter, what is it?'

Without a word her husband leapt out of bed and snapped on the bedside light. He stood there naked, his arms clasped round his chest, staring down at his wife. It was all she could do not to recoil, his brown eyes were so cold, empty.

'I . . . can't . . . do this.' He spoke slowly, carefully, as if he were feeling his way around the words.

She reached towards him, but he held out his arm, palm angled towards her, fending her off, although she hadn't moved from her side of the bed. With the other hand he reached down to pick up his navy pyjama trousers, which he clutched to his body like a shield.

'I don't understand, George. Tell me. Say what you mean.' Jeanie felt her breath catch uncomfortably in her throat as she sat up to face him.

George did not reply, just stood there. 'I mean . . .' He spoke like a drowning man refusing rescue. 'I can't do it any more.'

'Can't do what? George?'

He turned away from her, picking his glasses up from

the bedside table as he made for the door.

Jeanie jumped up and raced after him. 'Where are you going? George? You can't just leave me like that. Is it something I've done? Please . . . tell me.'

But George shook her off, barely glancing at her. 'I'll sleep in the spare room.'

I can't do it any more. His words haunted her as she lay alone in the crumpled bed, shocked and above all, bewildered. Their life together, twenty-two years of it now, was orderly, you might even say a little dull. They never argued, as long as Jeanie accepted George's apparently benign need to control her. Then tonight it felt as if she had been unwittingly perched on top of a volcano that had suddenly decided to erupt. What had got into her husband?

In the morning, George behaved as if nothing had happened. She came down to the sunny kitchen in her nightdress to find him laying out the breakfast cups and plates, the marmalade pot, the butter dish with its lid in the shape of a cow, just as he always did.

'What happened last night?' She slumped, exhausted, at the kitchen table.

He looked up from his task of filling the stainless-steel kettle as if her question was puzzling to him.

'Nothing happened. I was tired.'

'And that's it?' she demanded, dazed. 'That's all you have to say?'

Still clutching the kettle, he raised his eyebrows at her. 'Don't make your usual drama out of this, Jeanie. I've got a lot on at work. I said, I'm tired.'

He set the kettle on its stand and carefully flicked the button, smoothing his burgundy tie over his immaculate white shirt and into the band of his grey pin-striped trousers, held up with scarlet braces.

Jeanie waited, wondering for a moment if she had imagined it all. 'George, you ran away from me last night as if I'd suddenly developed ten heads. I don't need to invent a drama.'

George strolled nonchalantly round the table behind her, and she caught the mild scent of the shaving soap she had bought him for Christmas as he dropped a brief kiss on her head. 'I don't want to talk about it.' He opened the fridge. 'Juice? I'm doing you a boiled egg.'

George had never come back to her bed. Now, nearly ten years later, Jeanie lay and listened to her husband's firm tread on the floorboards above her head. It was hardly five-thirty, but this was late for George. She traced his usual path to the bathroom, heard the cistern flushing, the water running down the pipes, then the criss-crossing of the bedroom in search of his clothes. His routine had never varied for the thirty-two years of their marriage, but she had not been allowed to share it with him since that strange night. And to this day she was no closer to understanding why he had done it than she had been then. She had badgered him almost daily at first for an explanation. If he had performance anxiety, that could be dealt with. If it was something she'd done, just say. *Come back to our bed, please, George, please* – she had pleaded, cajoled, abased herself in her desire for things to return to normal.

The incident sat huge and painful between their every exchange back then, but through it all George said not a word, just point-blank refused to engage with her on the subject – there wasn't a reason, it wasn't her fault, and he would not, perhaps could not, talk about it. Jeanie got so tired of the constant tension that in the end she had simply given up, telling nobody, not even her best friend Rita, because in an odd way she felt ashamed. Surely, despite George's assurance to the contrary, it must be a poor reflection on her sexuality.

Her confidence crushed, Jeanie made no move to seduce him after that night. Only once, about a year later, when both had had too much to drink, did he follow Jeanie to what was now her bedroom, and they began a drunken fumbling, fully clothed, on the covers. But almost immediately, even through the haze of alcohol, she sensed a tortured indecision in her husband's caress. His hand fluttered, hardly committed, over her skin, his body held back from hers, even as he kissed her mouth. And then, as before, the shutters suddenly came down and he pushed her firmly away as if she were some corrupting temptress, quickly and silently dragging himself off the bed and out of her room.

Their marriage had adapted. Not all at once, of course: more a slow, painful fade of emotion, as Jeanie's anger at her husband's silence – which was much more tormenting even than the event itself – became contained, rationalized as an inevitable sacrifice to her marriage. Her childhood had been defined by sacrifice – *Jesus died that we might live. Remember this and be thankful. Amen* – had been her father's favourite grace. Fervidly pious, Reverend Dickenson based his life on harsh and joyless duty, and he expected the same of his family, the vicarage silent with anticipation of his rigidly imposed will.

George had bought her the shop premises soon after, perhaps with some cockeyed notion of compensation, and she had thrown herself into her business with energy and enthusiasm. And she was successful. The health-food shop, Pomegranate, sat halfway up Highgate Hill. It sold the usual vitamins, herbal remedies and dry goods, but also organic vegetables, cheeses, fresh juices and smoothies, delicious wholegrain breads and deli products. Jeanie had gradually built up a reliable set of regulars, some of whom came from quite a distance to shop with her, but also, especially in the summer, her deli sandwiches drew in passing trade en route to Hampstead Heath for picnics.

She must have dropped back to sleep, because the next thing she heard was, 'Morning.' She watched George carefully placing the hot mug of tea on the bedside table. 'It's a spectacular day.' He pulled back the heavy curtains enthusiastically, letting the early spring sunshine flood the room, then stood smiling down at Jeanie, hands on his hips. His grey hair was neatly combed, tortoiseshell glasses crooked as always – one ear was higher than the other they'd decided years ago, although it didn't appear so to look at him – giving him an intensely vulnerable air.

'What've you got on today?'

She yawned. 'Interview with a new girl for the shop.

Jola doesn't trust herself after she chose the last one. Meeting with a new supplier of vegan packed lunches; checking out a second-hand chill cabinet – the one by the window's knackered. Then Ellie.' They both smiled at the thought of their granddaughter. 'You?'

George moved off towards the door with his customary gangling lope. 'Not as much as you, old girl. Golf this afternoon. Give that adorable little girl a huge hug from her grandad.'

His tone was deliberately cheerful, but she detected – as always since the insurance company he'd worked for, man and boy, had 'offered' him early retirement five years ago – a desire to seem busier than he was. He had only once alluded to it, a few months after leaving his job: the feeling that he was now 'a bit of a spare part', as he put it. But it had changed things between them. She had felt almost guilty at first, getting off to work with her customary enthusiasm every day and leaving him to hover idle and lonely between golf games. He had rallied, however, taking up his boyhood hobby of buying old clocks, pulling them apart and mending them, and now the house was thick with them: every available surface tick-tocking, mostly out of synch, as if the shelves and bureau tops themselves were alive. Only in Jeanie's bedroom was there quiet. But she felt her husband's obsessive nature, contained in the face of a useful career, was slowly burgeoning. And with it an uncomfortably familiar need to control her. This had always been there between them, but recently it seemed to have lost its sense of humour.

2

As Jeanie turned the corner to her daughter Chanty's street that afternoon, she felt herself tensing. If Chanty had been there, it would have been fine: Jeanie and her son-in-law, Alex, knew how to comport themselves in company. But Chanty would be at work, at her documentary editor's position at Channel 4 – she seemed to work more hours than there were in the day. When it was just her and Alex it was more in the nature of a Mexican stand-off.

She walked up the steps of the Victorian terraced house, first moving the empty green recycling bin the collectors had casually slung on the path.

'Jean. Come in.' Her son-in-law managed a half-hearted smile as he stood back to let her pass.

Is it a sine qua non that artists smell? Jeanie asked herself, holding her breath against the whiff of stale sweat from his paint-spattered tee shirt. And for the millionth time: *What, exactly, does Chanty see in this man?* She could see he had once been a 'pretty boy': large blue eyes and jet-black curls, and he could certainly be charming when he chose. But she found his expression self-regarding and a little petulant, as if the world had not delivered on its promise. Now he was approaching forty, the looks he must have traded on had not kept up with him, though he still behaved as if they had.

Jeanie forgot her son-in-law as her two-year-old granddaughter came running towards her, a grin a mile wide lighting up her huge brown eyes, her arms outstretched: 'Gin, Gin . . .'

Jeanie bent down and lifted the child in her arms, wrapping her in a close embrace, burying her nose in the pure, sweet softness of Ellie's skin. 'How's it going, Alex?'

Alex shrugged his thin shoulders. 'Childcare was never going to be my muse of choice.'

Jeanie didn't rise; she couldn't afford to, not in front of Ellie. 'So when's the exhibition? Isn't it quite soon?' she said brightly. She hadn't meant this as a needle; she was merely making conversation, but his sardonic smile told her that he took it as one.

'I've postponed it.'

Jeanie turned away and began gathering Ellie's coat and shoes. 'Oh ... that's a shame,' she said mildly. 'Come on,' she addressed Ellie, 'let's get your coat on and we'll go to the park and feed the ducks.'

'There's no point in churning stuff out under pressure. It'll happen when it happens. I need space.' He stood propped against the mantelpiece in the sitting room, holding forth as if he were entertaining guests at a soirée. The room was sparsely furnished, the stripped floor covered with a pale sisal rug, bare of anything but the large brown leather sofa, a stylish dull-orange Conran armchair with wooden arms, a padded stool and a giant flat-screen television. Jeanie knew this was partly a style decision, the decoration being paintings, colourful and mostly abstract, and a modern rectangular mirror covering the area above the fireplace. They had obviously come to the conclusion that while Ellie was small it was pointless to deploy anything that might be knocked over, damaged or damaging to their child.

Jeanie felt her heart begin to race with indignation. 'Space'? He needs 'space'? This arrogant, weasel-faced layabout, who takes advantage of Chanty's misplaced love on a daily basis to feed, clothe and house him, never contributing a single, solitary penny, and resenting his own beautiful daughter, has the nerve to whine about 'space'! And to crown it all his paintings to date were, in her opinion, derivative, abstract, sub-Hodgkin crap.

'I'll bring her back around five.' She tried to smile but felt the anger sticking to her face like a neon sign.

'Sure . . . whenever . . . see you later, sweetie.' Alex bent to kiss his daughter on the top of her head, avoiding his mother-in-law's eye.

'Sing a song of sixpence, a pocket full of rye.' Jeanie took a deep breath and sang to her granddaughter as they walked up the hill to the park. She berated herself for her inability to be more grown-up. But she had been there when Chanty, eight months pregnant, had collapsed on her parents' kitchen floor, clutching the monstrous note Alex had left:

This isn't working for me,
I'm not ready to be a father, I have so much to achieve.
Please forgive me.
I love you, but this has all been a terrible mistake.
Alex x

The note wasn't scribbled in an agony of flight, which vastly added to the offence in Jeanie's mind. No, it was carefully penned with black, heavy flourishes on a thick cream card, set out in column format, for all the world like an invitation to a party.

Chanty had literally been unable to breathe, and by the time George had called an ambulance and they'd sirened her off to A & E, it was clear Chanty was in labour. So this man she was now supposed to like and accept – love, even – had put the very life of his daughter, and indeed Jeanie's daughter, in jeopardy through his selfishness.

Ellie took it all in her small stride, however. She'd spent forty-eight hours in an incubator to stabilize her breathing, but she'd never looked remotely frail. No thanks to Alex.

'Again . . . again, Gin,' Ellie was insisting. So Jeanie sang again, watching with delight as Ellie's blonde curls swung to and fro to the tune.

But if Chanty had chosen to forgive him, and George – not being the sort to dwell on these things much – had managed to get past it, Jeanie had not. Every time she saw him she was reminded of her daughter's face, permanently ravaged by tears, as she struggled to cope with her baby alone in the months before Alex had condescended to return.

The playground was empty except for one boy of about four and his father, who were racing round on either side of the roundabout, spinning it at high speed and shouting with laughter.

'Swin . . . swin . . . come on.' Ellie, released from her buggy, made straight for the swings. This, experience told Jeanie, could go on for hours, her granddaughter falling into an almost trance-like state as she swung, urging her grandmother, 'Higher, higher!' if Jeanie threatened to slack.

Today Ellie was spellbound not by the swing, but by the boy and his father. Her face lit up with laughter as she watched their antics. Then suddenly the boy let go of the blue-painted handhold and raced across the spongy playground tarmac towards his ball, cutting directly across the trajectory of Ellie's swing. Jeanie heard the shout, 'Dylan!' at the same time as she lunged for the swing basket, jerking her granddaughter to a halt as the boy sailed blithely past, quite unconscious of the inch of daylight that had spared him a nasty injury.

'Dylan!' Jeanie turned and saw the man's face, white

and shocked as he ran over to his son and, instead of berating him, just held him tight until the boy squirmed free and went back to his ball.

He rose to his feet, and although he was a thickset man, his movement was surprisingly graceful and fluid. Jeanie watched him brush his hand backwards and forwards across his greying, corn-stubble hair in a gesture that reminded her of a child with a comfort blanket.

'Thanks,' he said. 'Thanks a million.'

Jeanie shrugged, smiled. 'It happens all the time.'

'Well, it can't happen to Dylan, not even once.' His tone sounded almost desperate.

'Your son's OK, a miss is as good as a mile,' she said soothingly, thinking he must be a playground novice to take on so.

The man looked blank for a second. 'Oh . . . God no, this isn't my son, it's my grandson. Dylan's my daughter's boy. You've probably guessed I don't come out with him much. In fact, this is only the fourth time she's let me.' He breathed deeply. 'And it'd have been well and truly the last if that swing'd hit him.'

'Down . . . down, Gin,' Ellie was insisting. She had her eye on Dylan's ball. Jeanie lifted her out and she ran off to stand staring shyly beside the older boy.

'Let the little girl play too,' his grandfather called out, to which Dylan paid absolutely no attention.

'So how old's your daughter?'

Jeanie laughed. 'Touché . . . Ellie's my granddaughter . . . she's two and a bit.'

He laughed too, holding his hands up in protest. 'It wasn't flattery, honest. I just assumed.' He looked away, embarrassed.

There was an awkward silence and Jeanie glanced around for her granddaughter, who was now totally involved in chasing Dylan and his ball, shrieking with laughter whenever he allowed her to get close.

'Odd thing, grandchildren,' the man said, gazing after the boy. 'I didn't think it would be such a big deal.' It was almost as if he were talking to himself. 'But I find he means everything to me.'

His words surprised Jeanie, not because she didn't believe in their sincerity – or the sentiment, for that matter – but because it seemed such a personal remark to make to a complete stranger.

'I know . . . I know what you mean,' she found herself replying, because she too had been overwhelmed by her feelings for her granddaughter since the first moment she'd held Ellie in her arms, waiting as they prepared the incubator at the hospital for the little body.

It had literally been love at first sight. 'Perhaps it's because we don't feel old enough,' she said, smiling.

The man laughed. 'That's certainly true.'

'It's a bit like a drug,' she went on. 'If I don't see her for a couple of days I get withdrawal symptoms.' She laughed, shy suddenly, in a very British way, about the strength of her feelings. Because she hadn't been one of those mothers who pester their offspring to make them a grandmother. In fact when Chanty had told her she was pregnant, Jeanie had been a bit daunted, selfishly fearing the interference in her busy life.

Dylan came bounding up to his grandfather. 'Grandpa, she won't leave me alone . . . she keeps getting in the way every time I kick the ball.'

The man shrugged. 'She's only little, Dylan. Be kind.'

The boy looked up at him, a frustrated frown on his face, and Jeanie thought how exceptionally beautiful he was with his golden skin and bright, water-green eyes.

'Go on,' the man urged, 'play with her for a bit. It won't hurt you.'

Dylan stomped off, clutching his ball possessively to his chest.

'He's a lovely child.'

He nodded proudly. 'So's your granddaughter.'

Which was true. Ellie mostly took after her mother – strong, blonde and single-minded – but Ellie's was the cherubic blondeness of babyhood, coupled with George's vast, limpid brown eyes.

'I'd better be off.' Jeanie called to her granddaughter and moved towards the buggy.

'Maybe see you again,' the man suggested.

'Maybe.'

'I take Dylan every Thursday now. My daughter works and the childminder's going for radiotherapy at the hospital on a Thursday – she's had breast cancer.'

'Oh . . . I hope she's all right,' Jeanie muttered politely.

'It gives me a chance to see Dylan,' the man went on, then stopped. 'Sorry, that sounds callous. I didn't mean I was happy she had breast cancer . . .' He tailed off.

'No, I'm sure not.' She smiled at his confusion. 'Well, bye then.' Jeanie hurried off to scoop up her granddaughter in an effort to save the man further embarrassment.

3

Jeanie tossed the hot penne with the tomato and basil sauce and tipped it into a large blue earthenware bowl. It was quiet in the big kitchen, the sun casting a soft, golden glow on the garden beyond the French windows. This was the room she liked best, and where they spent most of their time. To Jeanie the Georgian house had a stiff, solemn nature, and although the rooms had high ceilings and good proportions, it felt somehow sad. But the kitchen was south facing and, since they'd put in the windows on to the terrace, full of light. George had wanted an Aga when they'd refurbished the old kitchen, but Jeanie had insisted on a sleek, modern Bosch gas range, and warm terracotta tiles to replace the dreary linoleum. It was now a bright, clean room, the glass-fronted dresser painted in National Trust Woodlawn Charm blue, the colour picked up on the cornices and door.

George had seemed very pensive since he got back from golf, and now he sat silently at the end of the kitchen table, a glass of red wine in one hand, his corduroy slipper flapping gently to and fro on his crossed foot. A copy of *Time* magazine was in front of him on the wooden table, but he wasn't reading it; he was staring at his wife.

'Why were you so late back?' he asked.

Jeanie's heart sank. *Here we go*, she thought.

'I went to look at a new organic salad producer. In Potter's Bar. I told you.'

'But you said that was at two. You can't have been there five hours, surely.'

Her husband's eyes drilled into her, as if he was trying to search her soul. The tension, even at a distance, was palpable.

'I went back to the shop afterwards. I needed to do stuff.' She sighed and plonked the bowl of penne on to the table with unnecessary force.

'Ah . . . so when did you get back to the shop?'

'Stop it, George, please.'

She always found herself responding to George's

ludicrous monitoring as a reflex, before she remembered that by answering she was giving his anxiety credence.

'Stop what? I was just enquiring about your day. Isn't that what husbands are supposed to do?'

Jeanie saw him take a deep breath, and knew that the inquisition was over for the time being. To give George his due, he did try and control himself once the involuntary spasm had passed.

'How was the game?' she asked, placing beside her husband a block of fresh Parmesan she had taken from the deli cabinet in the shop. George was usually full of his golf, regaling her with tales of skulduggery committed by his Thursday partner. Danny, if her husband was to be believed, enjoyed cheating more than he enjoyed the game itself.

But this evening George just pushed his glasses back up his nose and took the serving spoon his wife proffered.

'Oh . . . OK. Danny won as usual.'

'And?' Jeanie grated some cheese over her pasta.

She saw her husband take a deep breath.

'Jeanie.' He paused, then planted his hands squarely on the table on either side of his plate, his thumbs grasping the rough underside. 'I've been thinking . . .'

Jeanie frowned, waited. George sounded unusually ponderous.

'Go on then,' she said impatiently, when her husband said nothing further. 'You're making me nervous.'

'I've been thinking about this for a long time now, and it seems the right time, with you coming up sixty next month.' Again he paused.

Jeanie found her heart was beating hard. Was he going to tell her he was leaving her? Perhaps he'd had a mistress for the last decade and he wanted to spend his declining years in her arms, she thought whimsically. It might account for things. She shook herself. 'Yes?' she urged him on.

'You know we've been saying for ages we'll get a weekend cottage? Well, I've been thinking, and it seems daft to me, having two houses when there's just us.'

Jeanie nodded. 'Perhaps you're right. It would have been good to have somewhere to escape to, but there's always a pressure to go all the time, and my busiest time is the weekend.'

For a moment they ate in silence.

'I didn't mean that quite,' George went on, beginning to fiddle with the bread on his plate, breaking it into tiny pieces and balling each piece up before dropping it back on to the pile.

Again Jeanie waited, puzzled, as her husband slowly, meticulously munched on his pasta.

'I meant that instead of getting a weekend place, we should sell up and move to the country. Live there.'

'What?' Jeanie was stunned. 'Sell this house? Are you serious?'

George blinked and swilled his wine round his glass before taking a long sip. 'I know. It's quite a step.'

'But this house has been in your family for generations.'

'What difference does that make?' He sounded genuinely surprised.

'What country? Where?' Jeanie didn't know where to start, this was so totally out of the blue. George had been living in the rambling Highgate house when she first met him in the seventies. Back then he was camping on the sofa in what he called the morning room, amongst his deceased Uncle Raymond's books and paraphernalia, not having a clue how to proceed. It had been Jeanie who had taken it in hand, packing away the heavy Victorian furniture in the attic and bringing the house into the twentieth century with bright paint and modern fabrics. Despite her own reservations, Jeanie had always thought George loved living there.

'But there's the shop, I can't leave that,' Jeanie went

on, still in shock from her husband's announcement.

'Well, you'll retire when you're sixty, won't you. Any time now.' He grinned.

'Retire?'

'Jeanie, you're sixty next month. People retire at sixty, women anyway. You've often said what a nightmare the shop is, how tired it makes you. I've been retired for years,' George pointed out reasonably.

Jeanie got up and began pacing the tiles, her supper forgotten. 'For heaven's sake, George. Sixty is no age these days. And anyway, it should be my decision when I pack it in, not yours.' She glared at him.

'I'm not deciding anything . . . calm down, won't you, old girl.' George shook his head in bewilderment. 'I thought you'd like the idea. This is only a discussion. You always say you love the country.'

'Stop calling me "old girl". You know I hate it,' she snapped. 'Yes, I love the country for a weekend, to loll about in with a book, go for the odd walk. But I don't want to live there. What country, anyway?' she asked again.

George sighed. 'Dorset, I thought, near the coast, sort of Lyme way. It's beautiful there.'

Jeanie stared at him. 'You've really thought this out, haven't you?'

Her husband nodded. 'I want to get out of London, Jeanie – I don't see the point in us being here any more. It would give us a new start, you and me.'

'You were bored to death when you grew up down there,' Jeanie commented, ignoring the rest of his remark. For a long time now she had suspected that he resented her involvement in her business. He had never said as much, but there had been hints.

'Yes, but I was a teenager. Things are different now, obviously. At our age we want different things from our life.'

'You might. I don't,' Jeanie retorted. 'What about all our friends, your golf? What about Ellie?' She thought mention of her granddaughter would be the trump card that would put an end to this nonsense.

'Ellie can visit, come and stay for weekends and holidays. She'll love it, it'll do her so much good to get out of London. And we'll make friends. There are even golf courses in Dorset, believe it or not.' George grinned. 'Listen, Jeanie, just think about it, that's all I'm asking. It seems ridiculous, two old people rattling around in this vast house, and since Mrs Miller retired the place isn't even clean. We could put the money to much better use.'

'Money isn't an issue, as you well know. The cleaning's

gone to pot, but that's easily rectified. Jola has a friend who's willing to come a couple of mornings. I just need to get it organized.'

He looked at her, tolerantly amused, as if anything she said was of little importance. 'I've set my heart on this, old girl.' He spoke softly, with his usual deceptively mild manner, but Jeanie heard the finality with dread.

'I said stop calling me that. We're not old,' she muttered weakly. 'Really, George, we're not. Only middle-aged.'

With that the discussion was closed, but Jeanie spent a sleepless night. George always got what he wanted. It was his house, and finally, if he decided to sell it, there wasn't much she could do to stop him. He was old-fashioned in that way. Although she was the businesswoman who ran a successful health-food shop on the high street, it was George who took care of the business side of their lives. He decided how to invest their money, whether they needed repairs to the house or extensive garden, when it was time to get a new car, and he dealt with all the bills. She was perfectly capable, but he wouldn't have considered involving her. Would he really sell this place without her agreement, she wondered, as dawn began to lighten the sky and his cautious tread set off on its usual path.

Chanty opened the door to her parents. 'Shhh . . . Ellie's still asleep and she's been a nightmare all day. We're in the garden.'

They tiptoed through the house and out on to the fashionably faded decking. Easter lunch was laid for eight on the wrought-iron table – white cloth, polished glass and silverware glinting prettily in the April sunshine. It was surprisingly warm. Jeanie wished she'd brought her sunglasses.

'Hi there, Alex.' George moved to shake his son-in-law's hand. Alex had made an effort today. The habitual shabby tee had been replaced by a crumpled blue shirt, and to Jeanie's relief he smelt of soap rather than paint and stale sweat.

'Who else is coming?' Jeanie indicated the table.

'My oldest schoolfriend, Mark, and his wife and children. You won't mind it not being just family, will you?' Alex sounded almost defensive, as if he were challenging Jeanie to disagree.

'How nice. I don't think we've ever met them, have we?'

Chanty came out of the house with a tray full of glasses and a champagne bottle.

'No, you won't have.' She set the tray down. 'They've been in Hong Kong for five years. Mark's made his mint now and they've just bought a pile in Dorset.'

Jeanie shot a glance at George, suddenly certain that she was being set up. Chanty wouldn't meet her eye. Alex smiled triumphantly.

'How lovely.' She refused to rise to the bait, but Alex couldn't resist.

'We thought it'd be good for you to bond over West Country property.'

Jeanie accepted a glass of champagne and moved to one of the deckchairs in the shade of the cherry tree. This isn't fair, she thought.

'Isn't this lovely,' she repeated, but the tension could be cut with a knife.

Her daughter squatted down in front of her.

'Mum, Alex is just winding you up. We asked Mark and Rachel because we haven't seen them since they got back, not because of Dad's moving thing.'

Jeanie smiled, but she felt miserable.

'We can't talk about it now, but are you so dead set against it? Ellie would love it, you know . . . all that fresh air and freedom. You'd see more of her than you do now, what with giving up the shop . . .'

'If Ellie needs fresh air, then why don't you and Alex move to bloody Dorset?' she snapped.

Chanty looked patient. 'Don't be snippy, Mum, you know I can't be a commissioning editor from Dorset, and I have to work.'

Jeanie bit her tongue before she made some damaging slight about her idle son-in-law. 'And I have to work too,' she countered.

'Well, you don't *have* to.'

'Not financially, no, obviously not. But for me, I have to work for me.' Ridiculous tears welled behind her eyes. 'Your father seems to have written us off, Chanty. I'm not old; I may not be in my first flush, but there's life in the old dog yet.'

Chanty smiled. 'Of course there is, Mum,' she assured her unconvincingly. 'You look years younger than your age. But moving to the country isn't fatal. Loads of people live there quite happily, you know.'

'Yeah, yeah, and there are even golf courses.'

Her daughter looked puzzled. 'We all thought you'd appreciate being able to wind down a bit.'

The bell rang, and Jeanie heard Ellie cry out from her upstairs bedroom.

'I'll get her.' She hauled herself out of the deckchair and went to fetch her granddaughter.

Jeanie's shop suddenly took on a different significance for her. When she opened up on the Tuesday after Easter, she looked lovingly at the boxes of wheatgrass and spinach piled up outside the door, at the inevitable pool of water the chill cabinet had leaked across the wooden floor, the baby tomatoes that had softened into rot overnight, the endless sell-by dates which would have to be checked. And when Jola arrived and said the new girl had quit before she'd even started, she didn't even blink. Yes, much of the business of running a shop was frustrating, but she loved it. It was what she did and she was very successful at it.

She had refused to speak to George for the rest of Easter Day. The lunch had gone beautifully: the lamb was perfectly pink, the queen of puddings was a triumph, Alex's friend and his wife were surprisingly charming considering they were friends of Alex. And Alex himself seemed less edgy in their company. But Jeanie had just gone through the motions. No one would have realized, except perhaps her too-perceptive son-in-law, but that was one of the few perks of maturity: you knew how to dissemble.

Tuesday was busy. Everyone was back from the Easter break, and she and Jola barely had time to draw breath until the afternoon. But as she smiled and chatted to her customers, stacked shelves, organized deliveries, she was conscious of a shadow over her day, like a half-forgotten dream.

It was with some relief that she read the text message from her friend, Rita: *Court booked 4 5pm 2day. B there or b sqre. Rx.*

Rita, a tall, tanned, athletic South African, was already on the court when Jeanie arrived in Waterlow Park. The weather had clouded over and there was a cold April breeze, but Rita had stripped off to display her habitually immaculate tennis dress and sparkling white trainers. Jeanie, by contrast, wore grey tracksuit pants and a black tee shirt. They were evenly matched on the court, the weekly game a fight to the death. Rita, with her long reach and killer serve, hit harder than Jeanie but moved more slowly. Jeanie was quicker round the court, more creative with her tactics and marginally more accurate. Neither could claim to have the upper hand over the years, and so every victory was exhilarating and very sweet.

But today Jeanie felt stumbling and lumpen, as if someone had tethered her feet.

'Christ,' Rita shouted when she'd walked away with the first set. 'Wake up, Mrs L., this is like playing by myself.'

Jeanie waved her racket apologetically. 'Sorry, sorry, I can't seem to get going.' But the second set was no better.

They gathered their stuff before the hour was up and went to sit on their favourite bench with a view over the distant city. The sun was setting, bathing the park in a cool, soft light.

'Speak,' Rita demanded.

'You know we've been thinking of getting a weekend cottage for a while.'

Rita nodded.

'Well, George has taken it into his head that that's not enough. He wants to sell up and move out of London altogether. He seems deadly serious, and he's got the rest of the family involved. Chanty started getting at me at Easter. And Alex. They all see it as a fait accompli. Sell the shop, you're old, you don't have to work, etc.'

Rita snorted. 'Bastards! They can't tell you what to do with your life.' She peered into her friend's face. 'You're not falling for it, are you?'

Jeanie shook her head. 'They even invoked Ellie, saying it would be good for her to have fresh air and freedom.'

'Ridiculous. It's never about the children. George won't sell without your say-so.'

Rita was married to Bill, who did exactly what she said at all times, without even a whimper.

'I mean, what's he going to do?' Rita went on. 'Drag you off to some muddy cave by your hair?'

Jeanie laughed. 'Perhaps you'd respect him more if he did!'

She knew Rita tolerated George, even liked him, but had never understood why Jeanie gave in to him so much.

'No, seriously, darling, what's he actually said?'

Jeanie sighed. 'It's not so much what he's said about the country, it's his attitude to me, to us. He genuinely believes that we're old. He actually said it. "Now we're old . . . you won't want the shop forever." I'm sure he resents me working. He reckons that as soon as I've seen sense and quit we can sail off into the sunset and live happily ever after together. Being old.'

Rita began to laugh. 'Christ.'

'And it wouldn't be so bad if it were just him, but when your own daughter tries to shuffle you off, then you begin to think there must be some truth in it.'

She looked at her friend's concerned face. 'I don't feel old, Rita. I feel fit and full of life. OK, I get tireder than I used to, I forget things more, maybe, but I reckon that's just finding something to blame when in fact I've been tired and forgetful my whole life at times.'

Rita grabbed her hand. 'Look at me,' she ordered. 'You, Jeanie Lawson, are not old. You're middle-aged – which may be worse, come to think of it – but by no stretch of the imagination are you old. You can't be! I'm the same age.'

Jeanie squeezed her hand.

'I mean, look at you. You're beautiful. No one would guess for a second that you're nearly a senior citizen.'

They both began to laugh. 'Thanks a bunch.'

'But I'm serious. You could easily pass for forty-eight.'

'So what should I do?'

'This isn't about being old or moving to the country though, is it?' Rita's gaze rested for a moment on her friend's face, and Jeanie knew what was coming. 'Let's shift, I'm freezing.' Rita was seldom warm in what she termed 'this godforsaken climate'.

'Don't start,' Jeanie replied crossly.

'Well, darling, it has to be said again. You didn't hear me last time. Why . . . why do you let that man control you? Why do you let him get away with it all the time? You're a strong, intelligent woman, Jeanie. Wake up. They're sneaky, these people.'

'What people . . . what do you mean?'

'People like George.' Her friend ploughed on unapologetically as they crossed the park. 'Full-on passive aggressive . . . compulsive controllers. To meet George you'd think butter wouldn't melt. He's charming, polite, amusing in a quiet sort of way.'

Jeanie thought this summed up George perfectly.

'But Jeanie, he's . . . well, to put it politely, he's got issues. He's too smart to do it in front of me, but sometimes his guard slips. Remember the other week, when he tried to stop you having a drink, then dragged you off almost before we'd had pudding?'

Jeanie nodded.

'You didn't want to go, Bill and I could see that, but you let him bully you.' The frustration in Rita's voice was clear. 'Why?'

'Because . . . because he gets so anxious.'

'Anxious?' Rita spluttered. 'You kowtow to him because he's *anxious*? That's ridiculous. What's he anxious about?'

Jeanie shook her head. They had reached the top of Highgate Hill. This was where their ways parted, Rita

heading to her house on one of the leafy lanes opposite Kenwood, Jeanie to hers on the far side of Pond
Square. They both paused on the corner by the bus
stand.

'I don't know. It's just George. He wasn't always like
this.' She felt a strong desire finally to tell her friend
about that night when George had rejected her, when
things had changed irrevocably for them both. But she
didn't want to add to Rita's disdain for her husband.
Nor did she really know how to explain the enormity
of the event after all this time. Over the years she'd
begun to wonder if she'd exaggerated it. She knew
couples often stopped having sex and slept in separate
bedrooms; theirs was a long marriage. But another part
of her knew that something significant had happened
to George that day. Something that he was unable,
even with all the pressure she had put him under, to
tell her about. And she couldn't even imagine what
that might be.

'Well,' said Rita brightly, 'if he wasn't always like
it, then he doesn't have to be like it now, no?'

Jeanie shrugged. 'I suppose. But I don't know
why . . .'

Rita waited, but Jeanie didn't say any more.

'Look, darling, the bottom line is that you are not

old, you work, and you most certainly don't want to move to the country. So things are getting serious. If you get dragged away from a dinner party, that's tiresome but not fatal. But to be dragged to Dorset? The country's vile, don't forget: full of mud, the sartorially challenged and farm shops where a cabbage that's been sitting there for eighteen months costs twice the National Debt.'

They both laughed.

'So I tell him I'm not old, I'm not giving up my shop, and I'm definitely not moving to the country.'

'Hurray!' Rita held up her hand inviting Jeanie to a high five. 'Seriously though, Jeanie, it really is time to take a stand.'

'He's not a bad man, Rita . . . I really don't think he can help himself,' Jeanie finished weakly. Her friend just rolled her eyes and strode off towards the roundabout with a farewell wave, her tennis bag slapping rhythmically against her back.

Later that evening, as she stood alone in the kitchen preparing the salad for supper, George still closeted with his clocks, she remembered what her Aunt Norma had said about being sixty.

Her aunt was her father's only sister, recently turned ninety and still living, happily independent, in her house in Wimbledon. A quick-witted bird of a woman with the sharp blue eyes that Jeanie had inherited, she had been in MI5 in the war and then looked after her ageing parents single-handed. But by the time she was sixty they were both dead, and Aunt Norma, previously a stalwart gloved and hatted spinster of the parish, took on a distinctly bohemian air as she turned the dining room into her studio and began to paint. 'Sixty is heaven,' she had told Jeanie as they sat having tea. 'The world is done with you, you become to all intents and purposes invisible, particularly if you're a woman. I like to think of it as your third life. There's childhood, then adult conformity – work, family, responsibility – then just when everyone assumes it's all over and you're on the scrap heap of old age, freedom! You can finally be who you are, not what society wants you to be, not who *you* think you ought to be.'

'Isn't that a generation thing?' Jeanie had asked. 'Our lot are liberated now; since feminism we can do what we want.'

Aunt Norma had nodded wisely. 'Can you, now?

Can you really?' She had smiled, her blue eyes beady. 'It seems to me there are still expectations . . . family and such.' She'd shaken her head. 'But then, what do I know?'

4

Jeanie was late getting to the park on Thursday. It was cold and it looked like rain, but there were still a number of bored-looking mothers huddled in the playground with their children – and the man from last week. She'd hardly given him a thought, and was not altogether pleased to see him. She liked to potter on her own with Ellie and had never involved herself with the other playground adults. He was on his mobile, propped up at the head of the slide as Dylan threw himself head first, arms outstretched, down the metal run.

He waved and smiled when he spotted Jeanie, quickly finishing his call and putting his mobile back in his jacket pocket. 'Hey . . . how's it going?'

'Fine . . . you?'

Ellie demanded the swing, and for a while they were separated as they monitored their grandchildren's play. Jeanie deliberately avoided his gaze.

Dylan teamed up with another boy of his age, and they raced off round and round the perimeter of the playground.

The man wandered over to the swings. 'Listen, I'm sorry about the other day.'

'What do you mean?'

'I was . . . kind of intense . . . went on a bit.'

Jeanie laughed. 'Nothing to apologize for.'

'No, but you must have thought me a bit odd.'

She said nothing, not knowing how to reply. She had not thought him odd exactly, but there was an unsettling air about the man, as if he wanted something from her, and she wasn't sure what it was.

'It's just this whole playground thing is new to me and I'm not sure of the etiquette.' He laughed apologetically.

'Oh, there is no playground etiquette,' she assured him with a laugh. 'Except always making sure that whatever happens it isn't *your* child's fault!'

'Junior version of the blame game?'

Jeanie nodded. 'Do I sound cynical?'

He shrugged, grinned. '"Realistic" has a better ring

46

– anyway, I'll leave you in peace.' She watched as he pushed through the metal gate of the playground and went to lean over the fence round the duck pond.

'Down . . . down, Gin.' As Ellie stood up in the swing, Jeanie felt the first drops of rain. She searched in the bottom of the pram for the plastic rain cover, but it wasn't there, only a squashed packet of nappy wipes, one of Ellie's battered cardboard books and a rotting banana skin.

The playground was emptying fast. She heard the man shout to his grandson, 'Dylan! Dylan, come on, boy. It's about to tip down.'

She noticed the boy paid no attention to his shouts as she packed Ellie, protesting vehemently, into the buggy and hurried for the gate. As she was starting up the hill the heavens opened. Not just rain, but a torrential downpour, and she knew it would be stupid to attempt the fifteen minutes home until it had eased off. She changed course towards the cafe, only a short walk from the playground, Ellie still screaming her lungs out and struggling against the buggy restraints and the rain.

The cafe was empty. She chose a seat outside, but sheltered by the covered space in front of the building so Ellie could run about, and bought herself a cup of tea and a carton of apple juice for her granddaughter.

While she sat, already wet, looking anxiously at the sky and wondering how long it would last, Dylan's grandfather appeared with the boy.

'Me again.' He was out of breath from running up the hill but still seemed bent on apologizing to her. Her heart sank as she realized she was trapped with him for the duration of the storm.

Dylan began running up the buggy ramp into the cafe and down the steps, repeating the circuit with Ellie in hot pursuit, the pair of them laughing breathlessly as they ran.

'Phew.' The man shook out his wet leather jacket and placed it over a chairback on the opposite side of Jeanie's table. Seeing her fierce look, he grinned mischievously. 'All we need now is a shower curtain and a large knife.'

Jeanie couldn't help laughing.

'Well, you're eyeing me as if I'm an axe-murderer. Best-case scenario, a stalker.'

'Are you?' She found herself studying his battered, handsome face, and far from finding the sliding look of a stalker, saw an appealing openness, and a deliberate, almost learned calm, as if he had taught himself to be still.

'Not intentionally.'

'You can see my point.' Jeanie defended her position with a smile.

There was a scream and they turned to see Ellie flat on her face on the concrete. Picking her up, her little face suffused pink with shock, Jeanie cuddled her tight and waited for her screams to subside. Dylan hovered anxiously.

'I didn't do anything,' he muttered, eyes to the ground, as if he were used to being blamed.

'I know you didn't.' Jeanie smiled at him. 'Ellie hasn't got the running thing sorted quite yet.'

Dylan brightened. 'She's only small,' he agreed, from the lofty heights of a nearly-four-year-old. 'Come on.' He grabbed her hand and pulled gently at Ellie, eager to get back to the game.

The rain poured down, cooling the air and darkening the sky, the water dripping off the overhanging roof like a curtain, cutting them off in a damp, chilly world of their own. For a moment there was an awkward silence.

'Shall we sing? Like in the movies.' The man grinned. 'Ideally we need a nun with a guitar, a woman in labour, a precocious kid and a brute-turned-hero, but failing that, we could try something dramatic and gloomy of our own to pass the time till we're rescued.'

'Like what?'

'Oh, I don't know . . . how about . . .' He paused, straightened himself in his seat, his chest puffed out like an opera tenor, and began to sing the teenage tragedy tune from the sixties about the boy racer whose car crashes and whose dying words are: *Tell Laura I love her*. His voice was low but tunefully confident. As he finished they both began to laugh.

'The old ones are always the best ones,' she joked, and they sang the chorus again together, loudly this time, exaggerating the melodrama. The two children meanwhile had stopped playing, and were standing in front of them, wide-eyed at the spectacle.

'I'm Ray, by the way,' the man introduced himself.

'Jeanie,' she said, and they shook hands across the wooden table.

'Do many of your friends have grandchildren?'

Jeanie shook her head. 'None. My closest friend doesn't have children, even, but none of the others have yet. I suppose they have boys . . . takes longer.'

'Ellie's your daughter's child, then?'

'Yes, Chanty works full-time; her husband does most of the childcare.'

'So your help is much appreciated, I imagine.'

Jeanie shrugged. 'Not altogether. I don't get on too

well with my son-in-law, there's history.'

Ray sighed. 'Ah, families . . . can't live with them, can't live without them. But Nat, that's my daughter, seems to be coming round to me. She's even letting me take the boy swimming next week.'

'What did you do?'

'Oh, the usual, I left her mother. But being me I picked the worst way to do it. I fell in love with my wife's best friend's twenty-one-year-old daughter . . . didn't go down too well.'

Jeanie digested this information. 'How old was your daughter?'

'Nine. And Carol wouldn't let me see her after that. Called me a paedophile, etc., moved to Leicester, kept changing her phone number and sending back the cards and presents I sent Nat. Eventually I stopped even trying and we lost touch for years.' He rubbed his hand across his hair. 'Listen, I was a crap father. I don't blame Nat.'

'Why did she get in touch with you again?'

'She wouldn't have if it hadn't been for Dylan's dad. Ronnie's a musician, West Indian, does kids' education stuff. He never knew his father, and when Nat was pregnant he persuaded her for the baby's sake to get in touch.' He paused. 'You don't want to hear all this,' he finished softly.

There was silence as they both looked out at the sky and realized the rain had stopped.

'I'd better get Ellie home, I suppose, or said son-in-law will kick off,' she said, and was surprised at her own reluctance.

'Come and look at this.' George waved excitedly to his wife later that day.

Jeanie put the paper down and went and stood behind George at his desk.

'Get your glasses . . . you need to see properly.'

She looked at the screen and saw a photo of a huge country house.

'Isn't it beautiful? And look . . .' He clicked the mouse over the first of a row of smaller photos to show the interior of a spacious drawing room, sun streaming enticingly through the open window, then another click and a kitchen with a gleaming red Aga set in a slightly past-its-best Smallbone kitchen. Jeanie checked the estate agent's specification at the bottom of the page.

'It's huge . . . five bedrooms and fifteen acres. That's ridiculous, George, you said we were rattling around here, but that's just as big.'

George shrugged. 'Ah yes, but in the country we'll need space for the family to stay. Isn't it beautiful?'

'Yes, it's beautiful, but that isn't reason enough to buy it.'

'Well, check this one out.' The process began all over again. This time the house was a vicarage in Somerset. 'This has five bedrooms too, but we can each have one as a study. And it's just been refurbished. Look, can't you just see Ellie adoring that garden? It's even got a stream.'

'She'll drown,' Jeanie snapped. 'Listen, George, can we talk?'

George tore himself away from the screen and swivelled on his desk chair to face her, his eyes still alight with enthusiasm.

'Did you hear me when I said that I had no intention of moving to the country?'

George blinked. 'Of course I did.'

'Well, what are you doing then?'

'I'm looking for a house, because I just know it's the right thing for us. And of course you're going to take some time to get used to the idea. Chanty and I were having a laugh about that on Sunday. You always have to be carried kicking and screaming into a new venture. Remember the shop?' George was smiling at his wife with an affection which, Jeanie thought furiously, would have seemed touching to an untrained observer.

'You make me sound like a toddler,' she told him, ignoring the remark about the shop. He always threw this in her face as an example of how he knew her better than she knew herself. It had been George, ten years ago and just after the debacle in the bedroom, who'd suggested buying the premises. They were out for a walk one day and noticed the shop was up for sale. Jeanie hadn't taken him seriously. She was still angry with him, and thought this was a sop to her damaged ego. But he knew opening a health-food store had been something she'd wanted to do for years. In the end, yielding to the same dogged persuasion he was using now, she had agreed. She was heartily sick of being grateful to him.

George raised his eyebrows.

'Can't we rent somewhere first like we were planning before, see if we like it?'

He shook his head stubbornly. 'I don't want a weekend cottage – renting's such a waste of money. No, I want to move out of London.'

'And if I don't agree?'

'But Jeanie darling, you will. When you see some of the houses on offer, you'll be gagging to get down there. I mean, what's not to like?' He pointed at the house on the screen. 'Chanty agrees that it's a brilliant plan,' he added for backup.

'This isn't Chanty's life, George.'

'Just go with it, will you? Trust me. Come and see some properties and then we can make the decision. Yes?'

Jeanie gave up. For a second she had a horrible vision – herself surrounded by what Rita termed 'mud and the sartorially challenged' without knowing how she'd got there. And George, of course.

5

'Mum, we need to talk about the party, it's only three weeks away.'

They were sitting opposite each other in the small paved garden at the back of Pomegranate, in the half-hour before opening time. Jeanie had recently installed four tables for customers to sit and drink their juice and smoothies. She moved back under the umbrella, out of the morning sun.

'Haven't we done everything?' Jeanie found the whole idea of a gathering to celebrate her official decrepitude profoundly depressing. It had been Chanty who said it would be fun.

'Yes, but I'm away for a week, don't forget. Has everyone replied?'

Jeanie nodded. 'Forty-three, last count.' Her friends had been alarmingly enthusiastic.

'But we have table plans to do, decisions about speeches, what time we have dinner, what the quartet is going to play. If we leave anything to chance it'll be a disaster. I mean, has anyone checked if there are any special diets? We'll have to let the caterers know.'

'Special diets?' Jeanie looked blank.

'Yes, Mum, vegetarians, gluten allergies, nuts, that sort of thing.'

'My friends were born before the advent of nut allergies,' she said tartly, then paused to trawl through the guest list. 'No, everyone has their teeth as far as I know. I can't even drum up a vegetarian.'

Chanty laughed. 'OK, OK, don't start on about my "neurotic" generation.'

'How did Ellie get on at nursery?' Jeanie had thought her granddaughter too young, but it had been Alex pushing to have more time to himself that had swung it with her daughter. Jeanie didn't blame her: she realized Chanty must be frightened of losing him again.

'She loved it.' Chanty's face softened, 'They let her paint to her heart's content. Now, Mum, can we get on with it? I have to get to work, I'm late already.'

The following Thursday, when she arrived to pick up her granddaughter, she was surprised to find that Alex was uncommonly welcoming. He actually seemed to want to engage her in conversation.

'Chanty says the party is coming along well.'

'Uh yes, I suppose so.'

'You don't sound too keen.' He smiled sympathetically, his tone bearing none of the usual teasing malice.

Jeanie eyed him suspiciously. 'To be honest, I'm dreading it.'

Alex laughed. 'I don't blame you. My idea of a nightmare.'

'What, a party?'

'No, turning sixty.'

'And there was me thinking you were on my side for once,' Jeanie snorted, looking around in search of Ellie's shoes.

'I am,' he insisted, grinning. 'But I have to be honest, don't I?'

'Not relentlessly.'

'Sorry . . . sorry, I didn't know it was such a big deal. You look great for your age.'

There it was again: 'for your age' was probably Jeanie's least favourite phrase. But she was taken aback by her son-in-law's unique attempt at a compliment.

'Thank you.'

'You see, Jean, I reckon we got off to a bad start,' Alex was saying, as she took Ellie on her knee and struggled to exchange slippers for outdoor shoes.

Jeanie bit her tongue and waited, wondering where this was going. Was he having therapy? Did he need money?

'And I'd like it if we could have a truce and be friends.'

She realized in that moment that it's never easy to give up a habit, even a stupid habit like hating your son-in-law. Part of her enjoyed it, although it shamed her to admit it, and enjoyed the fact that she could justify her sniping. Every fibre of her being resisted now. It was almost painful to smile at Alex without giving it a sardonic edge, but she made the effort. 'The thing is . . .'

'I know, you don't trust me not to betray Chanty again.'

Jeanie nodded.

'The truth is, nor do I, but I'm giving it my best shot.'

'That's not exactly what a mother wants to hear, although as usual I can't fault your honesty.'

Alex's black curls were snared in a loose knot behind

his head. With his narrow face revealed he looked younger, more vulnerable.

'But there are no guarantees, are there? Not in relationships.'

Jeanie was forced to agree. 'Why now?'

If she hadn't caught the slide of Alex's glance, she would have decided reluctantly in his favour.

He shrugged. 'Does there have to be a reason?'

'There doesn't have to be . . . but there usually is.'

Alex shrugged, 'Have it your way. Does the truce still stand?'

He held out his hand to her and she took it.

When Jeanie drew level with the playground, she felt a twinge of disappointment not to see Ray and Dylan there.

Ellie had forsworn the swing today and was on one of her circuits up and down the slide. A child in front of her was trying one of those small boy show-off moves and came down head first on his back. Of course Ellie wanted to do it too, but couldn't quite work out how to position herself to achieve it. So she stood at the top of the metal run, her head down, hands hanging by her side, and howled. Jeanie took her off and hugged her, but the child, for some reason, was inconsolable.

'Let's go and have a look at the new playground,' she eventually suggested as a diversion, and Ellie was visibly cheered, taking off on her strong little legs at a run up the hill, her curls flying in the wind, while Jeanie hurried along behind with the buggy.

She saw them immediately as they rounded the corner. Ray was perched on the edge of the light-wood climbing frame, guiding his grandson's progress across the highest bar.

Ellie shrieked with delight at the sight of Dylan, and clamoured to climb up to where he was, but the frame was meant for much older children, and Jeanie began to regret her decision.

'It's too high, darling. You're not big enough.'

As her granddaughter stood crestfallen, clearly deciding whether a tantrum would help her cause, Ray lifted Dylan clear of the structure.

'Let's do the swing, boy.'

A gang of small children were already engaged in running backwards and forwards across the brand new rubber-covered mound beside the rope swing, and Ellie quickly forgot about Dylan and joined them.

Jeanie sat down on the grass and Ray threw himself down beside her, sitting cross-legged and picking at the grass and fallen twigs.

'How's it going?'

Jeanie shrugged. 'OK, I suppose. You?'

'That doesn't sound so good.'

'Oh, you know.'

He looked at her. His grey-green eyes, so similar to his grandson's, were very clear, very bright.

'No,' he said. 'Tell me.'

Jeanie didn't say anything.

'Listen, it's your turn, you've listened to my boring tales of dysfunctional families.'

For a moment she didn't reply. Then something suddenly snapped in Jeanie, as if years of holding on had finally turned her resistance to dust.

'Do you really want to know?' she said, hearing the defiance in her voice with surprise.

'Sure.'

He looked taken aback but Jeanie breathed deeply, determined. For days now she'd felt irritable with those around her, on edge, with an overwhelming desire to unburden herself. *You're it*, she thought, as she stared at this oddly sympathetic stranger.

'OK.' She took another breath, hesitated. 'Well . . . I'm sixty in a few weeks, and my husband and daughter have decided I'm now, officially, old. So they want me to give up the health-food shop that I own, that I love, that is bloody successful, and shuffle off to the country. They can't understand why I'm not jumping at the chance of retirement in some dozy Somerset village. Scones and jam by the fire, pottering around the begonias, church fetes, general innocent country jolliness. Am I . . .?' As she spoke, she found with horror that her throat was constricting with incipient tears, that her voice was faltering. Ray just watched her, seemingly without a trace of embarrassment, waiting for her to finish.

'Is that it, then?' She pushed through the tears. 'Am I supposed to just give in? Give up?'

'What would you like to do?'

'What I do now. I like my life. Well, most of it.'

'Which bit don't you like?'

Jeanie stared at him. 'What a strange question.'

Ray laughed. 'Is it?'

'Well, yes. Everyone has bits they don't like in their lives, but they don't really count, do they? I mean, I could go on forever about the bits I don't like.' She found she was gabbling and didn't know why. This man was unsettling in his directness, dangerously easy to confide in. 'You shouldn't go round asking people why they aren't happy. It's best not to think about it.'

'Sorry.' He looked baffled by her outburst and she had to laugh.

'No, definitely my turn to apologize,' she said. 'I'm behaving like a madwoman.' She searched for a tissue in her coat pocket.

'Surely your desires are important to your husband, aren't they?' Ray was saying. It was as if he could see into her soul with those bright, clear eyes. The tears began again.

'You shouldn't have started this,' she muttered, almost beyond embarrassment now.

'I didn't mean to, I just . . .' He looked away, and for a moment they both silently watched the children running to and fro around the playground.

'I don't feel old, I really don't.' She was trying, unsuccessfully, to gulp back her tears, but she had ceased to care what Ray thought; the desire to vent her feelings was too strong for her to stop now. 'I don't feel any different. I'm healthy and strong. I can't do it, I can't . . . rotting away with a man who doesn't even care about me enough to make love to me . . . hasn't for a decade.'

She gasped as she heard her own words, her face suffused scarlet with shame. She covered her face with her hands, wishing the earth would swallow her up.

She heard Ray draw in a long breath.

'That must be difficult.' He spoke slowly, carefully.

Jeanie shook her head in amazement at herself. 'Listen, I can't believe I said that . . . to you . . . a perfect stranger. I'm so sorry . . . it's the most embarrassing thing.'

Ray laughed. 'To you, maybe, but . . .'

A phone rang nearby, and Ray dived for his jacket.

'Saved by the bell,' she muttered ruefully.

'Hi . . . yes . . . yes . . . no, I won't be back today; I'll deal with it first thing. Thanks for letting me know, Mica . . . yeah, bye.' He slipped his phone into the pocket of his shirt. 'That was the club.'

'Grandpa! Grandpa! I need to pee . . . badly, Grandpa.' Dylan was standing in front of Ray, hopping up and down and holding his crotch. Ray jumped up.

'Come on . . .' And they headed off at a run towards the bushes at the edge of the park, leaving Jeanie feeling as if she'd just tottered off a switchback ride.

They didn't say much to each other after that. Jeanie clipped Ellie into the buggy, her granddaughter hot and pink-cheeked from the running game, and gave her a drink of water from her blue plastic beaker. Dylan scuffed along beside the pram, twisting his anorak up over his head like a cloak. At the park gates they said their goodbyes.

Ray hesitated for a moment. 'I'm sorry we didn't have time to finish our conversation.'

Jeanie tried to laugh. 'Just as well. Please forget every-thing I said.'

He smiled back at her, touched her arm before he turned away, just fleetingly, but it felt suddenly very intimate. And she found she liked it.

6

Rita bent to gather her racket cover, ball tin and jacket from the corner of the court.

'What's wrong with you, Jean Lawson?' She sounded cross but Jeanie knew better. 'You can't keep letting me win like this. I mean, I know I'm unbelievably good, but you're making me look like a superstar!'

Jeanie was leaning against the court netting, swinging her racket back and forth. She had thought about nothing for three days but Ray and what she had said to him. 'Bench?'

She waited till they'd settled themselves. The long evening shadows were creeping closer, and with them the spring chill, but they still had about fifteen minutes of the dying, dusty sunlight.

'Well?' Rita was staring at her friend. 'Something's up, I know it.'

'I've met this man,' Jeanie said quietly.

'Darling . . . no!' Rita's eyes widened with shock. 'What, you mean a real man?'

Jeanie laughed. 'Well . . . yes, to all intents and purposes, he's very real.' She outlined their three meetings, but there wasn't much to say. 'Look, it's nothing. I don't know him, I don't even know what he does . . . although he did mention "the club" on the phone.'

'What, a nightclub?'

Jeanie shrugged. 'I don't know.'

'A nightclub's not good.'

'Not good for what?'

'He might be sleazy.' Rita looked concerned.

Jeanie felt instantly defensive. She laughed. 'You mean he might be after my body, perhaps hoping to sell me to the white slave trade for a tidy profit? He's most certainly not.'

'It could be a sports club, or a health club, or. . .' Rita mused.

'I don't know. What difference does it make? I'm telling you, there's nothing to it. I've only met him twice, three times, but it's just . . .'

'Do you fancy him?'

Jeanie snorted. 'Rita! No.' Yet as she said it, she knew it to be a lie. She did find him very attractive – how could she not? – it was just that she wasn't in the zone, and hadn't been for so long, where she flirted. It was a muscle that had wasted away. She realized she was blushing under her friend's knowing gaze.

'Don't be daft, I'm married.'

Rita nodded wisely. 'I had noticed, darling.'

Jeanie took a breath. 'No, you don't understand. I . . . I told him . . . told him something . . . God, it makes me cringe to think about it. I don't know why I did it.'

'Told him what?'

'Told him that George hasn't had sex with me for ten years.' Jeanie spoke in a rush.

If Rita's eyes had been wide at the mention of Ray, this piece of news threatened to derail them altogether.

'What? What?' she shrieked. 'No! It can't be true?'

'Shhh!' Jeanie looked around at the last remaining stragglers on the nearby grass.

'You mean not at all, not ever? For ten whole years? Christ, darling, why didn't you tell me?'

'I suppose I kept thinking it would be OK, and then the years went on and . . . well, here we are.'

Rita was silent.

'I don't know why I told Ray. I didn't mean to, it just came out.' She wished Rita would say something. 'It's probably not such a big deal,' she went on quietly. 'Maybe there are millions of couples out there who never have sex.'

'So what happened? Why did it stop so suddenly?'

Jeanie sighed. 'That's the weird thing, I still don't know. He absolutely refuses to talk about it. I did try. When it first happened, I tried everything in my power to get him to tell me what was wrong. But he just clammed up, wouldn't say a word. He got really angry with me in the end, so I stopped. But it's driven me mad, not knowing.'

Rita shook her head.

'He was never that keen, it was always me.' Jeanie paused. This was new territory for her and Rita; they discussed every other aspect of life in the minutest of detail, but never each other's sex life. 'And never that frequent, but I could usually persuade him.'

'Was he any good at it?' Her friend's tone implied she knew the answer.

'OK, I suppose. I don't have a yardstick, I've never tried it with anyone else. George was my first . . . and last.'

The man responsible for closing the park came up

the hill, ringing his hand-bell in warning, and Jeanie realized the sun had almost gone down. She shivered.

'We'd better go.'

As they stood she felt Rita's strong arm round her shoulder and was grateful.

She finished the story about George as they walked up the hill.

'Christ! The bastard . . . you poor thing, that's so hurtful.' Rita stopped walking and turned to face her friend. 'He's gay. It's the only explanation.'

'What, suddenly gay? After twenty-two years of normal marriage? Was he just going through the motions all that time?'

Rita harrumphed. 'Pretty depressing to think so. I can't believe you've let it ride so long, darling. I mean, did George think you were happy not having sex? I'd have left him years ago.'

'It was a gradual thing, I suppose. You know, time passes without you realizing. I never thought it would go on this long, and then . . . well, it's just part of the marriage now. I do love him,' Jeanie insisted, 'we get on very well as a couple. Apart from the sex thing.'

'And the control thing.'

'Well, OK, that too. But honestly, I love George. I could never leave him, he'd fall apart.' Jeanie felt pathetic. She knew her friend would never have let Bill get away with such behaviour.

Rita shot her a shrewd look. 'Yeah, well, that's always a good reason to stay with someone, isn't it . . . to prop up their inadequacies.'

Jeanie winced at the sarcasm. 'Loving someone is a good reason to stay, though.'

'So the man in the park.' Rita changed the subject. 'What did he say when you told him?'

'Not much, poor bugger, what could he say?'

'George is a fool,' her friend commented thoughtfully.

Later that night, Jeanie stood naked in front of the bathroom mirror and looked hard at her body. She tried to imagine showing it, herself, to Ray, but the cold strip lighting seemed to mock her. It wasn't that her body embarrassed her. The pad of post-menopausal fat on her stomach drove her mad but refused to budge, her small breasts were definitely bigger since the hormone shift, but she was still slim and fit. Unlike some of her friends, she'd never considered HRT. She thought it was a sort of vanity if you weren't actually tormented with hot flushes, which she hadn't been. But would she look better now, younger, if she were taking hormones? She scrutinized her face. It was a little lined, but she had good skin; strong, slightly fierce blue eyes; and her dark auburn hair, though helped by the bottle, was shiny and well cut to her chin. No, the problem was that her sexuality seemed to have vanished. Here was a woman in the mirror who could be proud of a body, but that was all it seemed to be now, just a body.

7

Jola glanced up gratefully as Jeanie arrived at the shop. There was a queue at the counter, everyone juggling their purchases but looking smugly patient, as if the mere decision to shop in this healthy, organic, pure environment had made them better people.

'Morning.' Jeanie recognized one of her regulars as she hurried to open the second till. For a while she and Jola worked in silence to serve the customers, but soon there was a lull.

'Tea?' Jeanie moved to the back of the shop and the tiny kitchen.

'Can we talk?' Jola accepted the cup of tea, but seemed unusually tense. Jeanie groaned inwardly. For months now she had dreaded the conversation where Jola announced she was going back to Poland. She knew that Jola's boyfriend had been pushing for her to go home with him, and so far she had resisted. She was well paid by Jeanie, a hundred per cent more, she said, than she would get in Poland, and loved her job. But the boyfriend hadn't managed to integrate as well as Jola – he still hardly spoke English – and seemed to resent her success, even though (or maybe because) it was her salary that supported him. Jola was looking at her hard.

'Jean, I am thinking that something is not right with you . . . with shop.'

Jeanie looked puzzled.

'I cannot help hearing phone, last week . . . you say to your friend you don't want to move from London . . . but I don't know what you mean.'

She pushed her black-rimmed glasses back into place, her small face puckered with anxiety.

Jeanie thought back. What had she said? Then she remembered: she'd been ranting to Rita about George making an appointment to see a house the following week, and that she had no intention of going with him.

'You not go away? Leave shop?'

Jeanie shook her head vigorously. 'No, no way. I am not leaving the shop, Jola.'

She still didn't look convinced.

'I'll be honest. George wants to move to the country, but I have no intention of doing so. I promise you, Jola, I'm not giving up the shop.'

'But your husband?' Jola came from a much more traditional culture.

'He can't make me,' Jeanie assured her, although she felt a flutter of anxiety as she spoke.

Jola nodded, smiled. 'I am happy.'

'And Poland?'

'No, no . . . not yet . . . my boyfriend, he get job now. He happy too.'

'Don't forget we're away next week.' Alex had continued the friendship drive.

'I'm jealous. Brittany'll be wonderful at this time of year.'

Alex looked glum. 'I suppose.'

'Try to look more excited.'

'I'm just overwhelmed with work. The gallery've said if it's not ready for September, I'll lose my slot and they won't be able to fit me in till late next year.'

They stood in the hall, Ellie tugging on Jeanie's hand. 'Come on, Gin, let's go. Come *on* . . . stop talkin'.'

'I'm just coming, darling. Go and get your umbrella

and we'll take it to the park.' Her granddaughter was currently obsessed with her new umbrella, green and covered with small dinosaurs, which she dragged around with her wherever she went, putting it up and down regardless of the weather.

Alex seemed to want to say something more. This is it, Jeanie thought. I'm just about to find out why he's been so uncommonly charming of late.

'Umm . . . Jean, I was wondering . . .'

Jeanie raised her eyebrows expectantly.

'Well, basically I need more time.' He ran his hand through his dark curls, both spattered convincingly with paint in a variety of blues and greens, as he leant against the wall at the bottom of the stairs.

'I was wondering if you could do full-time with Ellie till the end of the summer.'

Jeanie gulped. 'What, you mean every afternoon?'

Alex pulled his mouth down in an apologetic grin. 'Well, that would be something. She's at nursery two mornings and you do one afternoon already, so it's not such a difference. I know it's a lot to ask, but Chanty won't hear of Ellie going to a childminder, and we can't afford a nanny, not in this economic climate.'

'But Alex, I have a shop.'

He shrugged. 'Yes, I appreciate that, but can't Jola run it for a while?'

Jeanie couldn't believe what he was asking.

'Er, no, she can't. She can do a lot, but she has no idea about ordering or accounts.' Jeanie stopped: she didn't need to justify herself.

Alex turned away, but Jeanie could see the muscle of his cheek contract. He was angry.

'I can do another afternoon if that'd help.' Despite her feelings for the man, she had some sympathy. 'I'm sorry, Alex, I'm not being awkward, it's just this is my business. I can't take my eye off the ball for three months.'

'But if you move to the country you'll be giving it up soon, anyway. George will cover any shortfall, won't he?'

'That's hardly the point.' She couldn't help raising her voice at his selfishness. 'And for your information, I'm not moving to the country.'

Ellie was standing by the front door, clutching her umbrella and watching the two of them.

'Oh, you know what, forget it,' Alex snapped nastily. 'Sorry I asked.'

'I would help you if I could.'

'Yeah . . . sure.' He glared at her then rudely turned away.

'Alex, please. I know we've had our differences, but that isn't why I'm refusing. I've said I'll do another afternoon.'

'Whatever . . .'

He pushed past her in the narrow hall and bent to kiss his daughter as she stood patiently by the pram. 'Have fun in the park, Ell.' Then back again, wrenching open the stair-gate and taking the stairs two at a time up to his top-floor studio without another word.

Jeanie gathered Ellie up and gave her a hug before tackling the pram and the steps.

'Daddy's cross,' the child commented, as if there was nothing unusual about this.

Jeanie didn't trust herself to reply.

It was a relief to see Ray. She'd been shaken by Alex's spitefulness.

'Hey, good to see you.' Ray rose from the bench on the wooden decking by the pond when he spotted her approach. He was looking particularly handsome, she thought, in a blue cotton shirt and jeans, very fit and spruce. She looked around for the boy.

'Where's Dylan?'

'His dad's taken him to a kids' music festival he's running.'

'But you came anyway?'

Ray smiled. 'Didn't want you to think I was avoiding you, after . . . well, you seemed in a bad way the other day. Hi, Ellie.'

Jeanie took Ellie out of the buggy and started to break up some bread for the ducks.

'That's bad for them, you know,' he said seriously.

'It's organic, I got it from the shop.'

He laughed. 'It's not its purity that's the problem, it's the bread itself.'

'Oh? I thought people had been feeding birds with bread for ever.'

Ellie was munching happily on the stale lump of rye loaf Jeanie had handed her.

'Throw it, darling, throw it to the ducks.'

Her granddaughter carefully passed a bit through the netting covering the fence, then stuffed the rest in her mouth.

'They have, but that doesn't make it good for them. Apparently it gets stuck in their guts and makes them ill. If you think about it, it's not surprising. I mean, bread is processed food.'

Jeanie thought about this. 'I suppose. . . I should know, I run a health-food shop.'

'For people, not ducks, though.'

They both laughed and for a second their eyes met. As the gaze held, Jeanie felt the breath stop in her lungs and her heart begin to race tight against her ribs.

She dragged her eyes away and sat down hard on the bench, realizing she was shaking. Ray remained leaning with his back against the fence, his elbows propped on the wooden railing. Disconcertingly, he continued to stare at her flushed face.

The little girl ran about the decking chasing pigeons, totally contained in the sheer exuberance of her freedom.

'I've just had another run-in with my son-in-law, Alex.' She began to talk, to say anything that came to mind, avoiding his eye.

'You mentioned the relationship was difficult.'

Jeanie nodded, willing her heart to quieten. 'He asked me to look after Ellie full-time so he can paint.'

Ray looked questioningly at her, a soft smile playing about his mouth.

'And that's bad?' He saw her rising indignation. 'No, no, I'm sure it is.'

'Well, obviously,' she replied tartly. 'No one seems to notice this fact, but I run a shop.'

'So you said no.'

'And he was vile to me . . . but now I feel guilty. I know he's a pain, but I suppose it can't be easy to look after a child when you're trying to get an exhibition together. Ellie looks as if butter wouldn't melt, but she's relentless.'

'Can't he take her to a childminder a couple of days?'

'Chanty won't hear of it – she does two mornings at nursery already.'

'You do what you can, but in the end it's their problem.'

Jeanie looked at him, nodded. 'You're right, it *is* their problem, I suppose. But I don't want him causing trouble with me and Chanty again, making it difficult for me to see Ellie.'

Ray shrugged. 'Maybe you should trust your relationship with your daughter more.'

'I sound paranoid, don't I,' she sighed. 'It's just it was hell when we fell out. I couldn't bear to go through that again.' She explained about Alex's behaviour before Ellie was born.

'Look, I'm no role model, Jeanie. I keep telling myself to do the same with Nat, to trust her. And in the end,

I believe they want us in their lives as much as the other way round.'

'Right.' Jeanie got up resolutely, anxious to avoid any further intimacy, yet she felt, ridiculously, that she had known this man for whole lifetimes. 'Let's go to the other play area, so Ellie has something to do.'

'Wobby log, wobby log,' Ellie chanted as they came up the hill.

'I'm impressed,' said Ray. 'Dylan can't manage the log.'

'She means the squared-off one, the safe one, not the very wobbly one!'

Jeanie's heartbeat had returned to normal as she held her granddaughter's hand along the line of suspended wooden bricks, but she didn't dare look at Ray.

'Go on,' she challenged him, 'you do it.' She pointed to the smooth, round log which swung lazily on its moorings, smugly challenging all comers.

'If you hold my hand,' he grinned.

'No chance . . . look, Ell.' She pointed at Ray. 'Ray's going to walk across the wobbly log without falling off.'

She never thought he could, but without a word Ray hopped gracefully on to the supporting block, stretched his arms out like a tightrope walker and stepped coolly on to the log. It hardly moved as he crossed, just shook slightly with his weight. As he reached the other end, Jeanie heard clapping, and turned to see a group of adults and children who had gathered to watch his performance.

A little boy was jumping up and down in excitement. 'Do it again, do it again.'

Ray hesitated. 'OK, once more.'

'Show-off!' she teased him, when the audience had gone.

'You made me.'

'True . . . so when did you learn to do that?'

'I ran away and joined the circus as a boy.'

Jeanie looked hard at him.

'OK, I'm trained in aikido – grounding and balance.'

'Martial arts?'

'Yup, but not very martial, aikido is as much about the spiritual . . . I'll explain it one day. I have a school, club, down at the Archway.'

Jeanie began to understand where that impression of learned calm came from – and Ray's obvious fitness.

Ellie had spotted a couple of older boys and was following them cautiously around the trees on the edge of the play area.

'Chanty and Alex are away next week . . . Brittany. So I won't be here,' Jeanie said, not looking at Ray. She felt jumpy, on edge with him so close.

'Meet me anyway.'

'What do you mean?' She stared at him.

'I mean . . . meet me, Jeanie.' His voice was suddenly low and intense, his grey-green eyes – Dylan's eyes – alight.

'I . . . I can't.'

'Can't or won't?'

Jeanie sighed in exasperation. 'Ray, I'm married, I can't just meet you. I hardly know you.'

'It's just a drink! I wasn't suggesting anything inappropriate, although . . .' He couldn't help smiling as she glared at him.

'Just a drink,' he repeated, clearly repentant. They both attempted to laugh, but the sound was forced and tense. Jeanie glanced quickly round the playground, and wondered that the others hadn't seen what was happening between her and this tormenting man.

'I'm sorry.' He saw her sudden distress. 'It was an impulse. I . . . well, it's a while since I've felt like this . . . I thought it might be fun.'

'I said, I can't.' But her reply held a certain reluctance, which he couldn't have failed to notice.

She watched as he reached into his jacket and pulled

out a card. 'If you change your mind,' he said as he handed it to her.

The walk back passed without Jeanie noticing. Her body, with Ray's card burning a hole in her jeans pocket, seemed to have come alive, as if every cell had suddenly been sparked out of a long torpor. The reality was that for the first time in a decade . . . no, she corrected herself, for the first time in her whole life, she was faced with a physical desire that threatened to stop her heart.

Her courtship with George had been sedate, she remembered. She'd been carried away by his quiet gallantry – every door held open for her, his refusal to allow her to pay for anything, to go home on her own – this in a time of bra-burning and rampant feminism. And he'd been a droll, amusing companion who planned every evening like a military operation, taking her to theatre in the park, foreign films, pubs by the river. Her work as a nurse was stressful and exhausting, badly paid, and it had been so restful to know that at the end of the day George would pick her up in his white convertible MG and whisk her off for yet another treat.

Then her father had died. Out of the blue, working

on yet another sermon, he had simply keeled over with a massive heart attack. Her distraught mother had found him when he didn't answer her call to supper, face down on his text, stone dead. George had taken charge, coming with her to Norfolk, finding the funeral directors, informing the relatives, organizing egg and ham bridge rolls for the wake, taking the death certificate to the town hall. He hadn't imposed on her and her mother's grief, just been silently strong and supportive. And Jeanie had fallen in love with him.

But the physical attraction had been different with George, and nothing, she thought now, that compared with the fireworks one look from Ray could arouse. She pushed open the white picket gate that led to Ellie's house, hardly able to deal with the complex emotions she was experiencing.

8

'We can't put Rita next to Danny, he's such a bore,' Jeanie remonstrated.

George pulled a face. 'That's not very nice.' He tapped his pen on the tidily compartmentalized diagram that he had spent hours constructing and that now lay between them on the kitchen table, finally circling Rita's name and drawing an arrow to the other side of table one. 'It's only dinner; they can move around after the main course. OK, let's put her between me and Alistair.'

Jeanie scrutinized the new order. 'No, that won't work because it leaves Sylvie next to Alistair and we can't have husbands and wives together.'

'This is a mess! We've been doing it for hours and

we haven't even sorted one table.' George threw his pen down.

'Tell you what.' Jeanie's face brightened. 'Why do we have to stick to this stupid man–woman–man placement? Why don't we just put all the names in a hat and pick the first ten for table one, second ten for table two, etc? It'll be original and everyone'll be amused. Let's live dangerously, shake it up.'

George looked anxious, then she watched him control himself.

'Hmm . . . OK. Yes, it could work. But what if I'm next to Marlene?' They both started to laugh.

'Tough.'

'And you get stuck with Danny . . . or Simon D.? Is that still tough?'

Jeanie frowned, 'Of course not. This doesn't apply to *me*, it's my birthday. If I get a rum pick I'll change it, but the rest of you will have to fend for yourselves. I'm over these tired, middle-class conventions.'

George grinned. 'OK. Could be explosive, though.'

'I hope it is.'

He got up and fetched the salad bowl from the side and they spent the next ten minutes cutting out the names to fill the four tables.

'Who've you got?' Jeanie closed her hand over her two choices.

'Your not-so-interesting aunt and Jola's boyfriend. That's not fair, he doesn't even speak English. You?'

Jeanie smiled. 'Bill and John Carver . . . how lucky is that?'

'You cheated.' George snatched the papers from his wife's hand and searched for any identifying marks.

They began to laugh again.

'Aunt M. is good value, she's the generation who knows how to sing for her supper.'

'Not necessarily conversation you'd enjoy, though.' George shrugged, smiling. 'Look, it's your party, this is a good idea; let's just finish the rest.'

'OK, but tea first.' Jeanie got up to fill the kettle. 'I wish Aunt Norma could come, I'll miss her. I can't believe she's doing a walking holiday at her age.' As she spoke she heard herself utter the dreaded phrase and roundly chastised herself.

Moving about the kitchen, gathering cups from the dresser, tea bags, checking the milk's sell-by date, she felt utterly discombobulated. She had agreed to meet Ray later. She'd told herself that this wasn't going to happen, that she would never go behind George's back. But the night after she'd seen Ray in the park, George had called her 'old girl' once too often, punctuating his relentless eulogies about the countryside with this patronizing epithet. It had been in a fit of 'What the hell?' that she had texted Ray.

She told herself it wasn't written in stone. She could back out any time. But her decision to meet him shadowed even the simple task of making tea for her husband. George seemed out of reach, distanced by her betrayal, and as a result she had an instinct to treat him better, more carefully, knowing as she did so that this guilt-induced behaviour was craven and contemptible.

They met at the park at six, in the usual place on the decking by the duck pond. Jeanie realized when she saw him that although she had spent the week persuading herself that she shouldn't go, in fact there had never been any real doubt that she would.

What about that drink? J she had texted him.

Hurray! When? he had replied.

Nothing had happened yet, she told herself firmly, and nothing would. It was a harmless flirtation. So she fancied a man in the park, so what? She was old and silly and according to her family no longer knew her own mind. But nevertheless, the guilt and the lying had already begun.

'I'm meeting Rita tomorrow,' she'd told George.

George had looked up from his crossword, nodded. 'What are you seeing?'

Jeanie had busied herself loading the dishwasher, rinsing off the cutlery and putting it handle-down in the basket.

'Not a film, just a girls' night . . . Lily might be coming too.'

'How is Lily? Shame she can't make the party.' He'd smiled a secret smile, pushing his glasses straight. 'Not long now,' he'd added with glee.

Jeanie was barely conscious of her impending birthday. It was the last thing on her mind. In fact the only thing on her mind was the lie she was telling. And Ray. It seemed that both were emblazoned on her forehead in neon lights. But, amazingly, George didn't seem to notice a thing.

'Coffee?' She'd moved towards the cafetière, knowing what her husband's response would be, since she knew all his responses as if they were her own. A few weeks before she would have considered this knowing a comfort, but now it was an irritation. She'd wished, unfairly, that just for once George would say, 'No, tell you what, I'll have a drop of nettle tea today, dear.'

Now, here she was, cold and almost sick with anticipation, being shepherded towards the west gate of the park, which led to the main entrance to Highgate cemetery.

'Where are we going?'

'I thought the new Greek at the bottom of the hill.'

Ray seemed as tense as she felt. Gone was the measured calm and the roguish smile, replaced by a shyness she had never seen before.

'Come back, grandchildren, all is forgiven.' He gave a short laugh.

'I think I need a drink.'

'I know I do.'

They both began to chuckle. 'This can't be a good sign, us needing medication to be together,' she said.

'It's just I've been building this up in my mind since your text,' Ray confessed, much to Jeanie's surprise.

They kept walking, not looking at each other. But hearing what he said, Jeanie took a deep breath and began to relax. Part of her had accepted that she was the silly one, the one with the fantasy, and that despite the obvious overtures, Ray was just going along for the ride. She didn't mind this, it was what she expected, but now she realized that perhaps he shared her sense of turmoil.

★

The restaurant was almost empty, except for one young couple by the window drinking beers from the bottle and sharing a plate of meze. Jeanie was relieved. She'd been checking every passer-by since meeting Ray, waiting for one of her many local acquaintances to spot them together and report back, en passant and quite innocently no doubt, to George. The restaurant felt very new, the waiters over-solicitous, the decor too pristine, as if the atmosphere were waiting to arrive. They were shown to a table close to the other couple – Jeanie supposed most people liked the illusion of company when they ate out – but Ray chose one at the far end of the room instead.

'What do you think?' He looked around.

'I don't really mind . . . it's fine,' Jeanie replied honestly.

Now they were sitting opposite each other, the essential bottle of wine ordered, she felt the fluttering, the churning, the out-of-control pounding of her heart begin. She wanted to catch his gaze, to feel again that first shocking intensity, but hardly dared, so she busied herself tidying the cutlery and unfolding the puce paper napkin, placing it carefully in her lap.

'Cheers.' They raised their glasses to each other and

took an appreciative sip. She hoped the wine might calm her.

'Tell me, then,' Ray was saying, 'tell me everything.'

Jeanie laughed. 'Everything about what?'

'You, your life, where you were born and who your best friend was . . . your favourite song . . . do you like carrots . . . just the normal stuff.'

'How long have you got?' They were both laughing now, the miraculous connection making it almost irrelevant what they said. It was enough just to be there as the light faded outside and the waiter lit the small table candle, to be allowed to watch each other without censure.

'Do you really want to know?'

Ray nodded.

'Born in Norfolk, near Holt, father a Church of England vicar . . . zealous, worthy . . . scary. He might have been happy if he'd thought it was God's will, but he saw life as grim sacrifice. I'm not sure he even noticed us, he was so totally wrapped up in his calling. Mother a parish worker, had a good heart but was annoyingly neurotic. One brother, two years older, who died when he was fifteen, and sent my mother off the rails. Both parents now dead a long time. Best childhood friend Michelle, who was half Canadian and went to live in

Toronto.' She paused for a moment, wondering what Michelle would think of all this. 'What were the other things?' She saw Ray about to speak. 'No, got it . . . I sort of like carrots . . . or maybe I'm indifferent to them . . . I prefer them raw, and my favourite song is . . . impossible to choose.'

'What did your brother die of?'

'Cancer. He'd probably have lived these days, there's such a good cure rate for children now . . .' She gabbled on about the wonders of science and the magical advances of chemotherapy to avoid having to address how she really felt about her beloved Will's death. It was something she had hardly talked about since the morning her father had come into her bedroom and told her he was 'now with God'. Neither of her parents had been able to help her, and there was no one else she'd felt might care.

'How horrible,' Ray was saying.

In her head she still heard Will's screams. At the end he'd been nursed at home by her mother and a woman from the village, but every time they moved him, day or night, she would listen to his exhausted howl of agony and feel her heart torn from her chest. 'He's on the mend,' her mother would reassure her brightly, and Jeanie went along with it, even as she saw the truth in her mother's tortured gaze. Because although she knew it was impossible that the yellow, emaciated figure that had once been her brother could ever be well again, she was unable to contemplate the alternative.

'You must have been devastated,' he said, and his face told her that he knew what she had gone through.

'It was a long time ago,'

'That doesn't make much difference.'

Jeanie nodded. 'It does and it doesn't.' She felt her throat tighten with decades of unshed tears. Ray's hand reached for her own, then the waiter arrived to lay the food on the table and they sprang apart like two teenagers caught in the front porch.

'Sorry, it still catches me unawares sometimes.' She helped herself to a hot pitta bread automatically, without really wanting it. 'Your turn now,' she insisted, swallowing hard. 'Tell me what happened to your girl-friend, the one you left your wife for.'

Ray looked away. 'We were together for eleven years . . . and then she died. A massive tumour on the adrenal gland. She said she felt tired, nothing more than tired, and a bit of what she thought was indigestion. By the time she saw someone they said it was the size of a grapefruit. Anyway, there was nothing they could do, and she died six weeks later.' He paused, looked at Jeanie with an echo of the original shock still burning in his eyes. 'It was the tenth anniversary of her death in January.'

'I'm sorry.'

'She smoked a lot,' he added, as if he were still trying to find an explanation.

Neither of them spoke for a while as they allowed the ghosts of the past to settle. The food lay almost untouched on the table.

'So where does your husband think you are?'

'Girls' night with my friend Rita and her friend Lily.'

'Will he ask about it?'

Jeanie shrugged. 'Depends. If he's on one of his compulsive benders, we could be discussing the whys and wherefores for ever.' She shuddered at the prospect, wondering how she had ever dared agree to this meeting with Ray.

There was an awkward silence at the mention of George.

'Sorry ... bad subject,' Ray muttered, offering Jeanie the saucer of hummus.

Jeanie scraped a small amount up with the pitta bread as she spoke. 'I could make the excuse that I have a dreadful marriage, that my husband is a shit or a bore, or both, that I don't love him, but . . .' she looked Ray straight in the eye, 'but that wouldn't be true.'

Ray waited.

'We've been happy.' She paused at the mention of the word, which suddenly seemed inappropriate. Thinking about it, she hadn't felt really 'happy' with her husband for a long time now. Whatever had happened to him all those years ago seemed to have changed his outlook on life. He no longer wanted to socialize, eat out, or go to the theatre or cinema, even when she offered to organize it – that's why she had taken to going with Rita. 'It hasn't been a bad marriage.'

'You don't have to convince me. Thirty-odd years of living with anyone is impressive.'

Jeanie sighed, 'Of course it's not you I'm trying to convince, is it?'

She saw his eyebrows raised in question.

This time Ray took her hand firmly in his. 'Jeanie, I don't want to be the cause of your distress. I can't say I'm not attracted to you, but it's early days: we can still walk away before we do any damage.'

Damage, she thought. Such a powerful word. But her mind refused to face what 'damage' might imply. Nothing had happened yet, nothing will happen, she repeated to herself like a mantra, but each time her assertion seemed weaker and less convincing.

'Can we just do this . . . now . . . and not think . . .'

He held her gaze and this time she made no attempt to look away.

'The park'll be closed . . . it's after eleven.'

They changed tack and began to walk along the road that traced the south end of the cemetery.

'How can it be after eleven?' Jeanie checked her watch, incredulous that they had spent over five hours together. Hours that had passed in a heartbeat.

She was a little drunk, and the darkness was cool and anonymous.

'Kiss me,' she said, turning to him as he walked beside her.

Without a word he steered her gently into the lee of a tree overhanging the cemetery railings.

Nothing had prepared her for this. As his lips touched hers she felt herself taken up in pure, exquisite sensation which seemed to appease a longing she had not known she possessed.

'God.' It was more a sigh than a word that she heard him whisper. 'You're trembling,' he added, putting his arms tightly round her body.

'Do you blame me?' Her laugh sounded soft and shivery in the night air. 'I can't go home . . . he'll see . . .'

'See what? He'll be in bed, won't he?'

Jeanie nodded with relief. 'I'd forgotten how late it is . . . I hope so, but I'd better get back. I don't want him phoning Rita in the middle of the night.'

They began to walk arm in arm up the hill, Jeanie grateful for the support.

'What does Rita think?'

'Oh, Rita . . . she's my friend . . . you'd love Rita.'

Silence fell as they both contemplated the possibility of their two worlds coinciding.

'Will you meet me again, Jeanie?' he asked quietly.

9

'So?' Rita's voice was charged.

'Ummm . . .'

'What happened? Come on, darling, every detail, please. No holding back.'

'I'm in the shop.' Jeanie moved to the kitchenette, but was aware that Jola could still hear. 'Can we talk later?'

She heard Rita growl with frustration. 'How can you do this to me? You know I don't do patient.'

Jeanie laughed. 'Meet me at Nero's in half an hour?'

'Done.'

Her friend's face was alive with anticipation as they settled with their cappuccinos. The small cafe was hot and packed as usual, a large contingent of mothers, or perhaps nannies, with their oversized buggies and roaming under-threes creating a pleasant chaos.

'Spill . . . now,' Rita ordered, rapping the round wooden table.

'God . . . where to start.' She looked at Rita, embarrassed suddenly. 'He's wonderful, we just . . . I don't know . . . connect. How can I describe how he makes me feel without sounding like Mills & Boon?' She tailed off. 'It's just so easy to be with him, we talked for hours.'

'Never mind the talking, did he kiss you?'

'Yes.' Jeanie found herself blushing.

'And?' Rita was leaning forward eagerly.

Jeanie took a deep breath. 'Heaven.'

Her friend clapped. 'Hurray . . . God, you deserve it, darling.'

'I do?'

'Well, doh. I should say so, with a husband who's withheld sex for decades.'

'Only one decade.'

'Splitting hairs, darling. Believe me, you deserve this. Is it just lust, or are you falling in love with him?'

'I can't even think straight. We agreed not to label it. Just let it be what it was.'

Rita harrumphed. 'Sounds a bit touchy-feely to me.

It's me you're talking to, Mrs L. You can agree all you like not to label it with this park fellow, but you can tell *me*. Are you in love?'

For some inexplicable reason, Jeanie found herself beginning to cry.

'Darling, what's the matter?' Rita reached for her hand, looking contrite. 'I didn't mean to be pushy.'

'It's not you, it's just . . . I don't know. Rita, I'm married, and George is a decent man. But Ray is . . . well, he's wonderful. I haven't ever felt so strongly about anyone, not even George, not in this way . . . and I don't know what to do.'

Rita handed her a tissue from a packet in her bag. 'Oh, darling . . .'

'And what if Ray's just playing with me? What if I fall in love with him and he's not serious? I don't know anything about him really, and I don't care, but suppose . . . well, suppose it's all just a joke for him. And then suppose it isn't? I can't leave George. I'm going to be sixty tomorrow.'

Rita threw her hands in the air.

'Christ, you're obsessed! What on earth's being sixty got to do with it? Love isn't age-specific. Listen, does it feel as if he's playing with you?' Her friend's face was a mask of concern.

'No, not at all, not one little bit.'

'Well, then. But Jeanie, it's early days, as you say: you've hardly known the man for more than a few weeks. Do you have to *do* anything at this point?'

'I should just shut up and enjoy it?'

Rita shrugged apologetically. 'Maybe, yes.'

'And go on lying to George? He was up when I got home the other night, almost insane with anxiety. Did the usual: searched my face, said I looked drunk (which I wasn't, not with wine anyway), gave me the third degree about which bar, why was I so late, why didn't Lily drop me home as usual. It was horrible. It sounds like jealousy, but it's not. He wouldn't even imagine me being unfaithful, I don't think. It's just he panics when he can't control me. But now I've got something to hide.'

'But telling him now, when there's nothing much to tell and it might go nowhere, would be a tad cruel, don't you think?'

Jeanie nodded. 'I suppose ... but it's like I'm ill, Rita. Oh, I almost wish I'd never met him ... then I could go back to my safe old life.'

' "Almost" being the operative word.' Rita raised her eyebrows and Jeanie laughed.

'Well, OK.'

'Exactly. Anyway, if you really feel like that you can just walk away, never see him again.'

There was silence for a minute.

'I thought not.' Rita sighed. 'It's not easy, I don't know what to advise. Did you find out what he does?'

'He owns an aikido school, sort of boys' club I think, in Archway.'

'So not a nightclub. That's good. We like martial arts, they're disciplined and character-forming.'

'I'm glad you approve.' Jeanie laughed.

'You know I only have your best interests at heart.' She clasped her hands. 'Now to get down to the really important stuff . . . who am I sitting next to at dinner?'

The *entente cordiale* between her and Alex was over. The holiday apparently had been a shambles. It had rained solidly, the roof leaked and Chanty had come down with flu. Now home, he faced a mountain of work without his recalcitrant mother-in-law to help, so Jeanie understood if he wasn't in the best of moods.

'Hi, come in.' He slammed the door behind Jeanie when she dropped Ellie back from the park, greeting his daughter with phoney enthusiasm.

'How was the park, darling? Did you go on the swings? Did you feed the duckies?'

Ellie put on her drama queen face for her father's benefit. 'Din didn' let me kick his ball . . . he soifish.'

Alex laughed. 'Who's Din?' He looked at Jeanie.

'It's Dylan . . . he's often in the park when we go on Thursdays.' Jeanie busied herself undoing the straps on the buggy to let her granddaughter out, but a blush crept inexorably to her cheeks.

When she stood up she saw Alex note this and look at her consideringly.

'Is this the boy I saw you with a couple of weeks ago?'

Jeanie held her breath. 'When?'

'I saw you walking up the hill with a man and a small boy. I was coming back from town.' He began chewing the side of his thumb. 'I'd forgotten.'

'Ray is Dylan's grandfather, he's doing what I do, looking after his grandson on Thursday afternoons. We got talking, and the children, despite what Ellie says, play together.'

'Sounds cosy.'

'Playground friends are a fact of life, Alex.'

Jeanie refused to be intimidated, but as she walked home she began to worry. Alex lived to make trouble.

She'd been dreading the park that Thursday, in case things had changed with Ray, in case she hadn't measured up, in case he'd gone off her and didn't show. But equally she longed to see him. She was living two separate lives now: part of her functioning, going through the motions in exactly the way she had for decades, with her real life, the life that lifted her soul, lived entirely separately in the secret place that Ray inhabited. She found herself annoyed when people demanded her attention; it interrupted her thoughts of him. The only exception was Ellie. Time in her company always had a certain magic where worries fell away and she could live like her granddaughter did, in the moment. Holding her breath, she'd rounded the corner to the playground. He was there as usual, and clearly looking out for her. Just a glance from his cool grey-green eyes made her heart sing. The next hour and a half flew in a haze of pleasure. They talked, they chased the children, Ray showed off on the wobbly log again, they had tea in the cafe. 'Another drink?' he'd asked as they walked towards the gate, but she hadn't wanted to commit herself till after the birthday. 'You'll be too old to go out with by then,' he'd teased, and she'd cuffed him on the shoulder. As they parted he whispered, 'I'd like to give you a birthday kiss . . . but it might be a tad inappropriate.' He indicated the children with a grin. 'Save it,' she'd whispered back.

10

'OK, Mum, what's the best plan for Ellie? I don't want her up during the party, so I thought if I come over early and we give her supper and put her to bed upstairs, she'll be asleep by the time the guests arrive.'

Jeanie was sceptical, but she'd learnt long ago not to interfere with arrangements for the child; it only caused friction. Anyway, Ellie was never left with any babysitter except herself, so there wasn't any choice.

'Fine, darling, you can leave her here while you go home to change. Don't forget the caterers are coming around four. Will that be a problem for Ellie's supper? They'll take over the kitchen.'

She heard Chanty sigh. 'Not sure what the best thing is, then. I'd forgotten the caterers. If there's stuff going on we'll never settle her. Plan B, we'll bring her over later when she's fed and bathed and so are we. It's starting at seven-thirty, so we'll be there about seven, and Alex'll bring the travel cot.'

'OK, whatever you think best.'

'I'm so excited, Mum. It's going to be a great evening.' Her daughter loved parties. 'Did you decide on the blue dress or the silver one?'

Jeanie laughed. 'Neither. The blue makes me look a hundred and fifty, and the silver has been seen by everyone at least ten times. No, I treated myself to a new one. A Crouch End special.'

'Fantastic, what's it like? Ell, no! Put that down, it's filthy. Sorry, Mum, Ellie's picked something up . . . Ellie, I said no, give it to me, let go!' There was a howl of rage from her granddaughter and sounds of a tussle. Jeanie smiled to herself. 'God, it's one of those horrible polystyrene takeaway things, covered in something unspeakable. London's so vile.'

Jeanie refused to respond to this ever-familiar mantra. 'It's black.'

'What's black?'

'My new dress. It's black, quite plain with wide-ish straps . . . quite clingy.'

'Oooh, sexy. Bet Dad likes it.'

'He hasn't seen it yet. But I feel good in it.'

Jeanie didn't care much for fashion. She appreciated beautiful clothes on others, but to have to work out what suited herself was a lifelong trial. Brought up by parents who thought frippery the work of the Devil, all her clothes as a child had been hard-wearing, mostly too big for her, practical and subfusc. Teenage rebellion had never materialized; she was too dazed by her brother's death, and somehow she had never regained lost ground. It was usually Chanty who coaxed her out to buy new things, always with a great reluctance on Jeanie's part. But she had chosen the black dress with care, had even sought the advice of the assistant in the small boutique, instead of doing what she usually did, which was skulking self-consciously around the racks, snatching the item of clothing that looked as much like the old one as possible then making a run for it, as if she were taking part in a heist. Standing in the dress in front of the mirror, with the assistant nodding her head in approval, she had thought of Ray, and tried to see what he might see.

'Great, Mum, this is your night. I'm sure you'll look gorgeous.'

'Oh Chanty . . . before you go.' Jeanie wanted to catch her daughter alone. 'Is Alex all right?'

'Yes. What do you mean?' Her daughter was still guarded when talking about him to her mother.

'Just that he seems stressed. You know he asked me to look after Ellie more full-time over the summer while he got his exhibition together?'

There was a pause. 'No, no, I didn't. What did you say?'

'Well, I said I couldn't. I can't leave the shop. Listen, don't mention it to him, darling. He was quite . . . disappointed I couldn't help out.'

'But you're getting on OK now, aren't you?'

'Yes, yes, fine,' Jeanie lied.

'I feel guilty making him do so much childcare, but what choice do I have?' Chanty sighed. 'Do you think it'd be OK for Ellie to go to a childminder? Just for the summer?'

'I suppose it depends on the childminder. It seems to work for lots of mums these days.'

She knew she sounded unenthusiastic at the thought of her precious Ellie left to the mercies of an unknown carer.

'But it's probably too late to find one at such short notice . . . a good one, at least.'

'I'm sorry I couldn't help out, darling,'

'No, no, Mum. It's not your responsibility. You'll have enough on your plate with the move, anyway.'

Jeanie gulped. The move. She'd forgotten about the still-hypothetical move.

'Speak tomorrow,' Chanty was saying. 'Can't wait, Mum.'

If her daughter felt guilty, so did she. Since becoming a grandmother Jeanie had found working out her family responsibilities confusing, as if she were on shifting sands. Was this really her 'third life' as Aunt Norma had insisted, or was she still primarily a wife, a mother, a grandmother?

But however confusing her responsibilities might seem to her, Jeanie woke the next morning to the peculiar certainty that she was an old-age pensioner – senior citizen, in today's parlance. *How did that happen?* she asked herself, remembering how she'd viewed people of a similar age even ten years ago. Rita said that their generation were different, baby boomers who didn't go gently into decrepitude, but didn't every generation think the same?

The door opened and George poked his head round it, a huge smile on his face. In his hands he bore a tray, immaculately laid with a red rose in a vase, toast in a silver rack, a glass dish of marmalade, a folded napkin beside a boiled egg, a steaming cafetière, blue china cup and matching milk jug. Leaning against the vase was a card and a long, gold-wrapped present.

'Happy birthday, darling.'

Jeanie struggled up into a sitting position to receive the tray. 'Thanks, George. How lovely.'

He drew the curtains as usual, and as usual commented on the weather. 'It's stunning out there, the perfect day.' He sat down on the bed. 'Come on,' he urged. 'Open it.'

Jeanie laughed. 'OK, OK, give me a chance . . .' She was touched by her husband's enthusiasm. As she reached for the present she pushed Ray firmly to the back of her mind.

The box was dark-blue leather with gold tracing, and inside was a beautiful analogue watch, silver-mounted, with a pretty, rectangular face and a silver-linked band.

Jeanie gasped. 'It's perfect, darling, just perfect.' She waved her wrist at him.

'I must say, it does look nice,' he commented, clearly pleased as Punch.

She reached to kiss him, and for once he enfolded her in his arms and held her close for a moment. She couldn't remember when he'd last done that, and it almost made her cry for what they'd lost.

'Did you guess? I mean I couldn't have given you anything else really, not with my clock obsession, even if you hadn't wanted it.'

Jeanie laughed and shook her head. 'I've wanted one for ages, but no, I hadn't really thought about presents. I love it.'

Now the tears came in earnest. George looked horrified, reached for her hand, 'What's the matter, old girl?'

Jeanie smiled through the tears. If only he wouldn't call her that. It seemed to represent all that was wrong with their relationship. 'Nothing. I'm fine . . . just a bit overwhelmed by it all.'

George nodded. 'It's a big thing, being sixty, especially for a woman.'

'Why for a woman?'

'Oh, you know . . . men can go on for ever.'

'Doing what?'

George looked embarrassed, not missing the touchy tone of his wife's question. 'Well . . . it's probably a matter of perception.'

On any other day she'd have had it out with him; she knew exactly what he was saying. But she bit her tongue and resolutely turned her attention to her breakfast, banging her boiled egg and pouring herself a cup of coffee.

'So what's the plan?' she asked, between mouthfuls of toast.

George had got up and was wandering aimlessly round the bedroom.

'It's your day, you choose. You're not going to the shop, are you?'

Jeanie shook her head, thought for a moment.

'No, Jola's got it covered. You know what? Since it's such a lovely day, I'd like to go to Kenwood, have lunch outside.'

George nodded approval. 'Kenwood it is.'

'Wow! You look amazing . . . sooo beautiful.'

George was leaning against the mantelpiece in the drawing room, avoiding the caterers. He was dressed in his ancient dinner jacket and black tie, his grey hair neatly parted and plastered to his head, monogrammed black velvet slippers on his feet. She thought his evening clothes made him look distinguished, a man who might have been a player but for that withdrawn, neurotic edge. Jeanie twirled round.

'Love the dress.'

'Good.' She waved her new watch and smiled her thanks.

George moved forward and took her hands. 'Jeanie, I want you to have the most perfect evening. You deserve it.'

She suddenly caught the vulnerability in her husband's expression. Was this his way of saying he was sorry, that he regretted wasting her?

The bell rang.

'That'll be Chanty.'

The dining room looked like fairyland. As the sun went down the ribbons of twinkling lights and the glow from the long, pale candles took over, bringing the normally dark room to life and enhancing the spotless white linen and crystal, the nests of pale pink roses, the bright party dresses of the assembled guests.

George caused a laugh when he admitted to the random nature of the seating plan, but it got the conversation flowing. Jeanie realized she was already drunk. Once Ellie had been safely stowed in one of the spare rooms, and the first guests had arrived, something in her snapped. She stopped thinking and allowed the tension of the past weeks to flow away on a gentle current of champagne. Nothing mattered, no one mattered. Tomorrow, in the immortal line, was another day.

Looking round the tables, she smiled at the strange blending of friends. Alex was doing his best to make nice to Rita; Jola was clearly bored to death by Danny's monologue; Marlene, her old tennis partner, was booming her right-wing opinions in the ear of their neighbour, Sue. Chanty had lucked out with the handsome husband of George's cousin. But generally they seemed pleased to be there, and she could sense their enjoyment as the smoked salmon, roast duck and finally chocolate cake with strawberries appeared in front of them.

'Are you having fun?' Bill, Rita's husband whispered in her ear. Jeanie liked Bill. He was relaxed and straightforward, a modest man despite the millions he had made from his garden centres. She wondered, fleetingly, if Rita had told him about Ray, but tonight she didn't care.

'Loving it.'

'Is that the watch?' He took her wrist in his hand. 'Good one.'

'You knew?' she asked, laughing.

'Blimey, everyone knew but you, Jeanie. George's been obsessing about it for months. He co-opted Rita,

Chanty, me, Jola; we all had to opine about what sort to get.'

'Did you agree?'

Bill laughed. 'Of course not. George, being the clock expert, pulled rank and insisted on a leather strap. Chanty thought you'd like Roman numerals. I . . .' he patted his chest, 'I suggested the link strap. It's more up-to-date, don't you think? One doesn't want to give in to the traditional just yet.'

'What was Rita's take?'

'Oh, Rita . . . she thought he ought to buy you an Aston Martin.'

'Too right.' John Carver, the gay and glamorous interior designer who'd helped them with the house, butted in. 'A girl can never have too many Astons, I always say.'

'I would like to say a few words about Jeanie.' George's words accompanied the commanding ring of Aunt M.'s fork against crystal for silence.

'Jeanie has been my wife for thirty-two years, and in my opinion she's the best wife in England . . .' Hear! hears echoed round the room as George pushed his glasses back up his nose and waited for quiet. 'We met, as many of you will know – but I'll tell the story anyway because it's a good one – in a cinema. The Screen on the Green in Islington, to be precise, seeing Julie Christie in *Don't Look Now* – my friend was obsessed by her. Halfway through the film there was a panicky shout from the row behind me. "Help! Quick, someone's collapsed . . ." and someone else shouted, "Is there a doctor in the house?" I didn't know what to do, so I'm ashamed to say I just sat there while the house lights went up. But suddenly, making her way down the row was this beautiful auburn-haired girl. Everyone else seemed to be paralysed. We all just watched this poor guy slumped and making choking noises in his seat. But without any fuss, she bent over and touched his arm. "Hello . . . are you OK?" she said. "You've had a turn." The man, he was young, immediately opened his eyes and looked around bewildered. "Are you epileptic?" the girl asked, but he shook his head. "No . . . no, I'm OK. I'll be OK . . ." But he was white and sweating and looked far from OK. She helped him to sit up and wiped away the sweat from his face.

Anyway, the ambulance had been called and eventually the man was carted away. But Jeanie, for it was she, had been so calm, so kind, so confident with him, and as she went back to her seat, everyone clapped.'

George paused; he looked as if he knew he had their attention. 'I was smitten. I told my friend I had to know who she was, and at the end of the film I scurried out before the crowd and waited on the pavement outside.'

Jeanie tried to remember the girl he was talking about. Responsible even then, she thought with a wry smile, realizing that although by the time she met George she was running as fast as possible from the gloomy Norfolk vicarage and its pervading sense of duty, she had never been light-hearted, carefree. It had been her brother Will who was the joker of the family, trying in vain to find the key to his parents' sense of humour. But he made Jeanie laugh till she could hardly breathe. She blew her brother an imaginary kiss, smiling at what he might have said about Little Sis making sixty had he been here tonight.

George was still talking. 'When she came out, me and my friend went up to her and we had a chat about what had happened. She was with another girl: they were both nurses, and we went for a drink nearby. The rest . . .' he held out his hand towards his wife, 'is history. This is not to say,' he went on when the cheering had stopped, 'that Jeanie is any kind of saint . . .'

'She's put up with you for thirty years, hasn't she?

Lucky bugger,' a male voice barracked and George grinned.

'Lucky bugger indeed, but rather her than a saint any day. She keeps me on my toes, she's feisty and doesn't suffer fools gladly, but she's as loyal, true and tolerant a friend as any man could wish for.' More claps and cheers greeted this statement. Jeanie had hung her head, struck, as if by a blow, by the cruelty of the present situation. She looked up and caught Rita's carefully neutral glance.

For a minute there was silence, and George looked as if he had temporarily lost his way. Jeanie could feel everyone holding their breath, when into the silence he spoke, quietly but firmly, looking earnestly round at their friends. 'I have nothing else to say, except I love her, I've always loved her, and I always will.' And with that he sat down as if the strength had gone out of his legs.

The silence gave due respect to heartfelt emotion. Jeanie saw Chanty's eyes had filled with tears, as had many others, including her own. She caught Alex's eye and saw him looking at her with new respect. She felt Bill's arm go round her in a hug.

'Let's raise a toast to Jeanie darling, who, I'm sure you'll agree, doesn't look a day over twelve.' John Carver had stepped effortlessly into the breach and they rose to their feet, glasses in hand. 'To Jeanie . . . Happy birthday.'

'Speech! Speech!' She heard shouts for her to respond.

Jeanie shook her head, laughing. 'I'll let you off, except to say thank you all so much for coming and helping me celebrate, and obviously a particular thank you to George for a beautiful speech.'

She went over and gave her husband a kiss. He looked drained. 'That was brilliant.'

He smiled. 'I meant it, Jeanie, every word.'

Alex threw open the French windows in the dining room on to the warm April night, and people began to wander out to the terrace where the caterers had placed lanterns and flares in the garden.

'What a fabulous party, darling.' Rita came up behind Jeanie and put her arm round her.

'How were your dinner companions?'

'Great. I know you and Alex don't see eye to eye on much; of course he's self-obsessed, but he's not bad company when he makes the effort.'

'Hope you put in a good word for me.'

'You'd think I was your agent, darling.' Rita looked round to see if they were overheard. 'Are you OK? . . . that can't have been easy.'

Jeanie shook her head. 'I feel like a total shit.'

'He really meant it,' Rita commented.

'Don't . . .'

'Mum . . .' Chanty hugged her tight. 'Wasn't that wonderful? Didn't you love Dad's speech?'

Jeanie held her close. 'I did. I've loved the whole thing. Thanks, darling, I'm so glad you made me have a party.'

Chanty made a face at Rita. 'I can't tell you the problems I had persuading her. "I hate parties . . . I don't want to celebrate . . . it'll be a palaver . . ." '

Rita laughed. 'She's a stubborn old thing but we love her.'

Much later, she and George were on their own again, sitting in their quiet kitchen, the doors still open to the cool night air, one solitary candle burning between them. The table was laden with plates of cling-filmed leftovers and boxes of glasses the caterers would pick up in the morning. George nibbled at a cold duck leg.

'This is the bit I like best,' George commented.

'When they've all gone?' Jeanie smiled, kicking her shoes off under the table. 'I know what you mean.'

'It went well, don't you think?'

'It was wonderful. You can never tell, but I think everyone enjoyed themselves.'

'Jola's boyfriend looked a bit baffled, and I'm not sure it was Bea's scene.'

'She probably can't hear what people say in all that noise. I'm glad she came, though.'

Bea was another neighbour, now in her nineties. They had known her for as long as they'd known each other.

They talked for a while, then George got up and took Jeanie's hands, pulling her to her feet.

'OK . . . bed.' Jeanie yawned, but George held on to her.

Suddenly he leaned down and kissed her on the lips. A lingering kiss. Jeanie froze. No, she thought, no, please . . . not now. She felt his arms go round her, his hands stroking her, pulling the strap from her left shoulder and kisses being pressed to her bare skin. His breathing was quick and uneven.

'George . . .' She pulled away slightly, but he paid no attention.

'Jeanie . . . come upstairs . . . please.' He kissed her again, a terrible, desperate passion in his mouth that made her wince. It was as if he were doing something he knew he must, and gritting his teeth to get it done.

He was pulling her towards the door, his hand firmly

on her wrist, then seemed to change his mind and made for the drawing room, pulling her down on the sofa. Ten years she had longed for him, but this was wrong. Ray wasn't the problem, she hardly thought of him; no, she felt furious, outraged that George should consider even for a single second that he had the right.

'George, stop it . . . please . . . not like this . . .'

And when he continued, 'George!' This time it was a shout.

She pushed him hard in the chest and pulled herself up off the sofa, breathing hard.

Her husband was slumped on the cushions, his glasses crooked, his face crumpled into the bleakest expression she had ever seen.

'Sorry . . . sorry . . .' George muttered as she stared down at him. 'You looked so beautiful tonight. Oh, Jeanie, I thought . . . after so long . . . it was what you wanted.' He blinked up at her.

Jeanie felt the strength go out of her and sat down again beside her husband. 'Not like this, George. Not suddenly. It's been ten years . . .'

George's owl-like eyes stared at her sadly. 'Ten years, is it . . . ? I didn't realize.'

There was silence.

'So you don't . . . you don't want to any more?'

'I do . . . of course . . . although it'd be odd after all this time. It was never my choice not to.' She sighed in frustration. 'But George, you still haven't explained what happened, why you suddenly didn't want to make love to me.'

She watched as her husband fiddled with his right cufflink, trying to push it through the buttonholes in his folded shirt-cuff. It was a heavy gold monogrammed disc, given to him by his father when he was twenty-one, and almost too big for the holes. She leaned over and did it for him, waiting for him to speak.

'Why, George?' she finally asked into the silence.

His eyes lighted on hers fleetingly, then flicked nervously away.

'There wasn't a reason.' His response was childlike, sulky.

Jeanie got up. 'I'm too old for this,' she muttered tiredly, feeling suddenly that she was indeed too old, as from today, to listen yet again to this ancient lie.

Her husband's look was dogged. 'There wasn't . . . I can't explain.'

' "Won't", you mean.' She snatched up her pale-blue wool wrap that lay over the back of the armchair. Making one last try, she stood with her arms crossed and addressed him as he sat, still slumped against the cushions. 'Look at it from my point of view, George. Suppose we'd had sex tonight. I think, "That's good, we're back on track." I don't ask any questions, just assume whatever it was that got in the way has gone. Then you leg it again.' She looked at him questioningly. 'I don't think I could cope with that.'

George nodded slowly.

'What I said about you tonight was true, Jeanie. I love you. I always have and always will.'

She nodded agreement because this, at least, was true.

'We're solid, aren't we . . . you and I?'

Jeanie just looked at him.

'I mean, I know the sex thing . . . isn't great . . . but apart from that. I couldn't bear to lose you.'

Jeanie turned away. She suddenly felt too tired to say one more word. They didn't seem to be on a level playing field any more. She knew he was still hiding something: she'd seen his eyes flick. And now so was she.

'Night, George.'

'Night.'

'It's like buses, nothing for years then two come along at once.'

Rita strode up the hill, Jeanie keeping pace. They reached the top of the path, buffeted by the wind, and drew breath, the landscape of London stretching ahead of them, panoramic, beyond the Heath.

'It's not funny,' Jeanie retorted, although they both began to laugh.

'Honestly, darling, we should be oiling our bath chairs, not fighting off the lustful hordes!'

Jeanie had texted Rita as soon as she thought it fair that morning. Despite her tiredness, she'd spent a sleepless night after leaving George. At five she'd gone down to the kitchen and watched the sunrise, picking at some of the strawberries left over from the night before.

'Should I have let him?' This was the question that had tormented her all night. 'If I had, maybe it'd simplify things . . . get us back on track.'

Rita took a long slug of water from the bottle she carried, wiping her mouth with the back of her hand. Even at short notice she looked immaculate in tight grey tracksuit bottoms and a pink lycra vest.

'If it felt wrong, it was wrong. End of.'

'That simple? Can we sit down for a moment?' Jeanie suddenly felt faint. The bench was damp and she wondered fleetingly if it had rained in the night.

'This is really getting to you.' Rita eyed her friend with concern as she brushed a twist of cellophane fastidiously off the seat before sitting down. 'It wasn't about

Park Man last night, was it? You comparing them?'

She considered this. 'It didn't seem so at the time. It seemed like an attack I was fending off.'

Rita raised her eyebrows.

'I know, it's George we're talking about, but you didn't see him, Rita, he was in a frenzy.'

'Of desire?'

'Not really . . . more desperation.'

'Not a good look. But Jeanie, what do you feel for George? Do you still find him attractive? Did you feel any desire when he kissed you?'

She shook her head. 'I used to, but I've stopped thinking of him in that way. And last night he didn't give me a chance to feel anything.'

'Except anger. So what did he say this morning?'

'I didn't wait. I couldn't face him.'

'Oh, darling.' Rita saw the tears almost before Jeanie was aware of them. 'Are you going to talk to him about it?'

'I don't see the point.'

'What, so you'll just go on as you were, as if nothing's happened?' Rita's look was incredulous.

'What else can I do, Rita, if he won't *talk* to me?' Jeanie snapped.

'OK, OK, don't get shirty.'

'Sorry, but you don't understand. You'd never get yourself into this ridiculous situation in the first place.'

Rita's silence seemed to confirm this.

'And Park Man?'

Something softened in Jeanie at the thought of Ray, and the hold she had kept on herself since George's attack seemed to fall away.

'He's separate from all this, Rita . . . he's just Ray.'

Her friend looked sceptical, taking another long swig from her water bottle, wiping the neck and offering it to Jeanie.

'Do you still have sex with Bill?' She suddenly wanted to know that the rest of the world functioned normally.

Rita laughed. 'It's not love's young dream, but yes, it's fun with Bill, we know what each other likes . . . and we find ways to rev it up, watch porn sometimes.'

Jeanie's eyes widened. 'Porn?'

'Don't look so shocked. You should try it, it's hilarious.'

She tried to imagine her and George, but failed.

'So will you meet Ray again?'

'I . . . seeing him seems both stupid and essential, and not seeing him the same.'

Rita stood up. 'Come on, this discussion is getting uncomfortably circular, you need to walk them both off.'

II

'Hi, darling, what's up?' Jeanie took her daughter's call as she balanced on a ladder, stacking the shelves above the shop's chill cabinet with surplus stock. It had been a frantic week in the shop following her birthday, Jola convinced that the sudden hot weather was making everyone self-conscious about their exposed bodies. Goji juice, anti-cellulite supplements, prunes, alfalfa, bran and salad vegetables had all been in high demand.

'Can you come over as soon as you've finished work?'

Her daughter sounded unusually clipped and tense. She wondered if Alex was playing up again.

'Is something the matter? Is Ellie OK?'

'Can't talk now.'

'OK, see you later. Oh, Chanty, shall I bring Dad?'

'No.' She sounded almost panicky. 'No, come on your own.'

She snapped her phone shut, checking her watch. It was only ten minutes till closing.

'Afternoon, Jean.' A plump, middle-aged woman in a large sun hat was peering up at her.

'Hi, Margot, what can I do for you?' She groaned inwardly as she came down the ladder, knowing she would be expected to listen for hours to a litany of Margot's ailments, from stiff knees to itchy patches to bloating. She must have tried every supplement under the sun over the years, but never for enough time to see any benefit, and now she'd be wanting to discuss the latest miracle cure she'd read about in the press.

Margot was fanning her face with the local news-paper. 'Well . . . I spotted this new research.' She was off.

'I'm afraid I don't have much time today, Margot, I've got to close up in a minute and I have to do the till.'

Margot looked crestfallen and glanced rather point-edly at the clock on the wall behind the counter.

'My granddaughter . . . I have to go round. Can you come back tomorrow?'

Margot made a play of considering this.

'I suppose so . . . no, no, you get off, dear, I know what it's like with the wee ones.'

Chanty and Alex were edgy.

'Where's Ellie?' It was only six-thirty.

'We put her to bed a bit early, we didn't want her hearing this,' Chanty replied ominously.

The three of them stood about awkwardly in the sitting room.

'What's going on?' Jeanie's heart was racing.

She saw her daughter's mouth twist. 'Mum, this is difficult . . .' She glanced at her husband, but Alex was just staring into space, propped, as always, against the mantelpiece, standing on one leg and rubbing one bare foot along the arch of the other.

'It's about Ellie . . . she's been talking about a man . . .'

No, thought Jeanie, looking immediately at Alex, who refused to meet her eye. She waited.

'She says this man, she calls him 'Way', holds her on his knee. . . touches her.'

Jeanie thought she would explode. She sat down hard on the sofa. 'I don't believe this,' she stated coldly.

She saw shock register on her daughter's features. 'Mum?'

'It's lies,' Jeanie said flatly.

'Mum . . . it's Ellie who said it. Are you saying you don't believe your own granddaughter?'

'Did she tell you this herself?' she asked quietly.

'No, she told Alex.'

'Right.' She took a couple of deep breaths because she knew she was on the verge of saying things that would never be forgotten.

'Obviously we're worried sick. Alex said that you and this man, Ray, have been meeting in the park.'

'Have *you* heard it from Ellie?' Jeanie interrupted.

She could see Chanty got it at once, and she watched her daughter's face harden.

'I'm not going to ask a two-year-old child to repeat something as upsetting as that. Are you suggesting Alex's made this up?'

'I'm suggesting he's mistaken.' Her words were slow and wooden with control. 'Alex?'

Alex moved. Jeanie thought he was finding his position in front of them too prominent, and he went to sit on the arm of Chanty's chair, behind his wife. 'I know what she said.'

'Which was what? Tell me exactly what Ellie said.' She knew her voice was threatening, but she didn't care.

Her son-in-law harrumphed. 'What Chant just said, that Ray took her on his knee and touched her.'

'Ellie said that? You are totally certain that she said that?'

Alex nodded, looked away. 'Not those exact words, I can't remember precisely, but the gist . . .'

Jeanie turned to her daughter, wondering how she couldn't see that her husband was lying through his teeth. 'I will say this only once.' She looked Chanty absolutely straight in the eye, and knew that her own would be sparking blue and intense in their need to communicate the truth.

'I have never . . . once . . . on any occasion whatso-ever, let Ellie out of my sight when she's in my care. And never once has Ray, to my absolute knowledge, so much as laid a finger on her. Not once, not ever, not held her hand, or picked her up or lifted her into the swing, barely even spoken to her except to say hi and bye and hand her an apple juice carton. Never, nothing.'

She took a breath. 'What's more,' she appealed to Chanty, who sat stony-faced as her mother talked, 'you must know that every cell in my body is devoted to Ellie, that I would happily lay down my life to protect her from any harm, however slight. So I don't see how you can possibly believe that I would allow a situation to occur where a stranger could molest my own grand-daughter in my presence.'

Chanty took a long breath. 'We weren't saying "molest" . . .' The look she gave her husband now was uncertain, bewildered.

'Yes . . . you were saying "molest". That's exactly what you were saying.'

'Mum . . . you must admit, it's worrying. I was frantic when Alex told me. These things happen without people seeing.'

'Nothing happened and I am not "people". I am your mother and Ellie's grandmother.'

'I know, Mum, and I do trust you. It's other people I don't trust. And it's easy for a situation to happen when you, say, go to the loo, or get a drink, and it happens when your back is turned, even for a moment. You might not be aware that you're doing it.' She looked at Jeanie questioningly.

'I'm not senile, for God's sake! I can still manage to track my own movements.' So that was it: they thought she was a dotty, incompetent old bat. 'None of those scenarios have taken place. I repeat, I have never, and would never, leave her with anyone to do anything at all, not even for a second. I just wouldn't. I'm far more paranoid than you are.'

Chanty looked as if she wanted to believe her. 'Maybe Alex got the wrong end of the stick . . .'

'I heard what I heard,' he repeated sullenly, but there was no conviction in his words.

'I just don't know why Ellie would say something like that if it didn't happen,' Chanty went on.

'Nor do I.' Jeanie looked pointedly at Alex. She sighed. 'Look, I can see why you'd be worried, darling, but whatever Ellie was talking about, it didn't happen on my watch.'

'Anyway, who is this man?' her daughter wanted to know.

'He runs an aikido school at Archway. He looks after his grandson on Thursday afternoons for his daughter. From what I can see he's an entirely decent human being. The children play together.'

She said no more, hoping it would be enough. What she was doing with Ray might be wrong, but it was a separate issue. She knew her cheeks were flaming, but it was from anger rather than guilt.

'Well . . . I'd rather you didn't hang out with him when you've got Ellie from now on, just the same.' Chanty's tone was preachy, that of a schoolmarm berating a wayward pupil. Jeanie's hackles rose.

'If you don't trust me, Chanty, then I won't look

after Ellie at all. I don't want you worrying every time I step outside the front door.'

She watched Alex, waiting for him to meet her eye. Why was he doing this? Couldn't he work out it wouldn't benefit him to lose even one afternoon's childcare?

'Alex?' Chanty had finally decided her husband should share the responsibility.

'I'm sure Jean has Ell's best interests at heart, but I would feel more comfortable if I knew this Ray man was nowhere near my daughter,' he pronounced rather smugly.

'He . . . hasn't . . . touched her. Haven't you listened to a word I've said?' Jeanie heard her voice rising and knew she had reached tipping point. She rose to go.

'Even so,' he added, 'you know nothing about him.'

Chanty also got to her feet. 'I'm sure you can see our point, Mum.'

Jeanie reached to give her daughter a formal kiss. 'If you don't trust me, you shouldn't let me loose with your daughter,' she repeated.

'Mum, I've said, of course we trust you, don't we, Alex?'

She saw him nod.

'Please don't let this be an issue between us. I had to find out what was going on.'

Jeanie looked hard at them both. 'And do you believe me when I tell you that Ray has never touched Ellie, even appropriately? Promise me you're not even thinking of taking this any further.'

They both nodded, but it was equivocal. She could tell her daughter was still uncertain what she should think.

'Please don't tell Dad, it'll only worry him.' Chanty lowered her voice as she escorted Jeanie to the door. And it was only then that Jeanie knew that Chanty had misgivings about Alex's account.

That Thursday, Jeanie took her granddaughter to a different park, one the other side of Crouch End. She didn't tell Ray; she didn't know what to say. 'We can't meet, my family thinks you're a paedophile.' How could you say that to anyone? She knew, however, that their short liaison had to end. If it could threaten her relationship with her daughter, stop her seeing her beloved granddaughter, jeopardize Ray's life and career, it couldn't be worth it. She still shook with anger when she pictured Alex's guilty face, worrying that she hadn't done enough to convince them. She wanted to talk to Ray about it, but not only was she hotly embarrassed by her relatives' behaviour, she also knew that if she spoke to him, if she heard his voice, she would weaken. She had to make the family her priority.

'Baa baa black sheep, have you any wool?' she began as they walked down Hornsey Lane in the hot May sunshine, waiting for Ellie to join in. '. . . One for the monster and one for the day,' the child sang, her sun hat bobbing from side to side, 'and one for the likul boy who live downa lay . . .' and Jeanie just smiled with pleasure, having no desire in the world to correct her.

As they reached the gates of Priory Park, her mobile beeped. Ray. *Are you coming? Got strawberries.*

Birthday strawberries. Resolutely she put her phone back in the pocket of her cotton trousers.

'Gin look . . . look, Gin.' Jeanie followed the direction of her granddaughter's finger.

'Sandpit . . . do you want to go in the sandpit?'

Ellie nodded. 'Buck . . .' She pointed at a discarded bucket. 'Owinge buck . . . sand fall down . . .' She began to busy herself picking up handfuls of sand and throwing it in the bucket, then tipping it out again. This occupied her for a while, until a small boy came over and snatched the bucket. 'Mine,' he declared, but

Ellie wouldn't let go of the blue handle. 'Gin . . . nooooooo . . . not boy's buck . . . moine, moine.' Her screams crescendoed as the boy successfully wrestled his orange bucket back. It took hours to calm Ellie down, by which time the little girl was red-faced and sweating, her fair curls plastered to her head, sand scrunching between her fingers and toes and coating her bare legs.

'Ice cream,' Jeanie announced cheerfully, but her heart wasn't in it. She kept looking around in the ridiculous hope that she would see Ray coming across the grass towards her.

'A'boy's horbor,' Ellie kept saying plaintively, her brown eyes still full of outrage. 'He did take my buck.'

'It was *his* bucket,' Jeanie repeated. 'We'll bring yours next time,' knowing this made no sense to a two-year-old.

They sat on a bench while Ellie picked delicately with a plastic spoon at a single scoop of chocolate ice cream in a waxed-paper cup, making it last for hours. By the end her small face was covered in a beard of chocolate.

'Anna-one?' she said hopefully, holding out the cup to Jeanie.

Jeanie laughed. 'No, darling, one's enough.'

'Where Din?' the child asked, then started hiccupping. 'I got neck-ups,' she announced, grinning.

'He couldn't come today.'

'OK . . . Din have play with me,' she said, and when Jeanie didn't answer she said again, 'Gin . . . Gin . . . Din play with me. An' my leg ouchy ouchy when a'ball hit me.'

'Yes, darling, but your leg's all right now, isn't it?'

Ellie looked doubtful and pulled up the hem of her skirt to point to an invisible wound.

'Ouchy leg like Daddy when he was a likul girl.'

'Little boy,' Jeanie corrected, smiling to herself.

She took her granddaughter on her knee and wiped the ice cream gently from her face with a wet-wipe. Ellie struggled and shrieked, but she persevered. Then she just held the hot little thing in her arms, stroking the damp hair back from her forehead. The thought that anyone could hurt her made Jeanie almost sick. What Alex had done was evil. Or had he really thought his daughter was being abused?

'I love you,' she whispered into Ellie's hair.

'I've found a house.' George was jubilant, jumping up from his seat on the terrace when he heard Jeanie and running into the kitchen, all gangly arms and legs, waving a sheet of particulars in her face.

Jeanie took out her reading glasses. The house was beautiful, an old rectory on the edge of the Blackdown Hills, it said: five bedrooms, morning room, etc. etc.

'It's so perfect, ticks all the boxes, and it's on the market for one point five.'

'Great.' At that moment, Jeanie didn't care if she lived in the Outer Hebrides. At least a move would take her as far away from Ray as possible. He'd sent two more texts, neither of which she'd replied to: *What's up? Xxx* and *Say something! X.*

'Think how wonderful it'll be to be in the country when it's hot like this,' George was saying, flapping a wad of printouts in front of his face like a fan.

'It's only this hot so early in May two days every decade. Hardly worth moving to Dorset for.'

'Somerset . . . this house is on the Somerset/Devon borders. Let me get you a drink, you look done in.' He scrutinized her till she had to look away. 'I've made some iced tea.'

Jeanie nodded.

'Go and sit down on the terrace, old girl, and I'll bring it out.'

His solicitousness was painful to Jeanie. She knew

where it was coming from. Since the night of the party he'd treated her as if she were made of spun glass.

'I put mint in it. So how was Ellie?'

'Fine . . . adorable as ever.' She told him about the boy and the 'buck' and they both laughed.

This is how it will always be, she thought as she sipped her tea, just this, just us.

'Jeanie.' George was looking serious. 'This move . . . you're OK with it now, aren't you?'

Jeanie shrugged.

'It's just I thought . . . I thought this could be a chance for us. You know, get away from it all, make a new life.'

'There's nothing wrong with this one, George.'

George looked relieved. 'No . . . well, it's good you think that. But think how much better it'd be to live here.' He pointed to the photograph.

'You haven't seen it yet: it's probably on the edge of a cliff.'

'Well, if not this one, then another one that isn't.' George grinned encouragingly and she wanted to be enthusiastic like him, wanted to stop being a killjoy, wanted . . . what?

'I'm going to see it on Saturday. Will you come?'

'Saturday's my busiest day.'

George's face fell. 'Well, Sunday. I'll change it to Sunday.'

'OK . . . I think I'll go up and have a cool bath now.' The sun was going down and the heat was finally beginning to lose its edge. As she turned to go she couldn't help seeing her husband's almost pleading glance, but she didn't feel there was anything, not anything honest, at least, that she could say to help.

The following morning she got to the shop early. She was on her way into town to see Tony, her accountant, and needed to pick up some documents. As she packed the papers into her briefcase she looked up and nearly jumped out of her skin. Ray's face was pressed to the glass of the shop door.

'Bloody hell, you gave me a fright,' she gasped as she opened the door.

Ray laughed. 'At least you still live,' he said.

There was a silence between them. 'Jeanie?'

'Look I'm late, I have to go.'

Ray looked puzzled. 'What's going on? Has something happened?'

'I can't see you any more,' Jeanie gabbled, unable to meet his eye.

'OK . . .' The syllable was drawn out. 'Will you tell me why?'

He was standing absolutely still in the centre of the shop, his arms folded, quietly watching her gather the rest of her papers which were strewn across the counter.

'I told you, I'm late,' she said. 'I have to go.'

Ray moved silently towards the door and opened it for her. She felt for her keys, couldn't find them in her pocket of her suit jacket, scrabbled in her capacious bag, slammed her briefcase on the counter again and dredged the corners. No keys.

'Christ!' She began again with her bag. She could see her hands were trembling, but she couldn't seem to do anything but this manic searching, a searching that felt like an end in itself that would continue for ever and ever, even after the keys were found.

'Are these them?' Ray was holding up her keys in his right hand.

Jeanie just looked at him, not trusting herself to speak, her heart thudding uncomfortably at the close proximity.

Ray didn't move, just held out the keys to her. 'They were on the shelf,' he said, his voice soft.

When she didn't take them, just stood gazing at him, he put them down on the top of her briefcase.

'I'd better go,' he said.

Everything seemed to slow to nothing as she watched him turn and walk towards the door. It might have been a hundred years till she heard a small voice say, 'Ray . . .' and recognized it as her own.

'I *do* have to go, I *am* late for the accountants.'

Ray nodded, smiled. 'I did believe you,' he said.

'Will you meet me later? In town? At least not anywhere near here?'

'Aren't you angry?' They were sitting in a Japanese cafe on the corner of Lisle Street sipping miso soup. The restaurant was heaving with the lunchtime rush but they'd found a cramped space in the corner under the coats, which suited them fine. Ray had taken a long time considering what she told him.

'Do you really think he made it up?'

Jeanie looked at him incredulously. 'Well, it didn't happen, so he must have.'

'It seems such an evil thing to do. I reckon he must have heard Ellie burbling on about something – you know how they do at that age – and got the wrong end of the stick.'

'Chanty said the same, but I don't even think that. You didn't see him. He wouldn't even meet my eye.'

'But Jeanie, unless the man's a moron, accusing you of being the conduit to his daughter's abuser is daft. Why would he do that?' Despite his robust tone, she could see he was worried. 'They aren't going to take it any further, are they?'

'They said no . . . I think I convinced Chanty.' She shook her head in exasperation. 'I still can't believe he said it . . . out of the blue like that.'

Ray took a drink from his beer bottle as they both sat in silence.

'It would ruin my life if there was even a hint,' he said eventually, passing his hand across his stubbly grey hair in a gesture Jeanie had come to love. 'Natalie would stop me seeing the boy, the school would be fucked – nobody has to prove anything, a rumour'd be enough to scupper me.'

Jeanie nodded. 'I'm so sorry.'

He gave her a wry smile. 'Like it's your fault.'

'They're my relatives.'

'So you don't think Ellie actually said anything?'

The waitress stood beside the table with their food, and both of them looked at it with the same disregard.

'She might have mentioned you. She adores you and Dylan, you make her laugh. But her stories involve all the people she knows and make no sense whatsoever.

She's too young to know that sitting on someone's knee might be a problem. Anyway, that's irrelevant, she's never been on your knee.' Jeanie wrenched her suit jacket off, suddenly boiling hot.

Ray shook his head, clearly bewildered. 'Do you think someone else, another man, could be involved? It *is* true, but she just got the man muddled up?'

Jeanie hadn't thought of this, and quickly trawled through the possibilities. 'She never sees anyone except me and George and Alex . . . not on her own.'

She picked at the rice and chicken with her chopsticks. 'Of course, they both have her on their knee all the time.'

Ray gave her a quizzical look and she laughed.

'No, no . . . I really don't think either my husband or my son-in-law's a child-molester.'

'Just a liar.'

'But the truth isn't always the point, is it?'

The words hung in the air. They both knew what she meant. The momentary ache of pleasure Jeanie had experienced as she sat down opposite Ray was lost.

'I've never been blackmailed before in my life,' Ray stated. He looked baffled, out of his depth, his studied calm temporarily deserting him, but she watched as he took a slow breath and seemed to retreat into himself for a moment. 'In aikido we're taught to see our attacker as someone who's lost touch with their own nature, not as evil. It's not about combat but self-defence; we use the attacker's body weight to deflect the attack.'

'Sounds admirable, but I don't see how it helps if he's not actually coming at you with a machete.'

Ray shrugged. 'He'll show his hand eventually.'

He made to take her hand, but she withdrew it, clasping them beneath the table.

'You know we can't meet again.' She heard the dull clunk of her words.

Ray said nothing, just lowered his head.

'More tea?' The waitress hovered with a large earthenware pot. They both nodded, although neither had finished the last cup.

'This thing with Alex frightened me, Ray. It's your life, my marriage. God knows how Chanty would react if she found out I was cheating on her father . . . I couldn't bear to lose Ellie again. It can't be worth it.'

She looked beseechingly at him, but his grey-green eyes met hers with what seemed like amusement.

'What are we like, eh? Two old codgers wracked like star-crossed teenage lovers.'

She found herself laughing, and for a moment nothing else mattered.

'Less of the old codger, please.'

'Jeanie, it's our turn, isn't it? We've both done our time with relationships and family, in my case not particularly successfully, maybe. But you've done the right thing, been there for them all. Then suddenly there's this powerful connection neither of us expected.' His voice dropped. 'I think about you all the time, Jeanie. It may not be cool to tell you, but hey . . .'

Jeanie found herself blushing.

'I know we don't know the first thing about each other, not really. But that doesn't seem to matter. I'm about to burst into cliché, but you make me feel . . . well . . . new. Like that ad: "You, but on a good day." Is this love? I've no idea, but it doesn't seem to matter what it is.'

For a moment there was silence. The word 'love' lay between them, too delicate to be touched.

When Jeanie didn't speak, he added, 'All I'm saying is . . .' He paused, threw his arms in the air in frustration. 'It's simple . . . not seeing you is a very bleak option for me.'

'What can I do?' Her voice sounded feeble and small.

Now he took both her hands in his, the food forgotten, the other customers dwindling to background noise.

'Jeanie, we can't *do* anything. There's no plan that will make this all OK. We just have to live with it, deal with things as they come up. If you have to walk away, then so be it, I'll have to deal with that.' He paused, squeezed her hands tight. 'But this seems so precious . . .'

She felt him gently wipe away the single tear that had escaped her control.

'I'm always bloody crying these days,' she muttered angrily.

Ray drew back. 'I've said, I'll never pressure you . . . it wouldn't be fair. You have a marriage to lose.'

'We can't meet with the children any more.'

'No . . . no, obviously not.'

He seemed to be waiting for her, but she didn't know what to say.

'Will I see you again, though?'

Jeanie shook her head. 'I say I can't with one breath, and with the next I can't resist you . . .'

He smiled at that, but it was a nervous smile. 'But . . .' he offered.

'But what will happen next? We meet for a drink, we want more. In the end we have more. What then?'

Ray smiled. 'I can't answer that, Jeanie.'

'It isn't funny.'

'It may not be, but it doesn't feel like a disaster either . . . does it?'

Jeanie shook her head, unable to think about it any more. She looked at her watch. 'I've got to get back in a minute. Can we talk about something else? Something normal, like . . .'

They looked at each other and began to laugh.

'Politics or the weather isn't doing it for me. All I want to do is kiss you.' Ray raised his eyebrows in question.

She looked around, panicky. 'Not here.'

'Where, then?'

'We're too old to kiss in public.'

Ray chuckled. 'I reckon most people are. That certainly limits the options in the middle of Chinatown, though.' He waved at the girl to bring the bill.

'So in theory,' he whispered, 'would you like to kiss me?'

Holding his gaze, Jeanie felt a wave of desire which, against her will, produced a small gasp. Ray's face told her he didn't need more of an answer.

12

'We could put the piano in here, for Ellie.'

It was as if George had bought the house already. As they entered each empty room, her husband started dragging virtual furniture from their Highgate house and installing it in the Old Rectory, Woodmanstead (pronounced Woomsted). The washed and brushed estate agent, James, was standing patiently by, toying with his cufflinks and agreeing with everything George said in an overly hearty manner. He had a glint in his eye, Jeanie thought, that must surely be the reflection of pound signs.

'This is the first house we've seen,' she hissed at George.

'But that doesn't mean we can't buy it, does it?' he answered mildly.

'Of course not, but we should at least look at others. This is very expensive.'

She knew it was a waste of time. George would either buy it or not, regardless of the price, regardless almost of what she thought.

'It's so perfect,' he kept muttering, as the glint in the agent's eye got brighter and brighter.

'Stop saying how much you like it, will you? It'll only up the price. He's not on our side, remember.'

Jeanie was tired. She had forgotten what it was like to have a good night's sleep. After lunch Ray had taken her to St James's Park. The hot weather had vanished as if it never was, and in its place was a sharp breeze and intermittent rain. The park had the usual trail of tourists, but not even many of them, and Jeanie and Ray had sat on his coat under a may tree, him cross-legged with an effortlessly straight back, her clutching her legs to her body, her suit skirt demurely pulled taut over her knees.

'You look strange in that suit,' he commented.

She felt a bubble of laughter burst up through the layers of worry.

'How rude! I'll have you know this is my venerated

Accountant Suit. I never wear it for anything else. Is it that bad?'

'I didn't say it was bad, just . . . not you. No, maybe it is bad. Wouldn't he do your accounts just as well if you wore jeans?'

'I've always thought not. It's an old-fashioned respect thing, I suppose.'

They watched as a large trail of teenage tourists shambled past, entirely unaware of the world outside their exclusive bubble.

Ray pointed at them, 'I blame central heating.'

'For what?'

'We're tougher than them by a mile. But we've molly-coddled them out of existence and as a result they have no backbone.' He began to get into his stride and Jeanie could tell this was not a new rant. 'I was brought up in Portsmouth, my father was in the Merchant Navy, and we had a draughty bungalow with a "turn-the-coals-up-Norman" fire . . .'

'The ones with the orange plastic coals on top of the bars?' she interrupted him. 'I remember them. They were better than the one we had, one of those grisly honeycomb gas jobs. It was either freezing or like a tropical rainforest.'

Ray chuckled. 'Exactly. None of this namby-pamby

heating. I used to hold my clothes up in front of the fire before I put them on in the morning, they were so bloody perishing. What do this lot . . .' he threw his arm dismissively in the wake of the foreign school children, 'know about that? It's our fault.'

'Ooh aye, and we had nought to eat but the neighbour's rubbish and one pair of shoes between twelve of us.' She pushed him playfully. 'It's just a changing world, isn't it?'

'No, but seriously, take people like your son-in-law.' Ray was on a roll. 'He obviously thinks he's God, and I reckon that arrogance comes not from self-belief but from mollycoddling and indulgence.'

Jeanie frowned. 'Please, let's not talk about him again.'

He grabbed her arm and pulled her close. 'OK, I'll shut up if you kiss me.'

The kiss, which she willingly gave, was long and very tender. For a moment she forgot she was in a public space. She just wanted it to last forever, to erase the painful decision she had made.

As they drew apart, Jeanie sighed.

'Ray . . . this can never work.'

She made to get up.

He rose with her, shaking his jacket free of grass. 'It's your call,' he said, reaching over and cupping his hand to her cheek as he looked down at her. For a moment she let it lie, her whole body luxuriating in his gentle touch, the pain of loss hovering beyond it like a predator. She bent to pick up her bag and her briefcase.

'I'd better go.'

'Can we potter about on our own for a bit?' George was asking James, and James obliged by going and leaning languidly on the open door of his Peugeot, his silver mobile pressed to his ear.

George took her hand and walked her upstairs to the stunning first-floor bedroom, the 'master bedroom', in agent-speak.

'Look at that view.' The house was situated at the head of a valley, and the window looked out towards the rolling Blackdown Hills. Sunlight dappled the hillside and the pink-white apple blossoms in the orchard. Sheep wandered in the fields. It was almost a caricature of the pastoral idyll. 'Imagine us waking up to that.'

'It's beautiful,' she agreed, but inside she was dead.

'Not too big, but lots of room for the family,' George was intoning. 'If we get going on the contracts James says we could be in by the end of the summer. There's no chain, the owner died over a year ago apparently, and his rels are anxious to get the estate sorted.' He put his arm round Jeanie in a totally uncharacteristic gesture. 'Can't you just see Ellie running about that garden?' He peered over Jeanie's shoulder and pointed. 'Look, there's even a swing on the old oak.' His delight was both touching and ominous. Jeanie knew she was already trapped. If she didn't say something, or do something, this would be her home for the rest of her life. What had Ray said? There was no plan that could make it all OK?

'Where's the nearest town?'

'James says Honiton and Chard. It's quite isolated, I grant you, but the village looks nice. And the sea's not far.'

Jeanie tried to imagine herself here. She'd left home for London at eighteen to train as a nurse, her first home being the nurses' home by Russell Square, a stark, dreary building, but situated in what seemed to her to be the centre of the universe. That was forty-two years ago. She watched her husband as he chatted seriously with the smooth young man. His certainty made it seem as if he'd been planning this for years.

George was bubbling with excitement as they drove home along the A303. He kept looking over at Jeanie and smiling encouragingly, until she felt so pressured she wanted to scream.

'We can put the house on the market immediately, but it doesn't matter if it takes a while to sell, we can bridge. Once we've got the Rectory we can do it up the way we want it over time; it's perfectly liveable in, don't you think?'

Then when she didn't answer, 'You seem a bit silent, old girl. I know you weren't keen on the idea at first, but seeing the house must've changed your mind, no?'

And when she still said nothing, 'Come on, Jeanie, spit it out. What's the problem? Is it the location? Or the size? Tell me.' He laughed. 'Turning sixty has put you in a very odd mood, I must say.'

She was almost too irritated to reply. But she knew her husband. He would go on nagging her till she answered.

'I've told you what I think, George. I don't have anything else to say right now.'

Jeanie waited every night, as if for a lover, for the moment when George went upstairs and she had the safety of her own bedroom. Then she cried – huge, almost silent sobs, muffled hot under the duvet, which left her gasping for breath. The tears weren't just for

Ray. They began for that reason, but then they seemed to morph into a much larger sadness that encompassed her constrained childhood, her brother's illness and death, the lie she had lived with her husband since he left her bed, the man that George had become. Tears should be cleansing, she thought, but these were not. These just seemed to intensify into something cruel, almost violent, until she felt she would crack apart. Yet every night was the same, every night she found herself crying – even looked forward to it – and couldn't stop until eventually she would sink into an exhausted sleep.

'Mum, you look terrible.' Her daughter peered into her face from the driving seat as Jeanie got into Chanty's car. Ellie was stretching out her hand from the back, trying to reach her grandmother.

'Gin . . . come too . . . look, I got my bag, an' my underbrella.' She waved a lurid pink bag towards Jeanie, into which was stuck the green dinosaur umbrella. Jeanie kissed the proffered hand.

Chanty was waiting, hands on the steering wheel, for her mother to fasten her seat belt.

'Shall I go in the back with Ellie? Keep her quiet?'

Chanty shook her head, her tight, blonde ponytail swinging behind her head. 'She'll be fine. I want her to sleep if poss. She'll be a nightmare if she doesn't.'

It was Sunday and they were going to visit Aunt Norma for tea. She always prepared a proper tea: fingers of white bread and butter with the crusts cut off and a magnificent wooden cake stand with biscuits on the top, fancies in the middle and a big, round fruit cake on the bottom, to be eaten in your fingers, of course. Oh dear, yes, Aunt Norma had a horror of cake forks, said they were a 'nasty continental invention'. They drank lapsang souchong, leaves not bags, naturally, out of fine bone-china cups and saucers, and Aunt Norma always trusted Ellie with her own china mug and a tiny amount of tea. A trust which, much to both Chanty and Jeanie's surprise, the child never betrayed by spilling a single drop on the cream carpet.

'Mum?' Chanty kept glancing over as they drove round beside Wimbledon Common. 'Are you sure you're OK? You look so tired.'

'I'm fine.'

'Are you still upset by the business with that man in the park?'

'I . . . probably best not to go into that again.'

Chanty's profile was tense. 'I had to ask, Mum, about Ellie. You'd have done the same if it'd been me.'

'It's not that. I'm fine, honestly, darling.'

'Tell me, Mum . . . please. I'm sorry I doubted you.

It wasn't you, really, it was just when Alex told me what Ellie had said.'

Jeanie laid a hand on her daughter's arm. 'I've told you, it's not that.'

'Well, what is it, then? Dad says you've been totally not-yourself, he's worried you're ill. Please tell me . . . is it the move? Dad said you loved the house.'

'It was a beautiful house, but that doesn't mean I want to live in it. I'd rather not have this conversation now, if that's OK. I'll be fine. I will.'

But her daughter was not a quitter. She pulled over to the side of the road in one of the streets behind Wimbledon Village and stopped the car.

'Sorry, Mum, we aren't going to Auntie Norma's until you've told me what's wrong.' She glanced over to check that Ellie was still asleep, then folded her arms and waited.

Jeanie was too exhausted to argue. 'OK . . . well, I suppose it is the move. I don't want to go, to give up my shop. I don't want to . . . well, give up on life.' She saw Chanty begin to line up her objections and held her hand up. 'Don't tell me the advantages of Somerset. I'm not a fool, I can see them for myself, but . . . well, I've felt recently that everyone has stopped listening to me. You, Dad, you don't seem to trust me to know my own mind any more. Take the park incident . . . or lack of incident, you could say. You implied I was dotty enough not to have remembered my own actions. And then not to believe me when I told you the truth. And Dad, well, Dad has just bulldozed me over this move. I said right at the start that I didn't want to live in the country full-time. I suggested we get a cottage if he wanted to spend more time out of London. God knows we can afford it. But he just hasn't listened. He's just gone ahead and offered for somewhere, and he doesn't seem to hear me when I say I don't want to move. In fact, over the last few years, since he retired, he's become more and more dictatorial. He never used to be like this, he was pretty easy-going before. Perhaps it's him you should be worrying about, not me. My problem is simple. I don't want to sell my shop. And I don't want to rot in the country with him.' Her voice was harsh and strident as she sat pressing her hands together in her lap, not looking at her daughter. 'I'm sixty, not a hundred and sixty, and I've done nothing to warrant this lack of respect from either of you.'

There was silence. 'Oh, Mum . . .'

'Please . . . please, don't . . .' She knew that Chanty's sympathy would be the last straw. She was only holding on to herself by sheer force of will. 'I'll be fine, I said. I'll get over it.' Despite her best efforts, the tears were close to the surface now. 'It's just been a difficult time.'

'I feel this is partly my fault.' Chanty paused, looking stricken. 'But you and Dad are OK, aren't you? I mean, you're getting on all right generally?'

It was the first time Chanty had ever asked her that, and she had a sudden powerful urge to tell her daughter the truth. *No, it's not OK, it hasn't been for years: your father's hiding something; I've met a man I want to run off with . . . the man in the park.*

'Dear Dad,' Chanty was saying, 'you always know exactly where you are with him. That speech he gave at your sixtieth was just heavenly, don't you think?'

Jeanie thought this was less than subtle as a ploy, but she nodded anyway.

'You must talk to him, Mum. Tell him how you feel. If you truly don't want to move, I'm sure he's not going to make you. And as you say, you could get a cottage for a while and see how it goes.'

'I'll be fine,' she repeated for what seemed like the hundredth time, and this time she tried to perk up, to let her daughter know that she did indeed feel better, when in fact nothing had changed at all except that Chanty's worst fears had been allayed.

'Yeah, but talk to him, Mum, promise?'

Jeanie smiled and promised and Chanty started the car.

She was in the shop on Tuesday morning when she looked up and was shocked to see Dylan standing there. He was with a woman perhaps in her late twenties, a pale, anxious-looking person with a nonetheless pretty face, who kept a tight grip on the hood of Dylan's striped sweatshirt, pulling him back whenever he took a step. Dylan grinned up at Jeanie.

'Hi, Dylan. How are you?'

The woman looked at her curiously.

'We meet in the park sometimes,' Jeanie explained, 'with my granddaughter, Ellie.' She knew this must be Ray's daughter, and she was finding it hard to still her heart.

'Oh, yes ... Dad said. And Dylan's mentioned her,' – she pulled an apologetic face – 'not always kindly.'

Jeanie laughed and was surprised at how normal she sounded. 'I'm afraid Ellie's obsessed with your son.'

Dylan grinned. 'She wants to play all the time but she can't because she's too little.'

'Yes, well, you should always be kind, you know

that,' the woman muttered sternly to him. 'By the way, I'm Natalie.'

'Jeanie.' They nodded, smiled. 'How is your father?'

The girl nodded again. 'Yeah, he's OK. Says he's very busy with the centre.' She looked at Jeanie. 'Do you still go to the park? Dylan hasn't mentioned you for a while.'

Jeanie pretended to be busy with the till. 'Not Waterlow . . . my daughter likes me to take Ellie to Priory Park instead, she thinks the play stuff is more stimulating.'

This sounded so patently ridiculous that she wondered Natalie didn't laugh in her face, but Natalie just nodded seriously.

'I know what she means . . . the new area in Waterlow is great, but it's not really for children your grand-daughter's age. Priory's a bit far for us, we're North.'

'Grandpa does the wobbly log,' Dylan interrupted, looking for confirmation from Jeanie.

'He certainly does, and brilliantly too.' She saw the pride in his eyes at her words.

Natalie was searching the shelves. 'Do you have any rice milk?'

'Rice milk, oat milk, soya . . .' Jeanie pointed to the shelf.

'Soya's bad for you, it gives you cancer,' Natalie announced in her light voice to no one in particular, 'unless it's fermented, which milk isn't. These look beautiful,' she said, indicating a basket of pears. She carefully selected two and put them on the counter.

'I had one for breakfast, they're delicious.' Jeanie wondered if Natalie knew about her and Ray, then remembered her expression of mild curiosity when she had greeted Dylan and thought not. She was sure Ray wouldn't have sent her, although part of her wished he had.

'Does Ray still take Dylan on Thursdays?' she found herself asking, then bit her tongue on the words.

'When he can. But the childminder has finished at the hospital, so he sometimes does other days. Do you have any spelt loaves?'

Jeanie picked one from the window, put it in a paper bag and set it beside Natalie's other purchases. The young woman bore little physical resemblance to her father, but Jeanie saw the same set of the mouth, implying control perhaps, or a determination to do the right thing.

'Give him my regards,' Jeanie said, no longer able to bear the reminder this woman and her child represented, however unintentional, yet at the same time wanting to talk about Ray till hell froze over. It was two weeks and four days since she had walked away from him in St James's Park, and true to his word, he had left it up to her to be in touch.

Jeanie felt she was involved in a daily battle of endurance, where she rose almost earlier than George, already exhausted, then used every means at her disposal to stop herself from thinking about Ray, from contacting Ray, and from comparing the way she felt about George to the intensity of her fleeting liaison with Ray. She failed on a daily basis on the first and last: it was only in her determination not to contact Ray that she succeeded. She felt this was no mean triumph, but the comparison threw into stark relief how intensely angry she was, angry in a solid, ancient, historic way, with her husband.

'Why don't you just leave him?' Rita demanded, finally losing patience with her friend. 'It's making you ill.'

They were sitting on Jeanie's terrace with a large glass of Sauvignon each, the only light coming from the kitchen behind and a candle flickering in the wind on the far edge of the table in front of them. Jeanie had a navy jumper on, but Rita was wrapped in a knitted throw from the kitchen sofa, only her strong, square face and her drinking arm visible above the mulberry folds. For once she was too focused on her friend's problem to request they go inside.

'Leave George?'

'Er, yes, George. Who else?' Rita shook her head. 'You make it sound as if the idea was ridiculous.'

'It is. How could I leave him? We've been together almost my entire adult life.'

'And that's a good reason to stay?'

They stared at each other in silence, both of them aware that this was not the first time they had had this unsatisfactory conversation.

'If you'd said, "I can't leave him because I love him", then that'd be a valid reason.'

'I do love him,' Jeanie said quietly, but with conviction.

She heard her friend's exasperated sigh.

'Yes, but does he love you? Bill wouldn't dream of even considering a move that I . . . that both of us . . . weren't totally happy with. You have to tell him, Jeanie.'

'About Ray?'

'No, not about Ray, you dozy mare. Tell him you won't, I repeat *won't*, not "don't want to", but *will not* move to the country.'

'But maybe it's for the best, Rita.'

Rita banged her glass down on the wooden table. 'Oh, for Christ's sake. Listen to yourself.'

Jeanie flinched. 'Shhh . . . keep your voice down.' She looked backwards to the kitchen.

'He's out, Jeanie, he can't hear.'

'He might come back early.' George had gone to a retirement dinner for a colleague at his old firm. Jeanie had thought it strange he should want to be reminded of the team who had chucked him on the scrap heap so soon, but George had been insistent he go.

'So he hears. I think it'd be great if he did, since you're clearly not going to mention it to him.'

'Please, Rita, don't be mean. I can't take it.'

Rita's face softened and she leaned towards her friend. 'Sorry, darling, but I can't stand to see you so down. This is really important. If George sells up and you go with him to the country, that's it. You'll have made your bed. This is the moment to make a stand. Just tell him, please. Or I will.'

Jeanie looked horrified at Rita's threat. 'Promise you'll do no such thing. OK, OK . . . I'll talk to him. But I know he won't listen. He's convinced himself, and Chanty, that I don't know my own mind, and that when I get down there it'll be bucolic perfection.'

Her friend didn't reply, just went on looking at her

as if there was nothing more she could say.

'And you know what? If I just go along with it, and get as far away from temptation as I can, perhaps I will enjoy it. Perhaps' – she paused – 'I'll forget this madness . . . forget him.'

'And that's what you want?'

Jeanie shrugged. 'Maybe, yes . . . the alternative seems just too extreme, too ridiculous.'

'What is the alternative? Seriously, what options are you throwing about in your mind?'

She took a deep breath. 'Well, leaving George, running off into the sunset with a man I barely know – not that he's asked me to – dumping my family and decades of what has been a good marriage. Not perfect,' she added in response to Rita's raised eyebrows. 'But I have been happy . . . content . . . you've seen.'

Rita nodded. 'Things change though, Jeanie. Don't forget, you've maybe got another thirty years of George.'

They both laughed.

'Put like that . . .'

'What's the joke?'

The two women jumped as George, smart in a dark suit and navy tie, suddenly popped his head through the French windows.

'Oh, we were just imagining what it would be like

to leave our husbands and run off with a tasty toy boy,' Rita replied comfortably, while Jeanie tried to still her heartbeat, grateful for the semi-darkness.

'That would be funny,' George said with a laugh. 'Can I get you ladies a nightcap?'

Rita yawned and began to unravel herself from the throw. 'Thanks, George, but I think I'll be on my way.'

'Now I feel guilty for breaking up your evening,' George said, swaying slightly. 'Please, stay, have one more. A brandy, perhaps? I've got some really good Armagnac . . .'

'No, I really must be off.' As she bent to kiss Jeanie goodbye, she hissed fiercely in her ear, 'Talk to him. Now.'

'I'm a bit tipsy,' George declared, unnecessarily, once he'd shut the door on Rita. He smiled loosely at Jeanie, waved his hand at the bottle of brandy he'd dug out of the cupboard. 'Come on, have a snifter.'

Jeanie knew it would be impossible to get any sense out of him in this state, but she suddenly wanted to be with him, to have fun with him, to test, almost, what was left.

'OK . . . just a small one.'

13

Tonight? The usual? Ray's text had said in reply to Jeanie's.

She had weakened. George had left that morning for a golfing weekend at Gleneagles. It was an annual trip that his golf-buddy Danny organized with six other men. They would fly to Edinburgh, where a chauffeur-driven people-carrier would pick them up and drive them to the hotel. They would spend the next two days playing an intensely competitive private tournament. The winner had the dubious honour of paying for everyone's dinner on the Sunday night. George wouldn't be home till Monday.

Having waved her husband off to the airport, his golf bag heavy on his shoulder, Jeanie had ploughed through the Friday morning at the shop in a daze. She told herself she couldn't, she wouldn't, while knowing all along that she could and she would. The text she sent as she'd sat on her lunch break in Caffè Nero, her hand shaking so much she could hardly fashion the words, had merely said, *Would you like to meet up?* and then she waited.

Nothing. She checked to make sure her mobile was working. It was. Nothing. Her heart wouldn't stop racing, she could eat nothing, but still the mobile stayed silent. By three o'clock she had begun to train herself into the possibility that he didn't want to see her again, that what had barely begun was now over. But she didn't believe it.

When his text finally came, she missed it. Margot was back, eliciting information from Jeanie about hyaluronic acid and whether it would help her skin rashes. She got back to the till and saw the message, and thought she might faint.

'Bad news, dear?' Margot asked kindly, watching her face.

The Greek restaurant was practically empty; it was early. Jeanie had left the shop deliberately late, so as not to have too much time to think, then hurried across the park, taking great gulps of the soft evening air. Her body felt pumped with freedom and exhilaration at what she was doing, her steps so light it was as if she were flying.

Ray was waiting for her, leaning against the wall of the restaurant, his face also alive with anticipation.

'Hi.'

'Hello.'

Both stood silently, suddenly shy, until she leant against him, feeling the softness of his shirt, breathing in the heavenly scent of his skin, and his arms went round her. From habit she glanced about.

'No one's looking,' he said softly. But she drew away from him.

'Drink?' he asked, and opened the door of the restaurant.

They ordered the house red. Jeanie pretended to study the menu, but the items danced in a blur.

'I can't decide . . . I . . . don't know what I want.'

Ray looked up at the waiter. 'Can we have a large bowl of chips, please?'

'Is that all?' The boy couldn't have been more than sixteen, and looked concerned, as if he might be blamed for this customer's vagaries.

'For now,' Ray added as a sop as he handed back the menus.

Jeanie breathed a sigh of relief. 'Just what I need.'

She quickly gulped a mouthful of wine. 'I shouldn't be here . . . but George went away for the weekend.'

Ray raised his eyebrows, smiled.

'I promised myself I wouldn't, but . . . well, here I am.'

'Let's not even think about why or how or what. Let's just have tonight, have now.' He fixed her with his light, laughing eyes, and she just nodded.

Their chips arrived, hot and salty, delicious.

Ray, when asked, told her about his family, his child-hood. 'Dad wasn't drunk or feckless, but he was away at sea most of the time, and Mum couldn't cope. She'd worry all the time, and I guess us boys didn't make it any easier. Jimmy was always getting into trouble, but then she never disciplined us.'

'Do you see them much?'

'All dead.'

'Even your brother?'

Ray nodded. 'He died two years ago, drink-related liver problems. He was only sixty-one.' He paused. Jeanie saw the look, knew it well, of a person telling a story they don't want to get emotional about. 'I hardly saw him once he left home. He went to sea like my dad for a while, but couldn't take it and went off the rails; took to the bottle and God knows what else. I didn't even know where he was for years, then we met up again about five years ago. He saw a piece about the aikido school in the local paper and got in touch. He'd given up the booze and sorted himself out but it was too late, his liver was shot. He was back in Portsmouth again and I used to go down at weekends sometimes and visit. I wish we'd linked up earlier.'

Jeanie said nothing.

'Families, eh? We've said it before.'

'At least you got close to him again.'

'I know. But I can't help feeling it was a life wasted. Jimmy was always such a live wire, he had such spirit. I'll never know what went wrong.'

'Perhaps he enjoyed himself along the way.'

Ray grinned. 'Oh, I'm sure he did.'

He finished the last of the wine in his glass. 'Where to now?'

Jeanie had stopped thinking; the wine was doing that for her.

'Do you live close?'

Ray held her gaze. 'About a hundred yards away.'

'Seriously?'

'When I last looked.'

They were both taken up in the moment.

'Er . . . you could come back to mine.'

'I could . . .' Jeanie held her breath.

'You don't sound sure.'

'I'm not.'

'Well, perhaps we should go for a walk on the Heath instead?'

She laughed. 'No, Ray, let's go back to yours.'

The flat was on the top floor of a thirties-style building on a side street leading up to the Heath. The outside had a rundown air, the paintwork in the lobby scratched and dirty, the lift rickety. But Ray's flat was light and had an atmosphere of calm, enhanced by the spare, pale-wood furnishing and Japanese prints. She was drawn to the window, which stretched the width of the room, standing for a moment to watch the softening greens of the Heath at dusk. This was the flat, she thought, of a man seeking peace. Ray had taken his shoes off when he came in, and she heard him padding about on the stripped wooden floor behind her, turning on lamps and rummaging for glasses and wine. She reached down to flick her pumps off, loath to turn away from the view, almost as if by doing so she would be irrevocably committing herself to him. When she did turn, he had laid a bottle of red wine and two glasses on the low table by the sofa, and was running his finger along the immaculate rack of CDs.

'Chet Baker?' he asked.

Jeanie shook her head. 'Don't know him.'

'You're in for a treat . . . if you like jazz.'

'Try me.'

Baker's melancholy trumpet filled the room with its gentle, sexy rhythm, and Jeanie sank back on the sofa and closed her eyes. This place, this man, this music, this moment, all flowed together, gathering her up in a quiet intensity that made her whole being sing with pleasure. She found she was smiling.

Ray poured her a drink, but she didn't touch it.

'Are you OK?' He perched on the sofa next to her.

'Very,' she replied. She saw him begin to relax, a smile also playing around his mouth.

For a while they said nothing, just sat side by side listening to the music.

'I've wanted to bring you here since the beginning. Just so that we could be alone.'

Jeanie reached her hand out and he took it.

'Not for nefarious purposes,' he grinned, 'but so that we could stop worrying about everyone else.'

'It's perfect,' she whispered.

Desire linked them, an unspoken certainty, but they

were in no hurry; the pleasure of touch, of scent, of just being close to each other, was enough.

'Ray . . .' She wanted to say everything, to explain, to tell him what he'd done to her, how he made her feel, but the words wouldn't come. She met his gaze and, no longer restrained by the outside world, allowed herself to fall at last into that intense space, a space she had glimpsed but not dared enter till now, where they were completely together. She felt his lips on hers and the desire was finally let loose, coursing through her body until she could barely breathe.

She had no idea how long they lay there; this was another place, without boundaries or time.

'Jeanie?' She saw Ray looked troubled, his eyes full of pain.

She pulled herself up. 'What is it?'

Ray gathered her to him, her face tucked in against his shoulder. Still in a daze from their kisses, she waited for him to speak.

'Jeanie, I want you so much, but this is huge for both of us. This isn't just a . . . just sex, at least not for me.'

She smiled up at him. 'Shouldn't that be my line?'

Ray's face cleared; she heard his chuckle rumble inside his chest. 'OK . . . but I don't think we should rush into it.' He looked down at her. 'It's . . . well, "huge" is the only word I can think of right now.'

'Have you not . . . had a relationship . . . since Jess?'

'Sex occasionally, nothing more.' She heard Ray sigh. 'It scares me, Jeanie.'

She sat up, reached for her wine. She didn't understand and was suddenly fearful that he was comparing her with his previous love.

'So what happened to enjoying the moment?' she teased, and he laughed.

'It's just I love being with you as it is, even if we are just eating chips or playing with Dylan and Ellie. If we make love . . . well, it takes it to another level.'

She waited. 'Are you worried it'll be no good with me?' she asked finally, when he didn't speak. 'I know I haven't had much practice this last decade.'

Ray looked horrified. 'Christ, no . . . but . . .' He shrugged hopelessly. 'I'm not explaining this very well, am I?'

'What, Ray? Please tell me.' His hesitation was causing echoes of George to spring to mind. Was it her, she wondered; was there something about her that put men off wanting to make love to her?

Ray got up and began pacing the length of the coffee table and back.

'I suppose what I'm saying is actually very simple.' He stopped, hands on his hips, and held Jeanie's gaze. 'I suppose I'm frightened that I'm falling in love with you, and that if we make love I shall be hooked. And . . . then you'll go back to your husband.'

Jeanie couldn't help smiling. It was from relief as much as anything else. So he did desire her.

'I found these last weeks very hard, when you wouldn't see me.' He held his hands up as she began to object. 'I totally understand why you couldn't, don't think I'm blaming you. But nothing's changed, Jeanie. We're still where we were three weeks ago.'

Jeanie realized suddenly that this was not just about her.

'Tell me about Jess,' she said, and saw the look of pained surprise in Ray's eyes.

He sat back down on the sofa and held his hands under his thighs, in a gesture which seemed very child-like.

'It wasn't Jess herself, so much as losing her,' he said, looking anxiously towards her as he spoke. 'Are you sure you want to hear about her?'

Jeanie nodded.

'I loved her very much. What's to say? She was young . . . which caused problems sometimes. It was just the

average life, I suppose. I had a successful print business with a friend, Mike – mostly stuff, brochures and
the like, for the marine companies in Portsmouth. She
worked for an IT company in HR – whatever that
means.'

'It was called Personnel in our day.'

'Anyway, Jess was good at it. And they worked her
to the bone. I thought she was tired because she worked
so hard. She got sick of me sounding off about her
hours. But it wasn't anything to do with her work, she
had bloody cancer all the time. And if I'd just had the
nous to get her to a doctor, they might have saved her.'

Ray talked as if this was now a story, a tale that had
an unhappy ending. His delivery was still angry, but
there was a quality of rote about it, as if he had repeated
the same sentences over and over again. She didn't know
if he had said them to others, or only to himself, but
Jeanie knew he didn't need her to tell him that Jess's
death was not his fault.

'She was so young, Jeanie. Only thirty-two when
she died. That's too soon to die.'

Jeanie nodded. 'Too soon indeed.' She watched his
face contort, battered and tanned as if by life, not the
weather.

'But I wasn't really telling you this so you could feel

sorry for me. The real point of my story is that I didn't deal with Jess's death, with losing her, at all well. In fact, I went to pieces. I began drinking heavily and neglecting the business. Mike put up with it for a while, but then he had to cut me loose, or the whole thing would've gone down the pan. And of course, thanks to the money he bought me out with, although it wasn't much, I could live without working for a while and drink myself into a stupor on a daily basis. God, how I wallowed.'

'It's understandable.'

'Yes, for a month or two. But this dragged on into years, two to be precise. Sometimes I didn't go out for days, except to get more whisky. I was probably months short of killing myself from liver damage like Jimmy.'

Ray reached over to take Jeanie's hand again. For a moment he played with it, turning it over in his own, stroking the fingers one by one, his mind still lodged in the past.

'So what happened? How did you recover?'

He chuckled softly. 'You're going to think me a crackpot, but I reckon I was saved by the universe.'

Jeanie raised her eyebrows, 'Are we talking God here?'

'I prefer to call it the universe. "God" always smacks

of organized religion, which doesn't do it for me, but call it what you like, it was just so fortuitous. I was in the usual mess, drunk from dawn to dusk, unshaven, gaunt, probably looking like one of those street people we avoid at the Archway on a daily basis. One day I had to go to the cash machine. We . . . I lived just behind the dockyard, and I walked along the waterfront in a daze to get to the machine. I didn't feel so well, so I sat down on a bench next to a man, fit-looking, but very old, like about eighty, who kept staring at me.

' "What are you staring at?" I asked him, pretty aggressively, but he didn't seem offended.

' "I'm staring at a man at the end of his tether," he replied calmly.

' "What's it to you?" I said, or something like that. I was well pissed off at being challenged.

' "It's everything to me," he said, "to see someone so beaten."

'I suppose it was the first time for an age that I had been spoken to at all, beyond the supermarket checkout girl telling me how much the booze cost, and it brought me up short. I had no one to care, my parents had been dead for years, my brother vanished and probably in much the same state as I was, my friends drifted away.

' "I am beaten," I admitted. "But there's nothing anyone can do about it."

' "That's true," said the old man, "no one except you."

'I laughed at that, not a good laugh; even in my dazed state it sounded cruel and cynical.

' "Right. That's right. No one but myself, and I don't give a fuck."

'The man nodded. "I can see that."

' "So don't give me any lectures about how I've got so much to give, how life is so precious."

' "I wouldn't dream of it," the man said. "But there is one thing I want to tell you."

'I had convinced myself that I didn't give a toss about anything at all, but I remember finding myself intrigued as to what he would say. He could see I was interested, and he seemed to measure his words, as if he wanted to be careful to get it right first time. Perhaps he knew there wouldn't be a second chance.

' "I have spent my life in pursuit of meaning. Like you, I went through a phase where nothing mattered except pity, for myself, not for others. When I was at rock bottom and close, I believe, to some sort of death, a friend suggested I go with him to the aikido school where he was taking classes. I pooh-poohed this. Martial arts? Me? I could hardly get out of bed. But he insisted, turned up at my house and virtually dragged me. I went because I had to. I was all of a tither, hardly able to stand without support, the tremor in my hands so severe I thought people must notice and judge. But I stayed because I wanted to. Since then it's been the central plank of my life, both physically and emotionally."

'He got up, and I remember a sense of panic that he was leaving me.

' "I would never presume to tell you what to do, nor even suggest it. I am merely telling you what happened to me."

'And with that he walked off, a tall, proud man, neither stooped nor stiff as his age would have implied. I wanted desperately to talk to him more − I had forgotten how much human contact meant to me − but my stupid pride stopped me from calling him back. The next day, and the day after, for a whole week I went to the same bench and waited for him, but I never saw him again. It was another month before I started checking out the local aikido school, and I half expected to find the old man there. He wasn't, but it didn't matter: like him I never looked back.'

Jeanie could see his eyes misting over as he remembered.

'He saved my life, Jeanie. Sounds like a cliché, but he did.' Ray smiled, shook himself. 'That's what I mean by the universe. When I think back to him now, it feels almost as if he wasn't real, just a visitation.'

'Maybe it doesn't matter.'

'But I told you the story for selfish reasons. I'm terrified of loss, of what it might do to me. You . . . that's why I'm trying to hold back.' He grinned ruefully. 'It's not working, of course, but I am trying.'

When she looked at her watch it was past three in the morning.

'It's happened again.' She began to panic, as if the hour was significant, somehow dangerous.

'You can stay if you like.'

'No . . . no, better not.' Suddenly she wanted to be on her own, to savour the evening, to have some break from the intensity of him.

'I'll walk you.'

They set off into the cold May night, up Swain's Lane, past the cemetery and on to Highgate Hill.

'We live so close,' she whispered as they got near. 'Don't come any further.'

Ray laughed. 'Nosey neighbours?'

'Nosey as hell.'

'If George is away, can we meet tomorrow?'

'I'm in the shop all day. Sundays are busy,' she told him regretfully.

'And I have to babysit Dylan in the evening.'

He pulled her into the shadow of the wall beside the church, kissed her softly. She had wanted to be on her own before, but now she clung to him, never wanting to leave the shelter of his arms.

She slept for only a few hours, and woke early, forgetting for a moment that today there would be no George with a cup of tea, smiling brightly and throwing back the curtains. She seemed to inhabit another world now, a world full of sensuality and indulgence, and to be another person. Instead of the normally practical Jeanie who leapt from her bed each morning at her husband's bugle call, who never lounged in her dressing gown, nor put off showering or bedmaking, who always had breakfast on the table by eight, she felt strangely centred and whole, as if that other woman were an impostor who had marched around her periphery putting on an act for years. She refused to get up, and snuggled down beneath the soft, warm duvet, still drowning in Ray's caresses. 'I'll have another hour,' she told herself, quailing at the thought of Saturday mayhem at the shop.

The next thing she was aware of was the phone buzzing on the bedside table.

'Jeanie?' It was George.

'Hi . . . hi, how's it going?'

'Did I wake you? Surely not, it's gone nine.' George sounded chirpy and robust.

'No. I was just off to the shop,' she lied. 'Sorry, I was deep in thought.'

'OK . . . We had a marvellous day yesterday: the weather's perfect, a bit windy, but you'd expect that at Gleneagles, and guess what? I won . . . me and Roger won. Isn't that fantastic? Danny was sick as a parrot, but serves him right. He can't cheat with this lot, they've got his number. I rang you last night, but you didn't answer.'

He was obviously waiting for an explanation, and Jeanie searched frantically for a plausible one. She couldn't use Rita, as she and Bill were in Antigua for two weeks at their timeshare, and George knew this.

'Jola and I went out for a drink after work. We'd had such a tough day and we both needed it.' This was true, in part at least.

'So what time did you get back? It must have been after eleven when I rang.'

'No idea . . . we didn't leave the shop till late.' Jeanie

was too tired to worry whether this lie would be sufficient to satisfy her husband. There was a pause at the other end of the line.

'Oh . . . OK. It's just you normally say if you're going out.'

'I said, it was a last-minute thing.'

'I'm not getting at you. I was just a bit worried.'

Jeanie refused to reply to George's lie.

'Anyway,' – his tone brightened – 'we're off out now. It's clouded over, but the weather forecast says it'll hold till tonight, so I hope they're right.'

'Don't golfers play in force ten gales?'

She heard him laugh. 'They do, all the time. But this one'd rather not. Bye, old girl, have a good day.'

'You too.'

Perhaps because she wasn't actually sitting opposite her husband, watching him eating his toast and marmalade and pushing his glasses up his nose, last night seemed far removed, separate from the reality of her marriage. And nothing about the day that followed seemed real either; she existed in a fog of tiredness and euphoria that left no room for guilt.

14

The deal was done: contracts on the Old Rectory had been exchanged. George had done it in record time, driven by Jeanie knew not what to get the house secured.

'We must get this on the market.' George was blinking over his breakfast cup at her. 'Soon as.'

She nodded. 'Have you decided on an agent?'

'Oh, I think we'll go with Savills; there isn't a branch in Highgate, but there's one in Hampstead. We need someone we can trust and I've never heard of half the ones on the hill.'

'Up to you.' She picked the edge off her wholewheat toast and crunched it slowly. She'd had no appetite for weeks now, but she'd always taken good nutrition extremely seriously and she knew she had to make an effort.

George had returned from Scotland triumphant. The weekend seemed to have sparked him up, given him energy he hadn't had in years. *Was winning that important?* she wondered. Since he'd got back she'd found herself able to go through the motions without a shred of irritation with her husband. His presence, so often recently a focus for her anger, no longer seemed to annoy her. In fact she felt strangely at peace. But then she wasn't really attending to him.

'Are you listening?' she heard George asking impatiently.

She smiled. 'Sorry, what did you say?'

'I think you live on another planet sometimes,' her husband accurately surmised. 'I was saying I'll make an appointment this week.'

'Fine . . . you're dealing with it, aren't you?'

'Yes, but it would be nice if you took an interest.' He sounded uncharacteristically tetchy.

'Well, I'm not very interested in selling this house, as you well know.'

George rolled his eyes skywards. 'Not this again, Jeanie, please. We've done this, haven't we?'

Jeanie couldn't be bothered to answer, but George persisted.

'You're not going to cause trouble, are you?'

Jeanie looked up, surprised. 'Trouble? What do you mean?'

George shrugged. 'With the agents, or prospective buyers . . . being negative. It's so easy to create the wrong atmosphere.'

'I'm certainly not going to buy fresh flowers and roast coffee beans under the grill if that's what you think, George, but I won't stop you doing so if you think it'd help.'

'Jeanie, please. What is wrong with you? I just don't understand you these days. I know you weren't keen on the move at first, but you loved the house, I know you did. Do you have to keep on being so bolshie?'

'It's not worth talking to you, George, because you never listen to a word I say. Or take my opinion into account.' The anger had gone out of her words; she knew she merely sounded tired.

George got up and came round behind her, patting her ineffectually on the back.

'Come on, that's not true and you know it. Of course I value your opinion, but you blow hot and cold. I don't know where I am.'

She wanted to ask him when she had blown 'hot' on this project, but she knew it was pointless. Chanty had insisted that her father would never move if Jeanie didn't want to, and she had talked to him, as Chanty had suggested, on the day he got back from the golf. She'd sat him down at the kitchen table and told him, in words of mostly one syllable, that she did not want to move to the country. She'd stated her case calmly, had taken his own position into account by suggesting they get a weekend cottage for now, and George had responded with the usual mantra: 'You'll like it when you get there; You loved the house; Chanty thinks it's the right thing to do; You often don't realize what's best for you (but *I* do).' (This last was couched in less inflammatory terms, but the gist was clear.) It was as if she hadn't spoken.

She got up. 'Do not mention the shop to Savills.'

'Of course I won't, the shop is yours.' George must have seen the dangerous look in her eye, because his tone was conciliatory. 'But what *are* you going to do with it, Jeanie? You can't run it from Somerset.' The bullying tone was back in his voice, and Jeanie could take it no longer. Without saying a word she left the table, and the room.

Lying inert on the bed, she was beyond even crying.

Rita's words echoed in her head. Why didn't she just leave George? For the first time Jeanie looked the possibility full in the face, instead of batting it away as she had done every time Rita confronted her. But her mind baulked at the suggestion: she found she was literally unable to place herself in this scenario. It wasn't about specifics – although she could see her father rising from his grave in protest at the word 'divorce'. It was less defined, more an amorphous, overwhelming presentiment of loss, such as she'd felt when Will died. And every cell in her body resisted that pain.

Thursdays were not the same any more. Jeanie continued to avoid Waterlow Park, not because she was frightened of Alex and Chanty seeing them together – Ray had told her he very rarely took Dylan on a Thursday any more – but because it reminded her of their days together, days when things had been so simple, so thrilling, when neither knew what could happen. But today Alex had specifically asked her to meet him there and take Ellie off his hands early. He was picking her up from nursery in Dartmouth Park, where she was staying three full mornings now, and he had to be in the West End by two.

The weather had swung again, and it was warm and

sunny – a perfect early-summer day. She and Jola had shut the shop for a stocktake that morning; Jeanie had been aware for a while that older stock was being wasted in the rush to get new stuff on to the shelves, but it had been too busy recently to monitor deliveries properly. Of course it had taken longer than either of them anticipated, and now she was late. She knew Alex would be champing at the bit to get going, and hoped he wouldn't be nasty. Since the incident with Ray, he had been sheepish with her, careful not to antagonize. But she hadn't forgiven him, and she kept their conversations short.

She arrived at the bottom of the hill where the old playground was, but couldn't see either Ellie or Alex. She searched by the ducks, but there was no sign of them. Checking her phone, she saw he had left a message that she hadn't heard amongst the traffic on Highgate Hill. He had taken Ellie up to the new play area.

Hot from her walk, Jeanie made her way slowly up the hill, but as she rounded the bend she was met by the most extraordinary sight. The playground was packed, children swarming all over the apparatus, mostly toddlers and the under-fives as the older ones were still in school, but in the centre of the playground stood Alex and Ray, face to face and shouting at each other. The other parents and nannies were pretending nothing was happening, but she could tell by their silence they were absorbing every word. Her first thought was that her son-in-law had somehow found out about her and Ray and was having it out with him. Her blood ran cold.

'You're a blasted idiot.' Ray's tone was cold and controlled. 'This isn't about me or you, you selfish moron, this is about your daughter's life.'

Oh God, no, she thought, not this. Please don't let it be about this.

Alex's pretty-boy face was suffused with rage, his arms were planted firmly on his skinny hips and he was leaning in towards Ray as if he were about to hit him. Jeanie looked around for Ellie and saw her slumped, oddly quiet, by her father's feet. She also noticed Dylan, hanging behind his grandfather, his eyes round with concern.

'You butt out. This is nothing to do with you. This is my daughter and you have no right even to speak to me about her, let alone tell me how I should parent her. Fuck off, just fuck off out of here. Leave us alone.'

There was a shocked silence in the playground, even the children watching now to see what might happen.

'What in God's name are you two shouting about?' Jeanie hissed as she drew level with them.

'This bloody man is interfering in the way I look after my daughter,' Alex huffed, immediately dropping his voice. 'You tell him, he's *your* friend. Tell him to bugger off and mind his own business.' He passed his hand over his sweating forehead.

'Hi, Jeanie.' Ray looked as if he were trying hard to contain himself.

'Will someone please tell me what this is about?'

'Ellie took a fall off the log. I was right there and I heard it. She hit the side of her head on the wooden stanchion as she went down and it was a nasty crack. She fell like a stone. I know she got up after a minute or so, but she looked dazed. She didn't even cry.'

'She's perfectly all right: look at her, will you? Do you think I'd jeopardize my own daughter's safety? She's fine, she's had a bump on the head, that's all' – he threw his arms wide to take in all the other children in the playground – 'like most of this lot have every day.'

Ray turned to Jeanie, his face full of concern. 'You didn't hear it, it was a real crack and she fell so heavily. I don't know if she was momentarily concussed, but even if she wasn't, she should go and be checked out at A & E. I know a good fall from a bad one, it's part of my work.'

Alex turned angrily away. 'Oh la-di-da . . . for

Christ's sake, give it a rest. I am not taking my daughter
to A & E over a small bump. They'll think I've taken
leave of my senses. Tell him, Jean, tell him how pathetic
he's sounding.'

Jeanie had bent down and taken a look at her granddaughter. Ellie smiled up at her wanly.

'Hello, Gin . . . my did fall on wobby log and it was
ouchy on here.' She rubbed her hand on her temple,
where there was already an incipient bruise. 'Daddy
bit silly cos he shout at Way.'

Jeanie knelt to kiss her. 'Do you feel all right now,
darling?' She stroked the blonde head, her heart
pounding at the thought that some harm might come
to her.

'Yers . . . but I did hurt my arm too . . . look, Gin.'

'You're OK now, aren't you,' Alex said soothingly,
picking up his daughter and looking at the bruise. 'You
just bumped your head . . . silly Ell.'

Jeanie took a breath and wondered how best to get
Alex on her side. 'There aren't necessarily any signs at
first, Alex. If she hit her head hard she should see
someone. They won't think you're mad, I promise.
Remember, I was a nurse, and we were always happier
to have a false alarm than see a child when they already
had brain damage . . . or worse.'

Alex looked at her hard. 'This is ridiculous. I have a meeting in town with a potential buyer, and it could be huge, and you're telling me I have to go and sit in that filthy hospital and wait for four hours so that they can assure me my daughter is absolutely fine and I've wasted everyone's time? That is soooo not going to happen.' He glared at Jeanie. 'You shouldn't listen to this man. I'd have thought better of you.'

Jeanie thought quickly. 'OK, you go, Alex. You're right, you'll be late.'

'Hurray, some sense at last.' She saw the smug look he shot at Ray, who kept silent as Alex handed Ellie over to her grandmother and slung his Eastpak over his shoulder with visible relief.

'I'll see you later, darling.' He kissed his child on her nose, trying to make her laugh, but Ellie just stared silently at him. Jeanie could see a flash of doubt cross his face, but he was too wrapped up in his own triumph over Ray to back down now.

They watched as he strode down the hill.

'Wait.' She shot a warning glance at Ray, who was about to speak. Alex looked back uncertainly, but didn't wave, and as soon as he was out of sight, she turned to Ray. 'OK, let's go.'

'Come on, Dylan.' Ray shepherded his grandson

down the hill towards the east gate, following in Jeanie's footsteps.

'Where are we going, Grandpa?'

'To the hospital to check that Ellie hasn't hurt her head too badly.' He turned to Jeanie. 'Do you want me to carry her?'

Jeanie shook her head. 'I'm OK.'

Before they were halfway down the hill, Ellie started to fall asleep on Jeanie's shoulder.

'Wake up, darling.' She shook her gently. 'Don't go to sleep, now . . . come on, Ell . . .' She brushed her cheek, talking to the child all the time. 'Shall we sing? Come on, let's sing. Sing a song of sixpence . . .'

She looked over at Ray. 'She mustn't go to sleep, we've got to keep her awake.'

'Give her to me, that'll wake her.' He took Ellie, but she seemed not to notice the change. Then the little girl suddenly looked white as a sheet and vomited all over Ray's shirt.

'Oh, God, Ray, I'm sorry. But that's not a good sign.' Jeanie was feeling as if a vice were tightening round her chest. *Let her be all right, please, let her be all right*, she intoned to an invisible universe. 'Hurry, we've got to get her there as soon as possible.'

Jeanie took Ellie as they pushed through the doors

of the Whittington A & E. She rushed up to the receptionist and told her what had happened.

'She's just vomited, she's sleepy,' she added. 'I'm a nurse, please can you get someone immediately.'

Time stopped for Jeanie. There was nothing now in the world but watching this little face, so unutterably dear to her, watching for any tiny nuance in expression, colour, response; nothing but the constant mantra that became central to every thought, her plea to any power for assistance. Within seconds a young doctor had appeared from the treatment area and was showing them to a cubicle.

'I'll stay out here with Dylan, go and wash this off,' Ray said, pulling his vomit-soaked shirt away from his chest. Jeanie nodded, although she would have liked him to come. The responsibility of this sick child seemed overwhelmingly hers.

Things moved fast. The doctor checked Ellie out, called another doctor, clearly senior to the first and possibly a registrar, who got a line into her small arm and fixed it with tape. Ellie just lay there, her eyes not focusing, her hand resting in Jeanie's.

'It looks as if there might be some brain swelling, but we want to check what's going on.' The registrar, a tall, ginger-haired man of about forty with a pale, tired face, hardly glanced at Jeanie. 'When did this happen?'

'About forty minutes ago I think; I wasn't there. Are you sending her for a scan?'

'Yes.' He met her eye, obviously deciding how much she could be told.

'I used to be a nurse.'

'OK. Well, we need to do a CT scan to check for a bleed. Lucky you got her here so quickly. If there is a problem, we should be in time to fix it. Are you her mother?'

'Grandmother.'

'Right. The nurse will take you up in a minute, and I'll see you later.'

Jeanie asked the nurse to get Ray.

'They're taking her up for a scan. Don't wait, please, take Dylan home. I'll call you.'

'I'll come back.' It wasn't a question, and Jeanie didn't argue.

'They should know . . . Alex and your daughter,' Ray said, never taking his eyes off the little girl on the gurney, his shirt wet from where he had washed off the vomit.

She nodded, everything forgotten in the panic.

Despite the sign banning mobiles, she flicked to her daughter's number. It was on answer. She left a message to come at once, but that didn't seem enough. She rang George. His phone was also on answer.

'George, Ellie's had a fall and she's being checked out at the Whittington. I can't use my mobile, so can you ring Chanty and Alex and get them to come at once.' She wanted to add that their granddaughter was all right, to be reassuring, but there was no evidence yet that she was. Jeanie knew when a doctor was worried.

'Well, good news.' The ginger-haired doctor, whose name was Rob, looked thoroughly relieved. 'The scan shows she has some brain swelling; it was obviously quite a bang, but there's no actual bleed.'

Jeanie took her first proper breath since the park. Ellie looked so pale, her eyes open but still no focus to their gaze.

'We'd like to admit her for twenty-four hours, keep an eye on her. The nurse will organize that – but I think she'll be fine . . . won't you, sweetheart?' He brushed the child's arm with surprising tenderness. He must have one of his own, Jeanie thought. 'We'll keep her lightly sedated.'

Ellie looked up at her. 'Gin . . . where's Mummy?'

Jeanie looked at her watch. It was nearly two hours since the accident, and still no sign of anyone.

'She's on her way, poppet. I'll give her another call.'

Determined not to leave the little girl for even a second, she flouted the rules and rang Chanty's mobile again. There was still no answer. Where was she? Where was everyone? She saw that George had tried to call her four times, but she didn't bother to listen to the messages. This time he answered, his voice breathless and panicky.

'I'm just outside the hospital. Where are you?'

'Still in A & E, but it's OK, George, I'll tell you when you get here.'

'Grandadz.' Ellie smiled up at George sleepily while Jeanie filled him in.

'Did you get hold of Chanty or Alex?'

'Finally. She wasn't answering her mobile, so I rang Channel 4 and they were idiotic, couldn't find her in the building, shilly-shallied until I nearly went down to get her myself. Obviously she was frantic when I did speak to her. She said she'd been in a meeting in Canary Wharf and her phone was on silent. She's probably on the Tube right now. I left a message for Alex, but no doubt Chanty will talk to him.' George shifted from one foot to another. 'Never liked hospitals,' he stated quietly.

'Who does?'

'You must have, you worked in one for years.'

She laughed. 'I suppose you like the work, not so much the place where you do it. Don't stay, she's been sedated and she should sleep now.' Ellie's little hand was beginning to relax its grip on her own, her eyelids fluttering softly.

'You're going to stay?'

'Until Chanty comes, yes.'

George looked uncertain. 'Are you sure you don't want me here?'

Jeanie shook her head, 'Go on, go. I'll let you know if there are any developments.'

He bent to drop a kiss on her head, then loped off. 'Call me.'

They moved Ellie up to the children's ward. She slept now, her beautiful face peaceful against the white sheet. Jeanie leant back in the hospital chair they had placed beside the cot and also closed her eyes, wishing her daughter would come.

'Jeanie?' Ray stood before her, his face as strained and anxious as George's had been. 'How is she?'

'Oh, Ray, she's all right. She's got swelling, but no bleed, the doctor said. They're keeping her in overnight.'

Ray grinned with relief. 'Thank God! Are you OK?'

'Not really, but as long as Ellie is, I don't give a stuff.'

'Quite. Where are her parents?'

Jeanie shrugged. 'On their way, I hope.'

There was a scurry at the ward entrance.

'Mum . . . Mum, what happened?' Chanty rushed past Jeanie and Ray, struggling to lower the cot side in order to stroke her child's hair as she slept and kiss the small face with a passionate ferocity.

'God . . . is she OK?' She turned to her mother, ignoring Ray. 'Tell me.'

Jeanie made her sit down.

'It was a fall. She hit her head in the playground.'

'What was she doing?' There was an accusatory note in her voice that Jeanie saw she was too wound up to control.

'I wasn't there. She was with Alex. Ray saw it, though.'

Chanty stared at Ray, comprehension dawning suddenly. 'You're the man . . . the . . . man from the playground.' She faltered, her gaze almost hostile. Ray just nodded. 'So where's Alex? I've tried him a dozen times but he isn't answering.'

'He was going into town to see an important buyer, he said.'

Her daughter took a moment to process this information. 'He left her?'

Jeanie shot a warning look at Ray. 'At the time he thought Ellie was OK.'

Chanty nodded. 'But then she got ill?'

'We . . . I thought it better to get her checked out. Head injuries can be deceptive; by the time they show any symptoms it can be too late.'

'I'll push off,' Ray whispered, and Jeanie nodded. It was clear his presence was not welcomed by her daughter.

'Well, thank God you did, Mum. If anything happened to her . . .' Tears had never come easily to Chanty – she'd been a tough little girl, very self-sufficient, someone who'd always known exactly what she wanted, and usually got it. But now she cried openly.

'I know, but she's going to be OK, darling.'

'What was that man doing here, Mum?' she demanded suddenly, wiping away her tears with irritation.

'Ray, his name is Ray. I said, he was there when it happened. He wanted to make sure Ellie was OK.'

'So that's the man . . . I thought you weren't going to meet up with him any more.'

HILARY BOYD

Jeanie tried hard to keep her temper, torn between a childish desire to dump her son-in-law in it by telling Chanty what really happened, and a more mature desire to help her daughter through her distress. Maturity won out.

'I wasn't there, darling. Alex asked me to meet him in the park early to collect Ell. He'd come straight from nursery. Ray happened to be there at the same time as Alex. Coincidence.' She paused. 'He has a right.'

Chanty nodded agreement, looked at her watch. 'Where *is* he?'

It was six o'clock when Alex finally put in an appearance. He looked stricken at the sight of his daughter. Ellie was awake, and although still sleepy, seemed more alert than she had since the fall.

'Daddy . . .' She reached up to receive her father's hug.

Alex straightened up and looked at Jeanie. 'What happened?'

'She wasn't right, Alex. She seemed dazed. I thought it best to have her checked out. Then on the way here she vomited.' She said no more.

Chanty explained to him what Jeanie had told her.

'So she's going to be OK? Completely OK?' Jeanie

saw Alex was shaking, his face suddenly white.

'Sit down, it's been a shock,' she told him, and dragged up another chair.

He slumped down, leaning forward over Ellie's bed, hiding his head in his arms. Jeanie realized he was crying.

'I should have listened . . . that man told me, he said . . . but I didn't want to believe it.'

Jeanie saw her daughter's puzzled look.

'You mean Ray?' Chanty asked.

Alex raised his head, and for the first time since she'd known him, Jeanie saw a look of pure vulnerability in the large blue eyes. The heavy mask of self-obsession which normally prevented any real connection with the rest of the world – unless they were talking about him – had fallen away.

'Yes, Ray. He saw her fall. He warned me, said he knew, and I just told him to bugger off.'

'Why didn't you say, Mum?' Chanty looked a little shamefaced, perhaps remembering her rude distrust of Ray.

Jeanie just shrugged.

For a while Alex lay there, and Chanty observed him, her look hardening as she thought the information through.

'So you knew Ellie had had a fall, and you knew it

could be dangerous, and you just walked away?' Her tone was steely, made worse by her own overwrought emotions.

Jeanie watched her son-in-law sit up to face the music.

'I thought she was OK, Chant, she didn't cry and she seemed fine.' His tone was unattractively pleading.

'But you didn't wait to find out.'

'I was late for Al Dimitri. He was only in town for a day, passing through to Cannes, and my agent had shown him my work on the Net . . .'

'Sorry,' Chanty interrupted coldly. 'But believe it or not I don't give a rat's arse about your sodding work right now. You left our daughter when it was clear she might need medical help.'

'It wasn't clear. I promise, it wasn't clear.' He looked pleadingly at Jeanie. 'You were there, you said it was OK for me to go.'

'It's not up to my mother to tell you what to do. You've never paid attention to her in the past. Mum, please tell me exactly what happened.'

'Ray saw the fall and because he's a martial arts expert he sees falls all the time and is trained to know a good one from a bad one,' Jeanie began reluctantly. 'He thought it was a bad bang and he told Alex that. But to be fair, none of us knew whether there was a problem or not. And people make this mistake all the time.'

'And die as a consequence?' Chanty snapped.

'Well, yes . . . sometimes.'

Alex was stricken again. 'I know, I know I'm to blame.' He laid his hand next to his child and ran his thumb down her cheek. 'Isn't she the most beautiful child in the world? And I walked away. She could have died . . . and I would have been responsible.'

His melodrama was unconvincing to Jeanie, but she could see her daughter softening, as always, at his manipulations. And perhaps — Jeanie gave him the benefit of the doubt — he had been truly shocked by what had happened.

'She hasn't died, Alex, she's going to be fine.' Jeanie's tone was practical, cutting through the thickness of his performance. 'I'm sure you'd have done the best thing when you saw she wasn't well.'

'That's hardly the point though, is it?' Chanty commented sharply, her husband still not forgiven. 'You left her.'

'Most people would probably have thought the same as Alex,' Jeanie insisted, truthfully. 'No one likes to make a fuss when there's no clear evidence for it.'

'So we have Ray to thank . . .' Chanty clearly didn't like this option.

Alex began shifting uncomfortably in his chair, then got to his feet. He seemed to be about to speak, darting anxious glances at both her and Chanty.

'Um . . . about Ray . . .'

Her daughter's eyes narrowed. 'What about Ray?'

Alex took a deep breath and straightened his shoulders, as if he were about to face a firing squad.

'Alex?'

Still he hesitated. 'Well, you know the thing that Ellie said . . . about Ray? It wasn't true. She never said it.'

He hung his head as if to ward off imaginary blows. And Jeanie thought for a horrible moment that Chanty *was* going to hit him. She was holding herself rigid in the hospital chair, her head lowered too (but not in fear), her hands clutching, white-knuckled, to her thighs, as if she were preparing to charge.

Alex, however, despite being at the bottom of the pit, went on digging. 'Ellie kept going on about him, how he could balance on the wobbly log without holding on and everyone clapped, and how he was brilliant at playing ball, with all sorts of funny games, and how he sang songs, bought her apple juice. And I was pissed off. I didn't want some man doing things with my daughter that I was crap at.'

Jeanie was shocked. Although she knew that he'd been lying, to hear his pathetic tale made her feel almost sorry for him. Imagine the hell of such an ego, she thought.

Disbelief had outrun Chanty's rage. She just sat there, stony-faced and silent, which was clearly more frightening than any blow to her husband.

'Chanty, I'm sorry. I know it was dumb.'

'Dumb?' Chanty sprang to life. 'Dumb? You call it "dumb" to accuse a man of molesting Ellie because you're *jealous*?' She was having trouble not shouting, but her face, normally fair, was suffused scarlet.

'I didn't exactly say child-molesting,' Alex countered petulantly. 'I just said . . .'

Chanty cut him off again. 'We know what you said, Alex. And we know what you intended to imply.'

'I didn't mean to say it, in fact I didn't really say what you think, not at first. I just wanted you to know about him, that he was playing with Ellie . . . and you over-reacted when I told you, and then it escalated and I sort of made more of it than there was. It got out of hand before I had a chance to explain.'

'So this is my fault?' Chanty spat. Then the strength seemed to go out of her. 'Just go away.' She waved her hand dismissively. 'Just leave. I can't stand the sight of you.'

Alex hesitated, but not for long. Jeanie watched him slope embarrassedly out of the ward.

'I can't talk about this now, Mum,' Chanty muttered.

For a while neither woman spoke. They both fixed their eyes on the sleeping child, who, despite being at the centre of all this upset, was mercifully unaware of the storm raging around her.

'Where's Dad?' Chanty sounded so sad, so disappointed.

'He was here earlier, when we were still in A & E. I told him to go home.'

'Oh?'

'He hates hospitals. And by then Ellie was OK . . . well, OK-ish. I'll call him in a minute.' She couldn't help her words sounding defensive, guilty almost. She told herself she hadn't got rid of George because of Ray.

For a second her daughter's glance rested on her face, and Jeanie, to her horror, saw the dawning light of comprehension in Chanty's eyes.

'How are we getting on here?' Sister Deehan must have witnessed the row, because her manner was politely disapproving. 'She needs rest and quiet.' She raised her eyebrows in Chanty's direction. 'You can stay tonight if you like.'

'Do you want me to come back later this evening? Take over?' Jeanie asked Chanty quietly, as they moved to allow a young nurse access to Ellie for the routine observations. Chanty hesitated.

'No, Mum, you go. I'll sleep here. I'll be fine. How long do you think they'll keep her in?'

'She seems a bit dazed still. They'll want her to stay quiet until the brain swelling has gone down. The A & E doctor mentioned twenty-four hours. See how she is in the morning, darling.'

Chanty sighed, obviously close to tears again. 'Oh, Mum, if you hadn't been there . . .' Jeanie put her arms round her. 'I know you think I don't value you, but I do, I really do. I'm so sorry for doubting you.'

'I can see why you did.'

She wanted to say more, but Chanty didn't need reminding about her husband's failings, nor would it help her granddaughter to have them at each other's throats. But she did wonder how Chanty put up with Alex's self-absorption. Someone that selfish could never be relied upon, unless his own interests were in parallel. She reflected on how solid George had always been.

So much so that Jeanie realized she took his probity for granted.

George had cooked supper. He had only one dish in his repertoire – spaghetti Bolognese – but he did it well, and, as was to be expected, was meticulous in his organization and presentation: everything measured out and lined up, the table set, the wine uncorked, the salad waiting for its dressing. But tonight Jeanie was grateful.

'Bit of a nightmare, eh?' he said, stirring the sauce fussily. 'Lucky you were there.'

Jeanie wondered if Ray's name would be mentioned by either Chanty or Alex in connection with today's incident. She had never told George about meeting Ray in the park with Ellie, not even in the early days.

'Pour the wine . . .' he pointed at the bottle, 'and sit down. You must be exhausted.'

'I was frightened out of my wits, George. I . . . I just kept on asking over and over again for her to be all right.' Once she was seated, she felt she would never have the strength to stand again. She reached for the wine and half-filled both glasses. (George was always very insistent that red wine should have room to breathe.) The full, fruity tannin hit her throat with an instant magic. She felt her body almost sigh with relief.

George looked at her sideways. 'Asking the God you don't believe in, you mean?'

Jeanie smiled. 'OK. But you would have done the same. It's a natural instinct.'

'Yes, but He'd have listened to me, I go to church.' He smirked smugly and they both laughed.

'Not much, you don't.'

And the laugh turned into more laughter, and in the end tears poured down her face as she gasped for air, clutching to her mouth the napkin George had so carefully placed by the cutlery, all the tension of the day washed away in the shared hilarity.

As she lay in bed that night, all she could see was her granddaughter's solemn brown eyes, huge and bewildered in her little face, as she lay on the hospital sheet. Nothing in the world could be more important than Ellie's safety and happiness.

15

Ray called her the following morning as she walked down the hill to the hospital.

'How is she?'

'I spoke to Chanty an hour ago and she's fine, by the sound of it. I'm just going down there now to give her a break. Not much appetite, and very sleepy, Chanty says, but that's to be expected with head trauma. Chanty sounded much happier.'

'Thank God . . . By the way, I love the thought of you as a nurse.' She could hear a roguish chuckle.

'Is it the black stockings? And they *were* stockings in those days,' she laughed.

'Ooooh, don't get me going. You must've driven your patients wild.'

'Thanks for the vote of confidence, but the majority were under ten. Remember I said I was at Great Ormond Street?'

'Still . . .'

'Ray.' Jeanie cut through the joke. 'I think Chanty knows . . . or at least suspects . . . about us.'

'Why, what did she say?'

'She didn't say anything, but Alex 'fessed up about you not being a child-molester after all. He'd been "misunderstood" apparently. This was after he'd mentioned that you'd warned him about Ellie and he'd refused to listen. It was serious Show Time . . .'

She heard Ray whistle. 'God. How did your daughter take that?'

'You can imagine.'

'At least he's told the truth at last.'

'Anyway, your name was very much on everyone's tongue, and there was this moment when she just looked at me . . .'

'You might be being paranoid. It wasn't exactly an easy day.' She heard him sigh. 'Jeanie, don't say more than you have to if she challenges you. You know, "never apologize, never explain"; it's a tried and tested motto, believe me. No one has any proof. And we haven't exactly, well, done the dirty deed . . . yet.'

'I can't lie to my daughter, Ray,' Jeanie said, ignoring the last part of his sentence.

'You have lied already . . . as good as.'

The baldness of his statement, despite being essentially true, was shocking to Jeanie.

'But if she asks?'

'With all that's gone on, she's hardly going to be in the mood to find out that . . . that we've been seeing each other.'

His sentence tailed off, and she understood why. There was no neat way of describing what was between them without resorting to labels that put their moments together under uncomfortable, slightly hysterical headings such as 'affair', 'unfaithful', 'cheating', 'in love' . . . And, of course, 'love'. None of which, and all of which, could apply.

'So how did it end with Alex?' Ray hurried on.

'He was sent packing. Stupid of him to tell her about you then, because Chanty had almost forgiven him for leaving Ellie. But boy, does he know how to manage her.' She paused, a passing bus drowning out her words. 'I suppose he felt hideously guilty. No matter, I'm sure she'll forgive him; she always does, no matter how heinous his crime.'

'And you too?'

There was silence.

'I don't think I've quite Alex's knack.'

She shared his unspoken fear that a revelation would spell the end.

'It isn't her business. But unfortunately she won't see it that way.'

'OK . . . well, let me know how it goes.'

'I will.'

They both lingered in silence at either end of the line.

'Jeanie?' He said no more, he didn't have to.

'Bye, Ray.'

Her daughter looked worn and tired, much worse than Ellie, who seemed almost back to normal, despite the hectic flush on her cheeks, which Jeanie thought was as much to do with the baking, airless atmosphere of the ward as with anything more sinister.

'Did you get any sleep?'

She shook her head wanly. 'No chance. But I wouldn't have, even if it'd been the Ritz.'

'I brought you a cappuccino.'

Chanty fell on the coffee like water in a desert.

'Oh, thanks, Mum. You'll never know how good that tastes.'

'Why don't you go home and have a shower and a sleep? I'll stay with her.' Jeanie bent to kiss her grand-daughter. 'Morning, poppet. Have the doctors pronounced yet?'

'They'll be here about eleven, according to Nurse Julie. Maybe I should stay till they've been.' She gazed at her daughter, a look both adoring and fearful. Jeanie knew she had looked down the barrel of the worst gun any parent could face.

'You gave us a proper old fright, you did,' Chanty told her gently, her finger brushing the hair from her daughter's forehead. Ellie twitched away from her mother's hand, ignoring them as she went on franti-cally building a tower out of junior Lego. 'Do you think she'll mind me going for a bit?'

Jeanie shrugged. 'See. You can always come back.'

The day passed slowly. Jeanie gave in to Ellie's request for a fourth repetition of the story she was reading, trying to make it just a tiny bit different every time to stop herself from going mad: 'Swish, swash, went the alligator's tail as it slid through the door, snip, snap went his teeth. Were the children scared? You bet they were . . .'

'Again,' Ellie demanded, pushing the book in Jeanie's face.

'You tell me the story this time,' Jeanie suggested, hopefully.

Ellie thought about this. 'Ummm . . . is bit too diffcu for me. You do it, Gin, is lovee for you.'

'Is it lovely for me? OK, well, one more time.'

'Sanks, Gin.' Ellie grinned in triumph, knowing she was winning where she normally did not, and not caring why this was so.

On the ward round that morning the doctors had declared her fit to go home by the end of the day, as long as she was kept very quiet at home, but it was nearly five and they were still waiting for the doctor to sign her out.

'All ready?' George appeared at the bedside, dangling the car keys as he gave a jolly wave to his granddaughter. 'Car's outside. It's in a dodgy parking bay – for deliveries or something – so we'd better get a move on.'

'We have to wait, she hasn't been officially discharged.' Chanty frowned, looking up at the ward clock for the millionth time. 'Where is he?'

'I'd better move the car, then.' George edged towards the door. 'Ring me. I'll go and sit in a side street. He won't be long, will he?'

'I think the paediatrician is a she,' Jeanie said, absently. Neither Chanty nor George seemed to hear her, and she wondered for a moment if she had really spoken, her mind consumed as it was with the possibility that the lid was about to be blown off her secret. Would her daughter mention Ray in front of George, to test her?

The mirror that night told her that the strain had pinched her features, accentuated the lines; her eyes drooped with tiredness. It felt as if her life were unravelling. On the way back from dropping Chanty and Ellie home, George had been disturbed by his daughter's treatment of Alex.

'I know she's been under a huge strain, but there was no need to be so nasty to poor Alex. He's under strain too.'

Chanty had snapped quite viciously at her husband when he opened the door and tried to take Ellie from her.

'She was angry with him for going into town after Ell had her fall.'

George had shot her a quick glance as he looked for a place to park. 'I thought you were with her when she fell.'

'No, I arrived just after it had happened. But Alex was told by someone else in the playground that Ellie might need checking out, because she'd really cracked her head, and Alex had pooh-poohed his advice and taken off to his meeting.'

George had nodded sagely. 'I can see why she'd be cross about that. When will that lad learn?'

Jeanie had been suddenly infuriated with George's endless tolerance of Alex. 'He's not a lad, he's a forty-two-year-old man.'

'OK, OK, keep your wig on. No harm done in the end, eh?'

Her phone had rung at the moment he was reversing cautiously into a space. She didn't have her glasses on, so she couldn't read the number, but she was sure it was Ray.

George had turned the engine off and was watching her. 'It might be Chanty,' he said, when she let it ring.

'It's not. I don't recognize the number and I'm not in the mood to talk to anyone right now.'

'Shall I answer it for you and say you're busy?' George had asked, reaching for the phone.

Jeanie had hurriedly dropped it into her bag. 'No! Thank you.'

George had shrugged, but as she got out of the car, Jeanie had had the depressing realization that all her

conversations with her family now had to be monitored and edited to avoid mention of Ray.

She smoothed cream over her face and neck, patted
another round her eyes, peered long and hard at her
complexion, brushed her hair, then sighed and turned
away from the visual reminder of her age. She must
be mad, she told herself, to think anyone, let alone an
attractive man like Ray, could find such an old crone
sexy. *Just don't ever let him ask to be my 'friend'*, she pleaded
into the darkness.

Rita was enviably bronzed from a fortnight on the
Antiguan beach, her body easy and confident in the
skimpy scarlet swimsuit. It was the first time this year,
however, that Jeanie had exposed her body to the naked
eye. She struggled into her black Speedo, horribly aware
of the see-in-the-dark paleness of her unbuffed skin
and lumpy cellulite. Every summer, Rita dragged her
friend for as many swims in the Hampstead ponds as
the weather permitted. The Women Only pond, Rita
insisted, was the best, and surrounded as it was by the
wild vegetation of the Heath, ducks paddling happily
amongst the swimmers, it did seem like a secluded
corner of country. Jeanie had the feeling of belonging
to a private members' club – despite the entry being

almost free: an elite whose membership were tough, fit, no-nonsense women of character.

The day was once again boiling hot. Jeanie knew that the water would be anything but. After the initial shock, though, it would be deliciously fresh and cool, without the claggy chlorine miasma of a pool.

Rita was in ahead of her.

'Come on, you wimp,' she shouted, as Jeanie hesitated, toes on the swaying wooden ladder, hands clutching the chilly metal handrail. The other swimmers turned to watch, leaving her no choice but to dive forward into the water.

'God!' she gasped, immediately piling into a fast front crawl to get the circulation moving again.

After a while they began swimming alongside each other, lapping the pond in the company of a male and female mallard.

'You poor thing.' Jeanie had just told Rita about Ellie. 'That must have been hell.'

By the time she had explained the rest of that day's dramas they were both sick of swimming.

'I can't leave you alone for a minute. I've only been gone two weeks and your life slides into meltdown,' complained her friend after they'd dried and were setting off in search of an ice cream.

The cafe near the Lido was pulsing, as usual, with children and dogs.

'Let's not sit here, we can walk,' Jeanie decided. 'I'll get them. Double or single scoop?'

'Oh, double of course, throw probity to the wind.'

As Jeanie wove her way through the tables, she noticed the back of a man's head in the queue and knew instantly it was Ray. He was with Dylan and another boy, the boys leaning against the tray ledge and swishing back and forth in their boredom until Dylan's friend knocked a tray to the ground, luckily with nothing more on it than a tuna and sweetcorn sandwich in a plastic packet.

'OK . . . out. Go and wait for me outside. But don't run off, stay by the tables.' Ray chivvied the boys in the direction of the door, and they obediently did as he asked. As he turned to check they had gone, he noticed her and pushed his way back out of the line.

'I'm with my friend . . . Rita,' she said at once, looking round nervously.

'And you don't want me to meet her?' His welcoming smile had faded.

'No. I mean, yes, I'd love you to meet her, but . . .'

Ray waited, looking a little hurt. 'You said she knows about me.'

'Yes . . . but it could be awkward.' Jeanie didn't know why she didn't want Rita to meet Ray.

He shrugged. 'OK, up to you.' He rubbed his hand across his head. 'Listen, I'd better get these boys a drink or all hell will break loose.' His smile was fleeting and forced.

'It's just . . .' *Just what*, she asked herself.

But Ray was gone while she deliberated, not even bothering to get the drinks, shepherding his two charges firmly away from the cafe at a brisk march. As Jeanie watched she could see Dylan's upturned face protesting at his grandfather's decision.

'Where are the ice creams, then? You've been an age.' Rita was by her side.

'That was Ray.'

'Where . . . which one? Which way did he go?' Rita was looking round eagerly. 'Why didn't you introduce us, darling?'

'I don't know . . . I . . . wait here.' And she was gone, running in the direction Ray had taken. It wasn't long before she saw them, meandering towards the Lido.

'Ray! Ray, Dylan.'

All three turned round. Dylan grinned widely, but Ray didn't.

'Hi.' She was out of breath, as much from anxiety as from running.

'Hi, Gin,' Dylan said, adopting Ellie's name for her.

'This is Ben.' Ray indicated the fair-haired boy. 'Dylan's friend.'

'Hello, Ben. Ray . . . can I have a word?'

They stood looking at each other for so long that the boys lost interest and went ahead.

'Please,' she went on, 'come and meet Rita.'

'You didn't seem so keen earlier,' he commented, his gaze non-committal.

'I didn't want you to be scrutinized,' she said softly.

'And found wanting?'

Jeanie looked at the ground. 'Not judged, I didn't mean that. And even if I had, I think you're the most wonderful man in the world. How could you think I'd be ashamed of you?'

Her words hung in the air between them and she realized what she had said.

'Jeanie.' Ray made no attempt to touch her, but she wanted desperately to take his hand in hers. 'If you're not comfortable introducing me, that's OK.'

She looked him in the eye. 'What we have is sacred. I didn't want anyone else, anyone from my other life, to be part of it, of you.'

He nodded, but she could see he didn't get it.

'Rita's my dearest friend, but she's only human, and prurient in her way.'

Ray laughed. 'You're not making any sense.'

Her own laughter was hesitant. 'You do understand. You'd be objectified as my lover, you'd be scrutinized, gone over with a fine-toothed comb. It's not the way it should be.'

'Listen, it's fine, this is getting way too intense.' He looked around for his grandson. 'I'd better go, they're getting away.' He gazed at her for a moment longer. 'I told you there could be no good plan.' As he turned he held his hand briefly against her bare arm.

'Bye.' She waited till he was out of sight, then plodded back towards the cafe, where her friend sat kicking her heels on the low boundary wall. Rita didn't speak, just raised her eyebrows.

'I've just messed everything up. He thought I was ashamed of him.'

'And were you?'

'Of course not!'

Now it was Rita's turn to be offended.

'So it's me who's the embarrassing one, is it? Not cool enough?'

'Yeah, right,' she said tiredly.

'Anyway, I saw him when you were both talking. He's cute all right.'

'Cute?' Jeanie was miles away, with Ray.

'Um yes, it's a modern slang term which designates the sex-worthiness of a member of the opposite sex, usually applied by moronic youth to their equally moronic peers,' Rita intoned.

'OK, OK.' Jeanie covered her face with her hands. 'Oh, Rita, I've blown it. He's hurt now. What can I do? Shall I ring him?'

Rita got up, grabbed Jeanie's arm and began dragging her along the asphalt path. 'No idea, darling. The pair of you are behaving like a couple of teenagers. I wash my hands of you both.'

It was a week since Ellie had come home from the hospital, and the little girl was full of beans, nothing remaining from the bang on her head except a small yellowing bruise on her temple. Jeanie had been round to the house many times, and seen both Alex and Chanty. In the time-honoured tradition of the Lawson household, nothing more was said about anything that mattered. Alex was subdued, it was true, and Chanty a little too bright for her mother's peace of mind, hardly letting a space occur in the conversation, as if she were frightened of what might pop in to fill the silence. Jeanie knew she was mulling something over in her mind, but there was much for her daughter to think about. The call Jeanie had dreaded since that moment in the hospital came when she was making tea in the kitchen of her shop.

'Alex has offered to babysit. Do you fancy supper tonight?' Jeanie heard her daughter pause. 'Without Dad.'

'I'd love that.' Jeanie felt her breath quicken. 'What shall I say to Dad, though? He'll want to come.'

'Say it's a girls' night. He'll understand.' Her tone was not hostile, but distinctly tense.

Someone spoke to her in the background, and Chanty became businesslike. 'Got to go, Mum. See you at eight, at the French caff on the hill?'

'Look forward to it,' she said, although nothing could have been further from the truth. She knew Chanty must be shattered from recent events, and understood that what she was doing would cause her daughter additional untold pain, but the fact seemed not enough to hold her back from seeing Ray.

The incident with Rita outside the cafe in the park had ruined the perfect accord that Jeanie had taken for granted between her and Ray. She knew it was fallout from the situation they were in, but seeing his pained expression when she refused to introduce him to Rita had been like a physical blow. Looking back, she couldn't understand, any more than he or Rita had, why she had made such a stupid fuss about it. And because Rita had lost patience, it was hours before she was alone and could ring him.

She and her friend had parted at the bottom of the hill, and she had raced home, holding herself together long enough to reach the sanctuary of her locked bathroom. Like the teenager that Rita had accused her of being, she had then given vent to violent sobs. When she finally called Ray's number, her voice was still choked with regret.

'It's OK, Jeanie,' Ray had assured her, but he had sounded raw. 'We knew this wouldn't be easy.'

'But you know I wouldn't hurt you for the world.'

'My ego was temporarily bruised. Serves me right for having one,' he joked.

'It wasn't about being ashamed of you.'

'Yes,' he said firmly, 'I know.'

'I hated seeing you upset,' she murmured, and couldn't help her tears.

'Oh, Jeanie . . . please don't cry.'

'What – as we've said before – are we like?' She laughed. 'Even Rita called us juvenile.'

'And like any teenager worth his salt, it may be hard, it's certainly intense,' he said quietly, 'but I wouldn't be without it.'

'Nor would I.'

The French restaurant was empty inside, but full and rippling with voices and the tinkle of glasses and cutlery outside in the small walled garden at the back. The sky looked thundery, but it was still warm, even sticky, and thunderflies hovered above the table candles. Chanty was already there, sitting hunched over her BlackBerry at a corner table, responding to the never-ending flow of work. She smiled at her mother as Jeanie approached and put away the device.

'Saved by the bell,' she said, obviously relieved to be given an excuse to stop.

Jeanie noticed a bottle of white wine already open in an ice bucket alongside the table; Chanty's glass was nearly empty. Her daughter waved the bottle and poured another glass for them both.

'This is nice,' Jeanie commented, and experienced a genuine sense of well-being as she sat in the fading light with her beloved daughter. Maybe Chanty felt the same, eager not to ruin the moment, because for a while neither of them spoke.

'How's Ellie?'

'Mum, you only saw her yesterday,' Chanty teased, knowing full well her mother could discuss Ellie till the end of time and still have more to say.

'Just checking. More to the point, how are you, darling? This last week can't have been easy.' She didn't specify which particular load on Chanty's shoulders she was referring to.

'I'm not really OK,' she replied, with her usual directness. 'I'm having trouble getting past what Alex did.'

Jeanie waited.

'I know you've always thought him an arse; you've made that pretty clear, so I don't want a rant about his shortcomings,' she warned, then added, 'I'm not stupid, Mum, I am quite aware he can be selfish at times.'

Jeanie thought this an understatement worthy of framing, but said nothing, as instructed.

'But this might have impacted on Ray's life in a way that could never be undone – the "no smoke without fire" syndrome. And I wonder at what point in the fiction he would have fronted up if Ellie hadn't got ill.'

'I'm sure he'd never have let you involve an outside authority.'

Chanty fixed her mother's gaze. 'Are you?'

'Yes . . . yes, I am. He's selfish, not evil, although I suppose selfishness is a kind of evil. He had a fit of pique when his ego was threatened by another man, and did a childish thing. He'd never have let it go any further.'

Chanty's laugh was wry. 'You support him at the same time as damning him, Mum . . . very clever.'

'I'm not trying to be clever. But darling, you can't have fallen in love and married this man because he was selfless and altruistic.'

'No. I've always known exactly what he's like. That's why I keep forgiving him, because I've no unrealistic expectations.'

Jeanie thought this sad. Why had she chosen such a man? He was hardly an echo of her father.

Chanty saw Jeanie's look. 'That sounds terrible, doesn't it?'

Jeanie nodded.

'Alex isn't second best, Mum. I love him, but I understand him, that's what I mean. He's damaged. He had a terrible childhood. His father left when he was four; he never saw him again till he was sixteen, and then only for a cup of coffee in a transport cafe on the A3. His dad had moved to Guernsey and ran a successful taxi business, but he was so scared of his ex-wife he made Alex promise never to mention he'd seen him. Alex said he liked him, he wanted to keep in touch, but his dad never contacted him again and wouldn't answer Alex's calls.' Chanty took a deep breath. 'His mother was the monster – totally obsessive and controlling. Alex says she monitored his every breath, always touching and stroking him, catering to his every whim. But even as a small child she made him feel responsible for her, so if she was sad or cross it was his fault. He had to help her choose her clothes in the morning, and praise her figure and the way she looked. Creepy. She even pretended he had a heart condition so she could keep him at home all the time and stop him from playing sport or taking part in any physical activity.'

'That explains a lot. No wonder he's so wary of me, a mother figure. Why didn't you tell me? I might have been more sympathetic.'

'He didn't tell me either, not till I got him to start therapy as a condition of him coming back after Ellie was born. The sad thing is he didn't think it was particularly odd till then. I mean, he knew she was clingy and possessive – she loathes me, as you can imagine – but it was his reality. Some of the stories he's been telling me recently beggar belief.'

For a second, Jeanie wondered if her son-in-law's confessions did indeed beggar belief, but Chanty, as usual, was one step ahead of her.

'No, Mum, he hasn't made it up. I've talked to his aunt. She had him to stay when his mother was ill – he was fourteen by then – and realized what was going on. The doctor tested his heart and the fiction was uncovered, but it was too late by then: the damage was done.'

'He still sees her, though, I remember you going over last Christmas.'

'That's it, Mum, that's the only time he sees her all year: an hour on Christmas Eve. And he goes into a decline for a week before the visit and is horrible to me, really snappish and tense. You know she drinks now, so we go early. She does nothing but lay on the guilt trip, says she was the 'best mother in the world' – the whole visit's a nightmare; she can't even remember Ellie's name. I think I told you, last year she revealed that his father was gay.'

Jeanie nodded, laughed. 'I remember. I suppose you'll never know if he was or not.'

'Exactly. Alex didn't believe her – she'd spent his whole childhood poisoning him against his father.'

'And the therapy?'

Chanty shook her head. 'He saw someone for about two sessions, but then refused to go any more. Said his work might suffer.'

'That old chestnut. Although he may be right. I mean, an artist's talent is part learned skill, part internal outpourings.' She patted her daughter's hand. 'Why couldn't you've married a brain surgeon, darling?'

'You reckon they're sane? Someone whose comfort zone is drilling holes in a person's skull and fiddling about with the part of the body that makes us tick? Who *dares* to?'

'OK, maybe not. What about a landscape gardener, then? Or a carpenter; there's good evidence they're reliable.'

The waiter stood smiling patiently with his carbon pad while they tried to control their laughter. Chanty ordered the chicken, Jeanie the salmon and lentils.

'Seriously . . . you probably need professional help to deal with this.'

'You mean marriage guidance?' She shook her head. 'Not a chance.'

'No, I mean getting him to go to therapy again.

Because you're right, what he did was very serious, and he did it on a whim. He needs help.'

She saw the tiredness in her daughter's eyes.

'You're right,' Chanty sighed. 'I keep hoping I can make him better, that if I love him enough he'll be OK.' She looked at her mother for confirmation.

'Loving him is fine, but it won't change him, Chanty, it never does. He has to do that himself.'

'Do you think he can?'

Jeanie shrugged. 'He's got a lot to lose if he doesn't.'

It wasn't till the mint tea was on the table that Chanty put her hands flat on the white linen cloth in a gesture, so like her father, that instantly implied gravity. Both of them were a little drunk by now, and Jeanie felt a devil-may-care insouciance for what her daughter was about to say.

'This has been great, Mum. Thanks so much for listening to me bang on . . . There's just one more thing.'

Jeanie held her daughter's gaze. 'Yes?'

'Tell me you're not having an affair with Ray.'

Jeanie knew in retrospect that she could have lied to Chanty. After all, what constituted an affair? She hadn't slept with Ray. Her daughter was so preoccupied with her own life that she didn't really want to hear the answer to her almost throwaway question. She was hardly listening when she posed it. Yet Jeanie couldn't stop herself from blushing. The awareness of her feelings for Ray was so strong, so near the surface, that it was almost as if he were standing beside her. For a fatal moment she hesitated, and as she did so she watched Chanty's face turn from distracted to shocked. And she knew it was too late to lie.

'Mum?' The word was like a pistol shot.

Jeanie genuinely didn't know how to answer.

'My God, you are! You're having an affair.'

'I'm not having an affair,' she eventually managed, but she knew it was unconvincing.

'I don't believe you.' Her daughter's face seemed fixed in that first moment of shock.

'I . . . won't say I don't have feelings for him . . .' How difficult this was, despite having run through the scenario a million times.

'Mum . . . it's very simple. Are you having a sexual relationship with Ray?' She was bent forward across the table now, her blue eyes wide and penetrating.

'I haven't had sex with him, if that's what you mean.'

This seemed to take the wind out of Chanty's sails for a moment.

'Well . . . thank God for that.' Then she thought about it. 'That's not what I asked.'

Jeanie knew that, but she wasn't prepared, even in the cause of honesty, to detail the precious intimacy that had evolved between her and Ray.

'No, well . . . it's not just about sex . . . I can't explain, but it's not.' She had never imagined this would be so difficult. How could she explain that her pleasure in Ray's company, the laughter they shared, was as significant as his kisses?

'You're not going to leave Dad? Mum, you can't.'

'I don't know what I'm going to do,' she said, which was the truth.

Chanty just stared at her, and Jeanie thought what a beautiful woman she was, with her high cheekbones and fine eyes caught in the candlelight. So strong, so honest, but surrounded by the most dismal, dissembling crew. Even Honest George seemed to be hiding something nasty in the woodshed.

Her daughter shook her head in despair. 'What do you mean, you don't know?'

'Exactly that. Chanty, it's difficult. I have a very powerful connection with Ray. We . . .'

'Mum, stop right there, I don't want to hear any more. You must end it right now.' She waited for her mother to agree, and when Jeanie didn't, she ploughed on desperately, 'Mum . . . listen to me. Dad doesn't deserve this. He's been the best husband anyone could ever have. You love each other, I know you do. Think about it. You don't even know this man.'

'I do know him.'

'How can you? What's it been, a couple of months at most? And you say you haven't even had sex? How important can it be? You've been married to Dad for a lifetime.'

'That's not the point.'

'What is the point, then? God, I can't believe this. You're sixty, Mum, not sixteen. You can't seriously be thinking of leaving a brilliant marriage for – what? A bit of . . . call it what you will . . . but it must be sex.' She spat the last word out as if it had been stuck in her throat. 'It's disgusting.'

Jeanie could see her shaking with indignation. The garden had emptied out; there was only one table left, on the far side – four men in their fifties, probably Italian, red faces glowing in the candlelight, their raucous laughter hiding the heated exchange from their own table.

'Does Dad know?'

'Of course not.'

'And that's OK, is it?'

'No, of course it's not OK.' She was tired, and felt herself sinking into a strange apathy. It wasn't fair to expect Chanty to understand or accept her position. And she wasn't going to betray George further, in the cause of mitigation, by telling her daughter the truth.

'Mum . . .' Chanty was taking a different tack, and Jeanie could almost see the effort it took to replace anger with reason. 'I'm not being funny, but you are old. You look great, of course, but the fact is that you're vulnerable at your age. This man is only after one thing. If you go that route and give up Dad and your marriage, where will you be in two years' time? Dumped, old and alone. It's horrible.'

'Horrible indeed.' She felt like pointing out that if Ray were merely after a bonk there were hundreds, probably thousands, of women half her age he could choose from.

'Don't be facetious, Mum.'

Jeanie took the rebuke seriously, 'Sorry, darling. I'm sorry for upsetting you, I really am. Believe me, I hate it. But I never meant for this to happen.'

Chanty's snort was cynical.

'I know, the whole thing's a cliché, I really am sorry you had to find out.'

'Sorry I had to find out, but not sorry it's happened?'

'Yes,' she answered firmly.

'Yes? Mum! How can you be so callous? This isn't like you. You've always been honest, so full of integrity. You know how much I admire you, but . . .' She drew a long, sad breath. 'Do you have any idea what this'll do to Dad? No wonder you didn't want to move to the country.'

'This has nothing to do with the move. Dad had already decided.'

When Jeanie fell silent, her daughter began again. 'You have to end this now, Mum. You do know that, don't you? End it now and Dad never has to know. I won't tell a living soul, not even Alex . . . especially not Alex.'

Her daughter's tone seemed to imply she was offering her a get-out-of-jail-free card.

'I can't,' she said simply.

Chanty turned away, her jaw clenched tight. Her anger was understandable; she and her father were so close, and Jeanie knew that if the shoe were on the other foot and it was George being unfaithful, Chanty would treat him with the same anger and disgust. 'So what *are* you going to do?'

Jeanie hung her head, feeling like a recalcitrant school-girl.

'Chanty, I've said. I don't know. Of course I know what I ought to do, but it's not that simple.'

'It's perfectly simple. Let me spell it out, Mum. You dump Ray and go to the country with Dad. End of.' She angrily gathered her bag up from the floor, signalling the end of their discussion. 'And what's more, if I find out you haven't, I'll tell Dad myself. However much it'll hurt him, I can't stand by and watch you deceive him. How would I face him, knowing the truth?'

Jeanie knew she meant it, and she understood where Chanty was coming from. Most children would do anything in their power to keep their parents together, but in Chanty's case she knew it wasn't purely for selfish reasons, to maintain the status quo. She was convinced her mother was being taken for a ride.

'I'll tell him,' Jeanie stated quietly, and immediately saw the concern in her daughter's eyes.

'You don't need to tell Dad if you're going to finish it, Mum. Once and for all. Never see that man or talk to him again. If you do that, then it'd be cruel and pointless to tell him.' Chanty stared hard at her mother, waiting for the assurance that Jeanie couldn't give her. How could she look her daughter in the eye and say she would never speak to Ray again?

'Don't bully me, darling. It doesn't help.'

And her daughter had to be satisfied with that.

16

Jeanie sat on a bench in the centre of Pond Square, only a hundred yards from her own front door. The square was quiet and dark; it was half past midnight, the restaurants that edged the square on one side all closed or closing, bin bags on the pavement, menu boards taken inside. Couples making their way home talked in low voices; a man on a mobile paced back and forth by the bus stop on the corner with the main road, clearly having a difference of opinion with the person on the other end. It was chilly now, but the thunder had held off. Jeanie's heart seemed to have grown to twice its normal size in her chest, pounding like a tom-tom as she tried to catch her breath.

'It's me,' she whispered into her phone.

'Where are you?'

'In Pond Square, on a bench.'

'Come down.'

'I can't. Ray . . . I've just had supper with Chanty. She knows. She's threatened to tell George if I don't break it off with you and never speak to you again.'

She heard the soft intake of breath.

'OK . . . so what are you going to do?'

'I don't have much choice. I'm going to tell him. It has to come from me.'

'Tell him what, Jeanie?'

'Tell him I've fallen in love with you.' She no longer cared about labels, no longer cared whether her feelings were reciprocated or how Ray would react; nothing seemed to matter in that moment but telling the truth, letting Ray know the truth, her truth, whatever the outcome. And telling it was like a cleansing breath. Her heart began to slow as she waited for him to speak.

'Jeanie . . . are you sure this is a good idea?'

'Falling in love with you? No, probably not, but it's what's happened.' She heard the reckless note in her laughter.

'That's not what I mean,' Ray chuckled. 'I mean telling your husband.'

She wanted him to comment on her words. Telling him had quickly become not enough.

'What choice do I have?' she asked.

'Would Chanty really do that?'

'Oh yes, you don't know my daughter. She's pathologically honest.'

'How do you think he'll take it?'

'Not well . . . obviously.'

Despite her bravado with Chanty, she couldn't actually imagine telling George.

'Think this through, Jeanie. What do you want the result to be?'

She brought herself back from thoughts of her husband. 'The result?'

'Yes, what do you see happening afterwards? You have to think of that.'

There was no 'afterwards'.

'I'm sure you could persuade your daughter not to tell.'

'And then what?'

There was a sigh on the other end of the line.

'I can't tell you what to do, Jeanie.'

'I wish someone could.'

'For what it's worth,' she heard him murmur, 'I'm in love with you too.'

★

'Can you open your mouth a little wider?'

Jeanie stretched her jaw and felt a pain run up the side of her face.

'That's as wide as it'll go,' she said as distinctly as she could with a cotton wad wedged inside her cheek and her jaw stretched to its limit. She smelt the familiar whiff of local.

'A little sting now, hold still,' she heard the dentist mutter before driving the needle into the back of her mouth. It hurt, but she didn't care. It was twelve hours since Ray had said he was in love with her, and the dentist could have pulled out every tooth in her head, including her implant, and she would barely have whimpered.

She hadn't told George. She was savouring Ray's words, holding them close, separate for the time being from the furore they would create when made public. She had given herself today.

'Bite down ... OK ... and again.' The dentist chomped his own teeth in example. 'How does that feel?'

'Fine. I can't feel a thing.'

The dentist's look was patient.

'But when you bite, it doesn't feel high over that tooth? Have another go.'

Jeanie bit down.

'It's fine.'

'Be careful not to drink anything hot for the next couple of hours. . . in case you burn yourself,' he added when he saw Jeanie's baffled stare.

She made her way from the dentist's surgery to her shop. Jola greeted her with sympathy. 'I have teeth done in Poland. Is very much pain. I be OK if you want go home.'

Home was the last place she wanted to be. George would be in his room, fiddling with his clocks, still innocent of the Scud aimed directly at his heart. Every time she saw him now, every time he smiled at her or called her 'old girl', her own heart would contract with shame.

'It's OK. It was only a filling,' Jeanie assured her, patting her finger gingerly over her cheek to see if there was any improvement in the numbness.

'That man come in, he ask for you.'

'What man?'

'He come in before with little boy, beautiful boy. You not here.'

'Dylan . . .' Jeanie said absently.

'I say you back soon, but he not wait. He say to ring him.'

'I can't speak properly.'

'Come anyway,' Ray said.

She met him at the cafe in the park after she shut the shop. The habit of worrying whether they would be spotted together no longer seemed relevant.

'Like old times,' he said, as he dangled the tea bag in his cup.

'Can we run away? We could go to Rio or somewhere they don't have an extradition treaty. I could get a cafe on the beach – they're supposed to be lovely, the beaches – and serve English sausages and Marmite. You could give aikido lessons to the Brazilians. We'd drink rum, or whatever they drink there, and just be happy.'

'Caipirinhas. They kill you but you die happy.' Ray laughed. 'You're on, let's go.'

They both went quiet.

'Don't say anything.' Ray held his hand gently to Jeanie's lips. She took it and held it between her own.

'I wanted to see you once more before . . .' he hesitated, 'before the shit hits the fan.'

'You make it sound so final.'

★

'George?' Jeanie called up the stairs. No answer. She mounted to the second floor and knocked on the door of George's clock room.

'Come in.'

He was sitting in the usual place at his workbench, the wooden surface strewn with tiny, intricate pieces of clock mechanism. The one he was mending had a pretty art deco case in smooth, grey marble.

'Hello, darling, what can I do for you?' He dropped the magnifying lens from his eye, caught it in his palm, pulled his spectacles from the top of his head and turned to greet her.

'Are you all right? You look worried.'

'George, can we talk?'

She watched him get up and stretch his long limbs, raising his hands above his head and yawning. He glanced at one of the twenty or so clock faces at his disposal. 'Gracious, is that the time already? I meant to get out in the garden and sort out the magnolia this afternoon.'

He turned Jeanie gently round and steered her towards the door. 'Let's get a glass of wine and sit outside. It's a lovely evening.'

Jeanie's hand shook as she took the glass of chilled white he proffered.

'Come on then, tell me what's up.' He took a leisurely sip and settled back in the garden chair, the look on his face one of pure pleasure. 'I hope it's not another rant about the country,' he added, his eyes, so like Ellie's, alight with mischief.

Jeanie, by contrast, sat bolt upright, her wine held away from her as if it were an unwelcome distraction. What she was about to say was so beyond anything she could ever have imagined herself saying that she almost laughed at the sheer implausibility of it.

'George . . . there's no easy way to tell you this, but I've fallen in love with someone else.'

There, it was done.

For a moment she thought he hadn't heard, or perhaps that she hadn't spoken after all. The sun didn't fall from the sky, George went on lounging there as if nothing had happened. Then he blinked, stared at her.

'What did you say?'

She put her wine down, frightened she might drop the glass on the stone terrace. It seemed very important not to do so.

'I met this man, a few months ago . . . and . . . well, we've become very close.' Even to her own ears this sounded coy, like a line out of some trite romantic melodrama.

George sat up.

'Jeanie, don't be ridiculous. You can't be in love with someone else . . . it's . . . well, it's ridiculous.'

She held his gaze.

'This is a joke, right?' She heard the anger building.

'I wish it were, George.'

Now he stood, smacked his glass down on the table and stood staring down at her.

'Stop it, stop this at once.'

She dropped her eyes.

'Who is he?'

'His name is Ray Allan. I met him in the park with Ellie.'

'I don't believe you.' His tone was stubborn and final. He began to walk away, back through the French windows into the kitchen.

'George, come back.' Jeanie hurried after him. 'Where are you going?'

Her husband went on walking towards the hall.

'I'm not going to stand around listening to this drivel,' she heard him mutter.

'George!' She reached him and grabbed his arm, swinging him round to face her. He tried to pull away, but she, in that moment, was stronger. 'We have to talk about this.'

Then he looked her squarely in the eye and she saw the pain. 'I don't want to talk about it.'

But Jeanie had spent a decade giving in to her husband's powerful denial, and it wasn't going to happen any more.

'No. No, George. We *are* going to talk about it. We have to.' She began to drag him back into the kitchen and pushed him down in a chair. Sitting down on the other side of the table, she watched his eyelids flutter across his blank, shuttered stare.

'There's nothing to say.' He wouldn't look at her, and began to flip the edge of his clock magazine back and forth between his thumb and forefinger. It was the only sound in the kitchen except for the clocks themselves. She snatched it away and threw it to the other end of the table.

'So you're just going to pretend nothing's happened?'

'Well, what do you want me to do? Shoot myself? Shoot him?' He paused, raised his eyebrow at her. 'Shoot you, even?'

'Please.'

He got up and stood for a moment watching her. 'Jeanie, I don't know what's been going on and I don't want to. I trust you to sort it out. Meanwhile I don't see the point in talking about it.'

And with that he turned on his heel and left her.

Halfway to the door he stopped and faced her again, a question, a comment obviously on the tip of his tongue. But whatever it was he couldn't say it.

Instead he nodded his head twice, briskly, and went on his way.

She sat at the kitchen table in the gathering darkness, numb. Once again he had refused to believe her, negated her feelings, leaving her in the limbo of the unheard. Yet he *had* heard her, she knew he had; she saw the pain, but it was as if nothing had changed.

The sound of her mobile roused her.

'Mum, it's me. Are you alone?'

'Yes, Dad's upstairs.'

'About last night: you haven't told Dad yet, have you?' Before Jeanie had a chance to speak, Chanty rushed on. 'Because you shouldn't, it would hurt him so much. I was being selfish. You shocked me and I wanted to get back at you, I wanted to blackmail you into dumping Ray. But that's not fair on Dad, is it? I was drunk and upset about everything. Don't tell him, Mum, please. I'm not condoning what you and Ray are doing, but if it's a passing whim then get on with it and don't ruin what you have with Dad.'

Jeanie heard her breath coming in short bursts as if she were climbing stairs. In the background was the ping of a lift. She heard her daughter say goodnight to someone. 'I've already told him, darling.'

'Oh no . . . oh God, this is my fault. What did he say?'

'He didn't believe me, then refused to talk about it. The usual. He said he was sure I'd sort it out. Chanty, this is *not* your fault. None of what has happened is your fault.'

'So are you saying Dad wasn't particularly upset?'

'He was very upset, of course he was, but he wouldn't admit it, probably not even to himself.'

'Don't say I know, will you? He'd hate that.'

'I won't.'

'You sound miserable.'

'I am, but it's my own doing. I just wish he would talk to me, even if it's to say he hates me.'

'I hope he doesn't hate you. Better go, I'm at the Tube. Talk later. Bye, Mum. Give Dad my love.'

Jeanie waited, hoping to catch George. Then she realized he was right: there really was nothing to talk about. What did she want him to say? Awkward questions about the detail of how, why and where were not

George's style. So she went to bed, despite it being hardly ten, and attempted to read a novel that Rita had lent her. It was an epic set in India, but there were too many characters for Jeanie's tired brain to get a grip on. She kept having to turn back to the beginning, and very soon she gave up, switched off the light and fell into an exhausted sleep.

She awoke to an odd sound. It was almost like a kitten, a sort of stifled mewling, and it was coming from the other side of the bed. Jeanie froze, her brain whirring with possibilities. Very slowly she slid her left hand out of the duvet and found the light switch. As she clicked it, the bedside light shone out, and there, lying curled in a foetal position on the end of Jeanie's bed, was her husband.

'George?' Jeanie, horrified, reached out to touch him. But he seemed catatonic, the rigid body tight-curled, the almost mechanical cries not coming from a conscious mind. He was icy to her touch, his hands clutched to his chest, eyes shut in a white, drawn face. Her heart racing, she automatically reacted without panic, as her long-ago training had taught her, quickly wrapping him in her duvet, dragging his long, pyjamaed body from the edge of the bed.

'George, darling . . .' she lay against him, cradling

273

him in her arms and rocking him to and fro like a child. 'It's all right, come on, open your eyes. Open your eyes, George.'

She gently brushed his hair back from his clammy forehead, as she so often did with Ellie, stroking his face and body firmly and repeating loudly, over and over, any words that might rouse him from this state. In time she felt him stirring in her arms and the whimpering stopped, but as he attempted to uncurl himself from the clenched knot of his distress, he began to shake uncontrollably.

When he opened his eyes, his gaze was blank and uncomprehending.

'Jeanie? Help me . . . I'm so cold . . . what's happening to me?'

'You'll be OK, you've had a turn.' She began to inch him round so that he was propped against her pillows and wrapped him more tightly in the duvet. 'Do you have any pain anywhere?'

'No, no pain . . . why am I shaking? I can't seem to control myself . . . I'm frightened, Jeanie.'

After a while the shaking lessened and colour began to return to his face.

'How did I get here?' His voice was breathy and faint.

'I don't know. I woke to hear this noise and it was you. You didn't seem conscious, you must have been in shock.'

'Shock . . . shock?' He looked at her, bemused. 'Why would I be in shock?'

Jeanie's heart sank. Please, she thought, please don't make me have to repeat everything all over again. She didn't reply, just held him close. He seemed to doze off for a while, his head sunk on his chest. He looked so old suddenly, naked and vulnerable without his glasses.

Jeanie waited for him to wake, guilt sitting heavy on her heart. For months now her feelings for Ray had made everything George said or did seem faint and lacking in reality. But now, lying in her arms, he was intensely present, his face almost as familiar to her as her own.

Jeanie left her husband in her bed and went downstairs to make tea. He had been awake for half an hour, physically recovered despite looking drawn and weak. She had gone up to fetch his glasses for him, still neatly folded by his unmade bed, and wondered at the mental processes that had led him, in the still watches of the night, to lie mewling at her bedside. She had never seen George cry, not once in the thirty-five years she'd known him.

'Jeanie, we must talk,' had been his first words on waking, as if he had fallen asleep in the middle of a conversation and was taking up where he left off.

Making tea was delaying the inevitable, she was well aware of that, but she hadn't had much sleep and felt hardly strong enough to hear what he needed to tell her.

She sat for a moment at the kitchen table, gathering her energy. It was six-twenty and a bright, sparkling summer morning, one she would have relished under other circumstances.

'Thank you.' George accepted the tea almost formally. 'Sit with me, Jeanie. I need to tell you something.'

'George, I'm sorry. I feel so responsible for last night. You were in such a state, and I know it's my fault, but why don't we leave it for now, wait to talk until you're feeling stronger.'

He shook his head firmly. 'This can't wait. It isn't about you. Please, listen to me, or my courage might fail me.'

Jeanie looked questioningly at him, but his face was set as he waited for her to settle on the bed.

'None of this is your fault. I've let you down badly because I've been such a coward.' He sat hugging his legs to his chest in an uncharacteristically childlike pose, his eyes, poking over the top of his knees, washed out and solemn behind his glasses. As Jeanie watched his face, she realized George had never looked young even when he had been. Measured and responsible in everything he did, he often seemed shut away from Jeanie and the rest of the world. Now his look was resolute; there was no longer any whisper of fear.

'Jeanie.' His gaze met her own puzzled one. 'I can find no easy way to say this, no way of making it more palatable . . .' he made a short, harsh sound, 'more palatable to you or to me.' She watched him take a deep breath and found her own heart beating loud in her ears, as if she too shared the as-yet unnamed dread. 'I was abused as a boy. It was my father's friend, Stephen Acland, the one who took me for the school holidays when I didn't fly home to wherever my father was being a diplomat.' The words, clearly rehearsed, came in a rush.

Jeanie stared at him. 'Sexually abused?'

George nodded.

'But . . . you went there for years.'

'And he abused me for years. From ten to fourteen.'

277

His face twisted in what looked like long-suppressed rage.

'God! Why didn't you tell me, George? All these years you've kept this horrible secret and felt you couldn't tell me?' She thought for a moment. 'But you said how wonderful he was to you . . . you said he was so clever, so cultured, so funny . . .'

George nodded again. 'Oh, he was. He taught me so much. Jeanie, it was my fault. I let him. I went to his study after supper when he asked me to – he was teaching me chess.'

Jeanie snorted angrily; her head was spinning. 'Ha! is that what he called it? The bastard, the sick, sick bastard.' She glared at her husband. 'Abuse is abuse, George, and it is never anyone's fault but the perpe-trator's. Christ, this is terrible! Terrible that it happened at all and even worse that you felt you couldn't tell me. What did you think I'd say?'

George shrugged, 'I was just so ashamed. I didn't want you to think I was gay. I'm not gay.'

'I didn't say you were.'

'And I thought you'd be disgusted. I've always thought it was my fault and I assumed you'd think the same. But there was no way I could tell my parents. My father would never have believed me in a million years anyway. Stephen was a fellow officer in the Gunners. They served together in Burma and were in the siege of Malta. Stephen was a war hero; he got the DSO for rescuing three men from a blazing tank in North Africa. My father thought he'd be an inspiring role model for me.'

'And his wife?'

'Caroline had no idea, I'm a hundred per cent certain of that. It was a different age, Jeanie. Nowadays it's talked about all the time; you've only got to speak to a child these days to be accused of abuse, but the fifties were more innocent. Someone like Caroline would probably hardly have known what it was, let alone suspected her adored husband was buggering me in the study after dinner. It was a large house, and she never disturbed him in his study. I'm sure she was tucked up in bed with cold cream on her face and a good novel from Boots Lending Library.'

Jeanie smiled. 'Boots Lending Library, I'd forgotten that.' She shook her head. 'Sorry . . . All this time . . . what, fifty years? And you never said a thing. God, George, I don't know what to say, except I wish you'd told me.'

They were both silent for a minute.

'So what happened? When did it end? Have you seen him since?'

George stretched his legs out in front of him, blinked a couple of times.

'It ended when Pa died. I was fourteen and at Sherborne by then, and my mother came home to the house we'd always had in Dorset.'

'But didn't you still see him? If he was so close to your father?'

'They went to live in South Africa. I suppose Ma might have met up with them when they made trips over, but people didn't fly about so much in those days. Anyway Ma, as you know, was the most antisocial woman on the planet. Always a joke that she'd been an ambassador's wife.'

Jeanie had liked Imogen. She was charming in a quiet way, gentle, very vague and never happier than when left alone to tend her beautiful garden. She'd died nearly fifteen years ago from complications after a fall. George had been devastated.

'Did you ever tell her?'

George laughed sadly. 'Can you imagine it? Anyway, even if she had believed me, what would have been the point? It'd just have upset her.'

'I suppose . . . but you could have told me. Didn't you trust me?'

George reached over and took her hand. 'It wasn't

to do with trust. I thought I'd lose you.'

'Lose me? You thought I'd stop loving you because you were the victim of child abuse? That's ridiculous.'

'It may seem so to you . . . and maybe now it seems stupid to me too. But at the time it was still so much a part of me. I thought about it all the time, every day of my life, and I thought you'd hate that, being made to think of it too, of me and him . . . but mainly I was ashamed. I still am.'

Jeanie was suddenly overwhelmed by such fury that she wanted to hit something. She got up and stamped around the bedroom, not knowing what to do with her emotions.

'You were so young. Ten years old. How did you cope with it alone? You can hardly have known what was happening.'

'He made it into a game.'

'Sick, sick . . . vile bastard.' She couldn't deal with the image, with the young boy in the study, vulnerable and without the necessary know-how or support to reject this man's manipulation, his casual pleasure.

'You see?' George was watching her. 'Don't you wish you didn't know?'

Jeanie went over to the bed and hugged him fiercely. 'That's not the point.'

17

She lay in the bath and watched the warm water lap to and fro across her breasts. Over and over in her head ran the same image – she'd seen a photograph of him in his school uniform at around that age: a gangly, shy boy swamped by a blazer that 'would last'. And George had lived with this every day, alone. She wanted to cry for him, his childhood stolen, and also for herself, because the tentacles of Stephen Acland's vile crime had ended up corroding their marriage. George had finally explained what had happened that day, over ten years ago, when he'd rejected her for the isolation of the spare room.

'I was having lunch with Simon in Primrose Hill,' George had told her. Even telling the story, Jeanie could see, was wearing for him, but she could also see that he was desperate to get it off his chest. 'And suddenly I heard a voice at one of the other tables. I instantly knew it was him; he had a very distinctive way of talking, very fast, very fluent, always loud as if he knew he had something interesting to say, and the remnants of his South African childhood in some of the vowels – it was unmistakable. I must have gone pale, because Simon asked if I was feeling all right. I pretended I was a little queasy and went to the loo. Acland followed me. He must have been in his seventies by then, but to me he looked no different. I really thought I was going to be sick. He caught me outside the Gents and acted as if nothing had ever happened. He asked me how I was, said how lovely it was to see me after all this time. Told me Caroline had died the year before and how much he missed her. I didn't say a thing, I couldn't. Then Simon, worried about me, pitched up too, and Acland, brazen as ever, started telling him what a wonderful time we'd had together when I was a boy, and how much my visits to his house meant to him. He said, he actually said, "You and I were such special friends, weren't we, George?" He used those words, Jeanie, "special friends" . . . can you believe the man's nerve, his sheer affrontery? But he looked at me . . . cowering there, white as a sheet . . .

and of course he knew I hadn't told and I never would.'

Jeanie had put her arms round him, still in his navy pyjamas after what seemed like the longest night of her life, and knew there was nothing on God's earth she could do to erase these memories.

'Did you think of him . . . what he did to you . . . when we were making love? Was that the problem?' she'd had to ask.

George's look was tormented.

'Yes and no. I wish I could say not at all, but I can't. I know it's so horrible to even think that would be the case. I did manage over the years to put it away in another part of my brain, I learnt to contain the thing . . . sort of. Sometimes it would ambush me and I'd be back there as if I was still ten, eleven, but mostly I lived with it. But seeing him that day finished me off. I suppose avoiding it couldn't work forever, and that night, when you and I were in bed . . . he was right there between us, smiling that smug smile. I panicked and ran. I should have told you then and there, Jeanie, it would have been so much better for us both, but I just couldn't do it.'

'You should talk to a lawyer, take the bastard to court . . . at least see a therapist.'

George had shaken his head. 'No, please don't say

that. I can't tell anyone else, ever. Please don't tell Chanty, Jeanie, I couldn't bear it,' he had pleaded. 'It's all so vile, what would she think of me?'

Jeanie had winced at the thought. She knew Chanty would feel only horrified sympathy for him, but surely no daughter should have to deal with such a revelation about their own father.

'Of course it's up to you who you tell. But please, you have to go to a therapist. Telling me won't change a thing, you need to sort this out with someone who knows about these things, or it, *he*, will haunt you for the rest of your life. Please, George . . . no more secrets.'

'Are you sure he's not invented all this to stop you leaving him?' Rita packed her tennis racket into its cover and zipped it up. Jeanie had played like a demon today, driving the ball to the line-edge with killer force, each shot discharging another bout of rage at what Acland had done to her husband.

Jeanie stared at her. 'You can't be serious.'

'Well . . .' Her friend shrugged, 'it wouldn't be the first time someone suddenly remembers something expediently.'

'He didn't "suddenly remember", he never forgot,

Rita; he told me he's thought about it every day of his life.'

'OK, just checking, sweetheart. Don't get me wrong, I'm not saying what happened, if it happened, isn't dire – no torture is bad enough for a paedophile. But George isn't stupid, you know. Even though he pretended otherwise, he must know you were contemplating leaving when you told him about Ray.'

'I can't leave him now.'

'So it worked, then.'

'Rita . . . please, stop being so cynical. You weren't there. He was in a terrible state. I absolutely know he didn't make it up.'

'You can't stay with him out of pity, Jeanie.'

She didn't know how to answer. Suddenly her friend grabbed her by both arms and looked her full in her face.

'Jean Lawson, this . . . is . . . your . . . life.'

'Meaning?'

'Meaning you know exactly.' She let go her grip, shaking her head as if baffled. 'Are you saying it's Goodnight Charlie for Park Man, then?'

'Maybe what I feel for Ray is just foolishness. Chanty said I'd be left alone and unloved . . . and old, if I broke up my marriage.'

Rita snorted, gathered up her things and began to drive Jeanie away from the court.

'Well, obviously she's going to say that. She's your daughter. She doesn't want either of you hurt. But that doesn't mean she's right, darling.'

'I know, but you didn't see George. He was so pathetic, so vulnerable. If I said I was leaving now I don't know if he'd survive.' She remembered his curled, shaking figure.

'He would,' Rita said firmly. 'People do . . . George does.'

Jeanie looked at her friend. 'Why are you so keen for me to leave him?'

'I'm not so keen for you to do anything specific. I just saw how you were when you met Ray. You came alive. I hate waste, and I feel you're wasted on George. He's not a bad man, but he lives beneath the surface. You're always dragging him through life, Jeanie. It must be tiring.'

She did feel tired, overwhelmingly so. And letting her guard down, she suddenly knew that she did want to leave George. The thought no longer spelt loss, but rather opened such a vista of freedom, such a scent of life, like breathing the fresh early morning air from an open window. Something had changed. Perhaps the burden of his secret had chained her to him, and now, ironically, when he needed her most, she was finally free. Yet the thought was transient. Responsibility tethered her obstinately to the present.

'I know what you're saying, Rita, I do.'

'But you're not going to take a chance?'

'How can I? I can't leave him immediately after he's revealed such a horrifying secret. It would confirm his worst fear, that I'm disgusted by him. I can't even think about Ray right now.'

Rita dropped her badgering tone; now she just looked sad. 'When will you tell Ray?'

Jeanie shook her head. 'I don't know. I haven't spoken to him since before I told George. He'll know something's up.'

'Poor man, he's been trumped.'

Jeanie looked sharply at her friend. 'You still think George is playing me, don't you?'

'He's no slouch at it, Jeanie. Don't forget he was quite happy to modify your marriage ten years ago without 'fessing up – he must have seen how unhappy that made you. He could have told you then, but he waited till he thought you were about to leg it. That smacks of self-interest, no?'

'I don't think these things are controllable. He told me when he could.'

Rita raised her eyebrows. 'Whatever. Listen, darling, you have to do what you have to do, and in the end I'm fully behind you . . . all the way, whatever it is. But please, *please* think twice before you pack your life back into last year's suitcase.'

'I'll be late tonight,' she told him. 'I'm meeting Rita.'

George looked at her sharply. 'You only saw her yesterday.'

'She's got tickets for the new Tom Stoppard play.'

This was true, but she wasn't taking Jeanie.

'Rather you than me,' he muttered, turning back to his crossword, a piece of toast dangling limply from the other hand.

'I'll go straight from the shop. I might be late; she likes to eat afterwards.'

She knew she should have just told him she was seeing Ray. But since the other night she had begun to view him differently, as if he were a hothouse plant that needed constant nurturing. She thought him too frail to deal with the truth.

'Enjoy,' he said, not looking at her. Then as she reached the door she heard her name. 'By the way, we have two people coming to view the house today. The agent says there's been a lot of interest.'

When Jeanie made no comment, he went on, 'It's exciting, Jeanie; it'll be a new start for us. I know we can make it, you and I. We've come this far and it hasn't been all bad.' He grinned winningly at her and she smiled back.

'I never said it was,' she replied. It was as if George's breakdown two nights ago had never existed, the pain she had witnessed on his face just a bad dream. He hadn't mentioned it since, but she couldn't believe anyone, not even George, had the perverse strength to bury a confession as momentous as that a second time.

'You're shaking,' Ray said softly.

She wasn't sure how she had arrived at his flat. The walk down the hill had passed in a pall of anguish. However much she told herself that this was the right thing to do, it felt entirely wrong. When they had talked on the phone, and Jeanie had told him about the abuse, Ray had been largely silent. Perhaps he'd known what it would mean to Jeanie.

'Ray . . .' She had hoped to be businesslike, to tell him the truth and hold her feelings at bay. Instead, as he gathered her into his arms, the pain of the last weeks instantly receded and she found herself delighting in the smell of him, the feel of his cheek against hers, the pure pleasure of his embrace.

'Don't,' he said, as she pulled away and began to explain. 'I know what you need to say, but please, don't say the words. I don't want to remember the words.'

Jeanie had no more desire to say it than Ray had to hear it.

'Let's just have tonight,' he whispered.

Two glasses and a bottle of wine sat waiting on the coffee table and Chet Baker's melancholy notes filled the room. But Ray took Jeanie's hand in his and drew her deliberately towards the bedroom.

The room was bathed in soft evening light. As she sat down on the bed, Ray knelt in front of her. He kissed her softly on the lips, his hands slipping the straps from her shoulders and moving them down across her naked breasts, her body. His touch was light, barely brushing her skin, but so sensuous and emotionally charged that she could hardly breathe.

'You're sure you want this, Jeanie?' he asked, looking intently into her face, his eyes alight with desire.

She nodded, trembling. And then his mouth was on hers, urgent and full of a long-repressed passion which was only equalled by her own. They sank back on to the bed, reaching for each other, giving and receiving the caresses of which she had hardly dared dream. And their lovemaking was beyond anything she could have imagined.

Chet Baker was a long time silent before either of them spoke again.

'What's the time?' she asked.

Ray glanced towards the bedside clock.

'Late.'

'I should go.' The words seemed to come from someone else. She heard Ray sigh beside her, but she was drugged with a pleasure so powerful and so unexpected that she could barely focus.

'We make a good team,' he chuckled, dropping a light kiss on the top of her head. 'And now you've had your wicked way, you're going to dump me.'

He got up, and Jeanie watched as he moved through to the other room and selected Miles Davis's *Kind of Blue* from the shelf. His naked body was strong and compact, yet he was light on his feet and as graceful as a dancer.

'I know who Miles Davis is,' she insisted when he got back into bed, kissing her as he teased her about her musical ignorance. The jazz was more lyrical, lighter than Baker, and she sensed Ray's joy in their lovemaking informing his choice.

'Tip of the iceberg . . . this is jazz lite. Wait till you hear some of my hardcore collection.'

Tears sprang to her eyes as she remembered why she had come. She sat up in bed, drawing the duvet round her breasts.

'I can't . . . I can't leave him, Ray, please understand. It's not to do with you or how I feel about you . . . tonight was unforgettable, for me unique.' She gazed at him, wiping the tears with one hand, the other clutching his own as if she were drowning. 'If he hadn't told me about the abuse . . . if . . .'

'Shh, Jeanie, shh, please, don't talk about it.'

'But I have to go, it's past eleven.'

Despite the hour, neither felt remotely inclined to move. For another half-hour they remained entwined, warm and sleepy, in each other's arms, until she forced herself upright.

Sighing, she dragged herself out of bed and began to gather her strewn clothes.

'I'll walk you home.'

They walked in silence, holding tightly to each other's hand. The night was cool and cloudy. At the top of the hill Ray bent to kiss her softly on the lips.

'*Dear Heart,*' he whispered, '*the thought of you Is the pain at my side . . .*

The shadow that chills my view.
I am afraid to lose you,
I am afraid of my fear.

You know where I am if you change your mind,' he murmured, and despite the deliberately casual tone, she saw in his eyes the bleakness of loss, reflected so clearly in her own.

The house was silent except for the loud, insistent ticking of the many clocks. The long-case in the hall wheezed the quarter as Jeanie passed up the stairs to her room. She no longer felt like crying; she just wanted to sleep forever and never wake. She didn't turn the light on, just shed her clothes as she walked towards her bed, lowering herself on to the smooth, cool linen and pulling the duvet close around her for comfort. But as she turned on her side she let out a cry. There, next to her, was George, fast asleep on the other side of the bed.

'Hello, Jeanie,' he muttered sleepily, woken by her cry.

'What are you doing here?' Jeanie was wide awake now, and furious.

George sat up in the half-light from the window, where the curtains were left undrawn.

'Sorry if I startled you. I thought it was time to start afresh, stop this silliness of separate bedrooms.'

Jeanie was nonplussed. 'Without asking me?'

'You're my wife, Jeanie; I shouldn't have to ask your permission to sleep in your bed,' he replied huffily.

'No, well, you shouldn't have left it in the first place,' she snapped. 'I'm tired. Please, George, go back to your room and we can discuss it tomorrow.'

Would he guess what she had been doing? Couldn't he sense it?

'OK, OK, if you insist. I thought it might be a nice surprise for you.'

'It was certainly a surprise,' she muttered.

'You're very late,' he said, as he stood by the bed, hitching up his pyjama trousers. She saw him staring at her.

'I said I would be. Rita hates eating before the theatre.'

'But it's nearly one.' His eyes continued to bore into her.

'Go to bed, George.' Jeanie turned her back on him. She was so close to telling him where she had really been.

Once the door had shut behind her husband, Jeanie hunched under the duvet, angry that his presence had dragged her so brutally from Ray, feeling as if her sanctuary had been violated. Fairness to George did not come into it.

★

Chanty called unexpectedly at the shop the next morning.

'Hi, darling, this is a nice surprise. Where's Ellie?'

'She's fine, she's at nursery. It's Wednesday.'

'Is it?'

'Are you OK? You look really tired.'

'I am. Late night with Rita.'

'Dirty stop-out, eh?' Chanty laughed. 'Hope it was fun.' She checked around to see if Jola was listening, then, despite the fact that Jeanie was alone in the shop, lowered her voice. 'How's it going with Dad?'

'It's fine,' Jeanie lied, the weight of George's secret sitting heavy on her mind. But it wasn't her secret to tell, and Jeanie realized with a shock that now she lived in a world of secrets. Chanty seemed happy to take her reply at face value, however.

'Good, that's good. Listen, Mum, Alex and I were wondering if you and Dad wanted to come over for supper this evening. We haven't seen you together for ages.'

'That would be lovely, darling. Why aren't you at work?' She thought her daughter looked unusually happy.

'I'm going in now. Had a few things to do this morning.' She seemed to hesitate, then reached across the counter to kiss her mother on the cheek. 'Tonight, then? Come around seven, then you can see Ellie before she goes to bed. If it stays nice we'll do a barbecue.'

After Chanty had gone, Jeanie slumped on the stool behind the till. She had had little time to dwell on the previous night, but the pleasure of their love-making, so surprising, so magical, still hovered around her tired body even as she worked, like a soft veil between her and the world. Ray had brought her alive, and every inch of her body reminded her of this. She refused to contemplate the probability that she would never experience it again. George had been his usual self that morning, hardly contrite about his trespass, and grilling her about every detail of the evening. By the time she left for work she was exhausted by her lies.

Ellie rushed along the hall to welcome Jeanie that evening, waiting to be picked up, then throwing her little arms round her neck. She was fresh from the bath, her hair still damp, her face glowing pink and clean. She pointed proudly to her pyjama top.

'Gin . . . look, Gin, it says I an angel.' She laughed and snuggled into her grandmother's body. 'Mmmmm . . . I bin waiting for you.'

'Your top is right, you are an angel.' Jeanie buried her face in the child's sweet-smelling hair.

'She's been dying to see you.' Chanty smiled, directing them to the garden. 'Dad's already here. Alex is doing a barbecue.'

Jeanie took Ellie outside and settled in one of the chairs on the wooden decking. George was hovering, a glass of wine in his hand, but he seemed uncomfortably on edge.

'We've had an offer.'

'A good one?'

'Amazingly, the asking price. They're only the fifth couple to see it. But the agent said there were two other people after it, and they panicked.'

'That's fantastic. I'm not surprised, it's a lovely house.' Alex avoided Jeanie's eye and addressed George. 'So you've accepted?'

George nodded, but he didn't seem to be as jubilant as Jeanie expected.

'You don't seem very happy about it,' Jeanie remarkd.

He stared at her vacantly. 'No, I am, I'm delighted. I thought it would be much more of a drama. I did call you to tell you, but your phone was switched off.'

Jeanie watched Alex poking ineffectually at the chicken pieces. It was clear the coals were not nearly hot enough, but he didn't appear to have noticed. There was definitely a strange atmosphere; everyone, including Chanty, seemed disconnected. She did a puzzle with Ellie on the garden table. Ellie knew the jigsaw back to front and triumphantly slotted the pieces in place as quickly as her small hands could manage. It wasn't till her granddaughter was tucked up in bed that Chanty emerged from the kitchen carrying a tray with a bottle of champagne. Jeanie saw her flash a smile at her husband.

'Are we celebrating the house?' George asked.

Neither Chanty nor Alex replied until the champagne was poured.

'We have something to tell you,' she said, and Jeanie could see that she could hardly contain her excitement. Alex had stopped cooking and stood beside her, looking sheepish, as he always did when faced with a family occasion. 'I'm pregnant.'

Jeanie was instantly lifted out of her tiredness.

'That's wonderful! How fantastic, darling. When's it due?'

'I'm about ten weeks already, so just after Christmas.'

She hugged her daughter, patted her son-in-law on the back.

'Ten weeks and you didn't tell us?'

'I didn't know till this morning. I suppose all the

stuff with Ellie distracted me, and it was only when I started being sick that I realized something was up.' Chanty leaned over and kissed her husband on the cheek. 'Alex worked it out.'

'But this is such bad timing,' Jeanie wailed. 'We'll be miles away when it's born.'

'You can stay up here. It'll be fine, Mum. I'll need you to help with Ellie big time.'

'Does she know yet?'

Chanty shook her head. 'The books say to leave it till much later; they have no concept of time at that age.'

Jeanie smiled. 'She ain't going to like it!'

The conversation, mainly between the women, flowed on, no one noticing that George had fallen silent and was sitting morosely nursing yet another glass of wine in the corner of the garden. When Alex announced the chicken and sausages were ready and they took their seats at the table, George didn't move.

'Dad? Come on, we're ready to eat.'

George looked round, but still made no attempt to join them.

'George?' Jeanie went over to him. 'Are you OK?'

'Not so . . . good, old girl.' She could hear the effort he was making to get the words out.

'Are you feeling ill?'

George stared up at her. 'I don't feel great . . . muss say.' He waved his glass at his daughter and son-in-law. 'Wonnerful news . . . give me a grandson . . . why not . . .'

Chanty looked crestfallen. 'Dad, you're drunk.'

George laughed and nodded. 'I s'pose I am . . . sorry 'bout that . . . but it's been a helluva week.'

'George, let me take you home . . . come on, get up.'

Jeanie gestured to Alex to help her, but George was having none of it and jerked his arm from her grasp.

'I'm talking . . . I'm telling them 'bout my week.'

'Stop it, George. You're not making any sense.'

'I'm making perfect sense . . . they should know about my week . . . because my wife is having sex with another man . . . and I told her . . . told her about Missa Acland . . . so she knows now . . . and it's been a helluva week for all of us.'

There was a shocked silence.

'Who's Mr Acland?' Chanty looked to Jeanie, accusation in her eyes, as George had slumped into silence, his glass hanging loosely in his hand.

'It's a long story and one best told another time,

darling,' Jeanie whispered, signalling to Alex to take George's other arm.

'Missa Acland ... Stephen Acland Esquire ... buggerer esstraordinaire, played with me ... chess.' He pointed drunkenly at Jeanie. 'She knows now ... helluva week ... helluva ... sorry ...'

Then George began to cry, weak, plaintive whimperings it was an agony to listen to.

'Mum? What's he talking about? What's going on?'

Jeanie gave up trying to move her husband. 'It would be better coming from him, but seeing as he's in no fit state ...'

The chicken and salads sat untouched on the table between them as she told them the story, watching their faces register bewilderment, then disgust, then harden gradually into anger.

'A war hero,' Alex muttered through clenched teeth.

Chanty looked devastated. 'That's so horrible, Mum. I can't believe he never told anyone. Poor Dad ... how do you deal with something like that?'

George suddenly staggered to his feet. 'Did you say something 'bout food?' He stood, swaying for a moment, staring unfocused at them, then slid gently to the wooden decking, spilling what remained of his wine and knocking his glasses to the ground. Chanty burst into tears.

'I've never seen Dad like this; it's dreadful, just dreadful what happened to him. Help him, Alex, get him inside.'

Alex came home with Jeanie in the car, and together they undressed her husband and put him to bed. He was barely conscious, only occasionally rousing himself to mutter another raft of incoherent syllables.

'Will he be OK?' Alex pulled the duvet over his father-in-law with surprising gentleness. He looked at Jeanie. 'Shouldn't we walk him up and down or something, give him black coffee?' He smiled apologetically. 'I'm not much of a medical whiz, I'm afraid.'

'I think he's better just sleeping it off. I don't think he's actually drunk that much; most of it's shock, him not dealing with the abuse thing. I've tried to get him to see a therapist, but he refuses.'

'It must be terrible, suddenly confronting your past like that. God, he's going to have one stonking hangover tomorrow.'

They left George and went back downstairs.

'Thanks so much for your help, Alex.'

'Are you OK? This can't be easy for you either.'

For the first time in her relationship with Alex, she felt a genuine warmth for the man.

'Let's just say things have been better.' She patted his arm. 'Look after Chanty . . . and Alex, that's such great news about the baby.'

His face lightened. 'It is, isn't it? I never thought I wanted one, let alone two, but hey . . . I'm thrilled.'

18

Jeanie ached for Ray. It seemed to her that she wanted him more than breathing. But a crowd of dreary, but imperative, practicalities lined up and took over her life. So she carried him silently around with her, refusing to believe she would never feel his touch again, never experience the gentle intensity of his lovemaking. And despite reaching for her mobile a hundred times a day to call him, she resisted, because what did she have to offer him while she stubbornly stuck to her sense of duty?

The truth was that George needed her; he had sunk into a deep, reactive depression. Since the night at Chanty and Alex's house he had become largely unresponsive, shuffling aimlessly round the house like an old man. He didn't change his clothes unless Jeanie removed the old ones; he only shaved when she reminded him. He shut himself up in his clock room all day, but when Jeanie went to see if he was all right, he was just sitting in front of the same clock pieces that were there the day she had gone to tell him about Ray.

'You've got to see Andrew. You're not well,' she told him every day.

'I don't need a doctor. I'm a bit low, that's all. I'll be fine when we get to Somerset. Just can't seem to get my energy up,' George would invariably reply.

The new house seemed to be his answer to everything. Jeanie had rung the doctor herself. Andrew Hall had been their GP for over twenty years and was a bluff, dependable bear of a man with two impressive cauliflower ears acquired in his tighthead prop days on the rugger field.

'I can't do a thing unless he wants me to, Jean, you know that,' he'd said.

'But that's the nature of depression, isn't it? He doesn't realize how ill he is.'

'Has something triggered it, do you know?'

'He'll have to tell you that . . . but yes.'

'Fine, fine, quite understand. Get him here and I'll do what I can. But unless you feel he's a danger to himself or others there's not a thing I can do without his consent. Is he suicidal at all? In your opinion?'

Jeanie considered the doctor's question for a moment.

'No . . . no, I don't think so. But how can you tell? God, what am I to do? I'm at my wits' end with him.' She had fought back the tears, but the doctor knew her too well.

'Shall I drop round? Do you think he'd open up to me in a casual sort of way?'

George had greeted Andrew with a weary smile.

'What are you doing here? The old girl been on to you, has she?' He cast a shrewd look at his wife.

Andrew's hearty guffaw rang hollow. 'Course she has, that's her job, and a jolly good thing she did by the look of you.'

George had thrown his hands up in frustration.

'I know Jeanie worries, but I'm fine, honestly I am. Just a bit tired, that's all. It's always nice to see you, Andrew, but go away, please, and look after someone who's really ill.'

Andrew had signalled to Jeanie to leave them alone, but when he spoke to her later he was uncharacteristically gloomy.

'You're right, he's in a bad way all right, but he

wouldn't talk to me at all. Went on about his handicap and Somerset, but got irritated when I said he looked rough. Sorry, Jean. All you can do is keep an eye on him and if you think he's getting worse, or might do himself harm, get on to me at once. These things tend to be self-limiting; they wear themselves out over time, but it could be a while. Don't give up on him.'

So Jeanie resigned herself to waiting and watching. And although she saw no signs that George was getting worse, she didn't like to leave him for long periods and decided to take on someone to help Jola in the shop earlier than planned. She would have had to do so when they moved – before George's collapse they had agreed she should come up three days a week until the business was sold.

As August approached, the days – baking hot, they kept saying, like no summer since the dawn of time – were filled with small, round, coloured stickers. Red for Somerset, blue for storage – the Old Rectory was smaller than their Highgate house and had no attic for Uncle Raymond's vast stock of Victorian furniture, which George refused to sell – and yellow stickers for the Sally Army, who most obligingly came round with a van and a team of eager helpers to take away everything that filled neither of the other categories. The more Jeanie looked at the quantity of stuff to be processed, the more she despaired. If you counted Uncle Raymond's tenure, the house had not been properly cleared for over eighty years. George would have been good at this, she realized, with his obsessive, methodical attention to detail; he'd even have enjoyed it. But there was no help from him and some days she had an overwhelming desire to find some giant bin-bag and just empty the entire contents of the house into a skip.

'How's Dad?' Chanty whispered, looking around the kitchen for her father. Jeanie noticed her daughter seemed to talk constantly in whispers these days.

'Don't worry, he's in his room, he can't hear.' Jeanie moved to fill the kettle. 'And even if he was sitting right there at the kitchen table, he probably wouldn't react.'

Chanty looked horrified.

'What are you going to do, Mum?'

'I can't do anything.' Jeanie sighed. 'I've spoken to Dr Hall, and he says that unless he is a "danger to himself or others", as he put it, he couldn't help him until he asked him to.'

'That makes him sound like a lunatic. What does he mean?'

'He means suicide, Chanty. Depressives are vulnerable, obviously. But Dad's not suicidal,' she hurried on, seeing the look on her daughter's face, 'really he's not, darling.' She wasn't lying; she thought this was true.

'But how can you know?' Chanty's voice rose in panic.

Jeanie handed her a cup of tea and pushed the milk carton across the table. She remembered that Chanty was pregnant and more sensitive than usual.

'I can't, not for sure, but he seems to be marking time till we get to the country. He talks about it all the time. He believes things will be OK then, so I'm hoping they will.'

But Chanty was a doer, and she clearly found Jeanie's laissez-faire attitude baffling.

'What if they're not, Mum? You've got to do something now, not wait on the off-chance. Suppose he does decide to . . .' She couldn't say the word.

She got up and began to stride restlessly around the kitchen.

'God, it's hot. I wish this bloody weather would break.' She turned to her mother. 'Maybe you should give up the shop and Ellie and stay here with him, Mum.' Her look was one of entreaty but also of desperation. 'I mean, you're giving up the shop soon anyway. I know it'd be hard for you, but there's so much at stake.'

'Darling, please, calm down. It's quite understandable that your father is depressed, given the circumstances.' She noted her daughter's accusatory glance. 'Blame me all you like, but we have to deal with what's happening now. Go up, talk to him, see for yourself. I'm looking after him all I can, but he doesn't want me hovering about him all day; he tells me to go away.'

Chanty glanced towards the door, then at her watch. Jeanie could see her reluctance.

'Go on, he won't bite. It'll put your mind at rest.' She smiled understandingly and Chanty smiled back.

'Sorry, Mum, for getting at you. It's just Dad's always been so solid, so unflappable. Nothing ever seemed to faze him. I hate it.'

'So do I, but I have to believe he'll be all right. In time.'

As Chanty got to the door she hesitated. 'That man . . . Ray. Are you still seeing him?'

Jeanie shook her head and got an approving nod. It made her furious. She wanted to haul Chanty back and tell her the truth about her feelings. Tell her how sick she was of considering her family above herself. But this is my choice, she reminded herself firmly as she gathered her daughter's empty mug. Her father had always told her and her brother Will that a thing was not worth doing if it wasn't done with grace, and she knew he was right. What worried her was that she had placed herself between a rock and a hard place. She was capable neither of looking after George with grace, nor of leaving him with it.

'Can my have some blarna, Gin?' Ellie had spotted the banana Jeanie had tucked into the hood of the pram.

'You can have some later, in the park.'

It was almost too hot to be out, but Jeanie had decided to take Ellie to the paddling pool at the Lido. These days, whenever she walked anywhere, especially the park or the Heath, she looked for Ray. She longed to catch sight of him as much as she dreaded it. Nothing had changed, but even the pain of seeing him when there could be no follow-up seemed better than this terrible, empty longing.

'No . . . now. My want blarna now.'

Ellie began to whimper and Jeanie gave in and handed a chunk of fruit to her granddaughter. These times with Ellie were so precious to her. She felt, ridiculously, that the child somehow shared in her courtship with Ray, that she had given them her blessing. The thought that she should give up the visits to entomb herself with George – who wouldn't care, or even notice her presence – was unthinkable. But there was always the guilt at leaving him, and when she returned home it was with a certain apprehension.

She reached down to put Ellie's red sun hat back on.

'No . . . don't want it.' The child snatched it off again and flung it on the pavement.

'You must, darling. The sun's very hot, it'll make you ill.'

'No . . . noooooo . . . don't want it . . . Noooooo.' Ellie struggled and squirmed as Jeanie tried to tie the strings beneath her chin, the protest quickly escalating into a full-scale tantrum. The hat was on, but her granddaughter still wrenched at it as she screamed, her little face red and sweating, her huge brown eyes awash with rage.

'Let's not go to the park, let's go to Gin's house.' She made a quick decision, not having the energy for this battle today. At least the house would be cool. She repeated it over again to the toddler until she heard through her screams.

'Gin's house . . . yers, let's go to Gin's house, see Grandadz.' The tantrum stopped abruptly. The only sign was the occasional heaving breath beneath the sun hat, which Ellie had now forgotten about.

Jeanie gave her a drink of water and some more banana as soon as they reached the house.

'Let's do sticking.'

'Sticking . . . yers . . . hurray, my love sticking.' Ellie clapped her little hands with excitement and went straight to the cupboard where the box was kept. George had made a huge collection of things for Ellie to stick, from loo rolls to foil, burnt matches and dead flowers. 'Save that,' he'd command as Jeanie was about to thrust something in the bin.

'Where's Grandadz?'

Jeanie called to George but got no response. She settled the child at the table with the glue stick and paper and went up to the clock room. Her husband was asleep in his chair, his head lolled to one side, his hands clasped across his stomach.

'George . . . George . . . Ellie's here.'

George jumped and stared at her uncomprehendingly.

'Come down, she's asking for you.'

316

He got silently to his feet. 'I must have dropped off.'

Ellie jumped down from the table. 'Grandadz . . . Grandadz . . . come and huwp me stick. Look . . . I got a feather.'

Jeanie watched as George lifted the little girl for a hug, the man and child still for a moment in their close embrace, then sat beside her, picking different bits from the box and handing them to her to paste. Ellie heals us all, she thought, as she noticed her husband silently listening to Ellie's flow of insistent questions. His face, recently so blank and wooden, had been softened into life by his granddaughter.

Jeanie typed up the letter giving their tenant above the shop formal notice. He was a student in his last term at Byam Shaw art college and was due to leave in a couple of weeks anyway, but Jeanie wanted to make sure he did, as she intended to paint the place up and stay there herself on the nights she was up for the shop. George, before he got ill, had been nagging her almost daily to sign up with agents and set the sale in motion. But although it preyed on her mind, she had done nothing about it. Now she guiltily took advantage of George's lack of interest, and made a decision to postpone the sale. She told herself it was too much to deal with at the moment, but the truth was the shop was the only thing keeping her sane. And the only thing which would give her an excuse for leaving Somerset each week.

'I go for lunch now?' Jola put her head round the office door.

'Yes, of course.' Jeanie stretched. 'Is it that time already?'

'You want me wait for you check on Mr Lawson?'

She shook her head. 'No, I'm sure he's fine. I'll go when you get back.'

Jola had been very philosophical about George's illness.

'He get well soon. You see, this not last long. My mother, she have depression two, three times already. Now she take pills, she very happy.'

'But George won't see the doctor,' Jeanie told her, at which Jola shook her head.

'No good, you tell him. Pills very good, he must see doctor. You take him, no nonsense.'

Jeanie went through to take over the till, dogged by a habitual restlessness and distraction. The move was barely ten days away and seemed increasingly unreal. But it was true that over the previous week George had begun to focus intently on the packing, taking over from her the distribution of coloured stickers. Jeanie would come home to long, carefully written lists allocating every chair, lamp, clock, etc. a place in the new house.

She had watched his face light up as they drew on to the gravel drive of the Old Rectory the week before, watched the way he straightened his shoulders as they greeted the spruce James with his Peugeot and took possession of the keys to their new home. James showed them round again, and explained the boiler and the window locks, the septic tank, but it was the garden George seemed most taken with, spending ages, while Jeanie half listened to the agent, pacing round the lawn and the shrubs, peering closely at the plants, touching some of them gently as he passed as if they were long-lost friends. Finally the impatient rattling of the agent's car keys prompted Jeanie to tell James he could go. It had been a strange feeling as she clutched the envelope of keys and realized that this was now, officially, her home. She wanted to run down the drive in the wake of the fast-retreating car and stop him so she could hand them back – this alien house certainly did not feel like home.

On the drive back to London, George had said not a word, slumping into his familiar blankness, and Jeanie had wondered what the house represented to his disturbed mind. She worried that whatever magic he attributed to it would prove ineffective in reality. It wasn't possible to heal psychological trauma by avoiding it, displacing it, despite George's valiant efforts over the last fifty years.

The bell on the shop door roused her and she looked up to see Natalie and Dylan.

'Hello, Jean.' Natalie smiled, apologetic, as if she thought she had no right to be where she was.

'Natalie . . . Dylan, how nice to see you.'

'I'm going to big school,' Dylan announced proudly. 'This is my school bag.' He handed over a blue backpack with the school logo emblazoned in white on the front for her inspection.

'Wow . . . that's very smart.'

'My friend Sammy's going to the same school as me, but he hasn't got his bag yet.' His eyes, Ray's eyes, were laughing and bright, animating his perfect features, and Jeanie wanted to wrap him in her arms, to breathe in the essence which would somehow be his grandfather's also.

'That's great,' she said instead. 'It's good to have a friend when you start school.'

Natalie laughed. 'Such enthusiasm.'

'Long may it last. How's your dad?' She put the question with her head lowered, tidying the perfectly tidy pile of biodegradable brown bags on the counter.

'Oh, he's away. He's been gone for weeks now. He suddenly took off on a friend's boat. They're sailing down to the Dalmatian coast. I'm not a sailor, but all Dad's side of the family are. He loves it.'

'I love it too. I haven't sailed since I was young, but I grew up by the sea in Norfolk; my friend Wendy had a small sailing dinghy. I lived for the times I was out on the water.' She didn't know why she was telling Natalie this, she just wanted to keep them there for a bit longer. 'The Dalmatian Coast is beautiful, I'm told,' she added, hearing the longing in her voice.

'Dad's going to teach Dylan to sail when he's a bit older. It terrifies me.'

Jeanie watched her anxious face with sympathy and remembered her own mother's constant neurosis and fits of rage when Jeanie disobeyed her and went out on her friend's boat.

'I'm sure he's a brilliant sailor,' she said, forgetting to conceal her passion. All she could think of was Ray, tanned, salt in his hair and on his lips, face towards the sun and the clean, sharp breeze off the sparkling

Adriatic. Her desire to be with him was like a deep pain. She realized Natalie was looking at her closely.

'Sorry, I was miles away . . . it's an age since I've been out in a boat.'

'Um, well . . . I didn't come in for anything really, we were just passing and Dylan saw you through the window.' She turned to her son. 'Say goodbye to Jean, Dylan.'

'We're moving to the country, to Somerset, next week,' Jeanie suddenly blurted out after their retreating figures.

Natalie looked surprised. 'Oh, Dad didn't say. So you're selling up, I suppose.'

'No.' Jeanie's tone was firm, and she realized any intention of putting the business up for sale in the near future was just a fiction.

'Good, it'd be a shame to lose the shop,' Natalie called over her shoulder as Dylan pulled her purposefully on to the pavement.

'Hmmm . . .' Rita's beady gaze rested consideringly on her friend's face. 'So you'll still be up each week, eh?'

Jeanie nodded.

'Would this have anything to do with a certain Park Man?' She raised her eyebrows. 'You're still seeing him, aren't you, you dirty dog.'

'I wish. He's away, sailing. But even if he weren't, I wouldn't be seeing him.'

'So how do you know he's sailing then?'

'His daughter dropped by at the shop.'

Rita's face fell.

'So you're really going through with this, this ludicrous commitment to die in Dorset.'

Jeanie couldn't help laughing at her friend's tragic countenance. 'It's not the dying that concerns me, it's the living. And it's Somerset.'

'Whatever. So what does His Nibs think about you deserting him for the shop every week?'

'He doesn't know or care at the moment. I did tell him, but he didn't take it in. It's just for a while, Rita, until I get used to being there. I just can't do it all at once.'

'Darling, you don't have to justify it to me. I don't think you should do it at all, ever, let alone in easy stages.' She paused. 'We'll have to move our tennis to one of the nights you're up.'

Jeanie suddenly felt overwhelmed. Chanty had been round again that morning, fretting over her father, fretting over Alex's September exhibition, worrying about how they would cope when the baby came.

'I wish you weren't going, Mum,' she had admitted, much to Jeanie's irritation.

'You and me both,' had been her tart reply, which had caused her daughter to burst into tears and declare that 'everything seems to be falling apart in this family'.

Now Jeanie looked across the cafe table at her friend. 'I've made a mess of things, haven't I?'

Rita's face was full of concern. 'Oh, darling, you have rather, but I'm sure you'll sort it out somehow.'

Jeanie's tears turned to laughter at Rita's brutal honesty.

'Thanks for the vote of confidence,' she said, but Rita wasn't listening.

'By the way, does Ray's daughter know about you and him?'

'No . . . no, I'm sure not. She thinks we're just friends . . . we're not even that now.'

'Hmmm . . . I suppose there's no reason you couldn't take up with him again, sort of on the side, when you come up. It'd be the perfect solution, no?'

Jeanie looked shocked.

'On the side?'

'Well, don't tell me it hasn't crossed your mind.'

Of course it had, she was only human, but she knew seeing Ray like that would never be enough.

'Ray isn't someone you have "on the side". He's not like that.'

'All men are like that,' Rita assured her cheerfully. 'I know I encouraged you to run off with him at one point, but this may be the better option in the short term. I mean, George isn't well at the moment, but he's a tried and tested safety net, so to speak.'

'You've changed your tune,' Jeanie snapped.

'As I keep telling you, I've only got your best interests at heart, and I've thought a lot about it all. Age is no bar to an affair, I stick by that, but risking your whole way of life . . . you know I'm right, or you would have legged it long ago.'

And Jeanie realized that Rita was right. She was a coward through and through, clinging purely for security to a dying marriage there was little hope of resurrecting, while making out to everyone, including herself, that she was being noble, looking after George and putting the family first. And now it was too late: she'd been punished for her cowardice. Ray was getting on with his life. She thought of the boat again and almost enjoyed the masochistic stab of pain the knowledge brought. He was probably sharing a chilled glass of white wine with some lithe bit of boat totty as they spoke.

19

'George! George.' She could see the back of his head bent over a patch of shrubbery at the far end of the lawn. It was the first she'd seen of him all day. The old friend of his mother's stood beside her, waiting patiently, breathing heavily from her walk up the drive. Lorna was a large, ponderous woman with sparse grey hair gathered in an untidy bun. She could have been seventy or ninety, with her swollen, purplish feet beneath the brown wool skirt pushed uncomfortably into pumps. Jeanie was sure they were put on specially for the visit.

'I live, oh, hardly three hundred yards away.' She waved her thick arm towards the village. 'Four at the most. I can't believe the coincidence, Imogen's son buying the Old Rectory.' She laughed, the sound more like a hearty wheeze. 'I heard the name Lawson, but I thought no, it couldn't be. It's been empty for so long, it must have been waiting for you.'

'It is a beautiful house.'

Lorna shrugged. 'Was. It used to be much more beautiful before that dreadful Barkworth man ruined the front with those ghastly Victorian-style bays.' When Jeanie looked a bit baffled, Lorna went on, 'Victorian? On a Georgian rectory? I told him, but he wouldn't listen, said it didn't matter and that different styles were always added at different times. Of course this is true, but Barkworth isn't exactly Victorian, is he?'

Jeanie assumed not, but didn't feel qualified to comment on what she considered rather pretty bay windows on either side of the front door.

'Spoils the whole thing, in my opinion' – Lorna sighed heavily – 'but then what does my opinion count for in the end? People do what they want these days, don't they?'

'Come inside and have a drink. I'll give George another shout.' She was worried that if her neighbour didn't sit down soon she might keel over.

'George, didn't you hear?' She tugged at his sleeve. 'Please, come on and meet Lorna. She's an old friend of your mother's. Do you remember her? She says she met you often when you were young.'

George stood looking at her, making no move towards the house.

'We've still got another hour of light,' he muttered, casting a regretful eye at the shrubs he was pruning.

'Look, I didn't ask her here. But you must come; it's so rude to leave her sitting there all alone.' Jeanie was exasperated, but hardly surprised. They had been in the house for nearly six weeks, and George had spent almost all of that time in the garden. His previous obsession – the scores of clocks he had collected over the years – had been ignored since the move and were still in packing cases stacked against the wall in his new study. These days he would eat breakfast with one eye on the door, then be out until dark – in every weather – only returning in the early afternoon to raid the fridge for a cheese sandwich and a cup of cold coffee left over from breakfast. When he came in at night he was exhausted; he'd pour himself a large whisky and sit silently over supper before shuffling off to bed. He was perfectly civil to Jeanie, but seemed hardly to know who she was. Jeanie knew he was still depressed, but oddly he didn't appear unhappy, just fixed in his own tiny world. She thought about what would happen if one day there was no cheese for his sandwich. Would he go and buy some? Because he never left the house. She had tried again to get him to see a local doctor, someone he didn't know. She'd thought it might be easier for him. But the same answer came back. 'Nothing wrong with me, just a bit tired.'

'George, dear.' Lorna struggled to the edge of the sofa.

'Don't get up,' Jeanie insisted, since George didn't.

'How long is it since we saw each other?' Lorna went on, leaning back gratefully on the cushions. 'Your dear mother's been dead such a long time now, but I see you've inherited her passion for the garden.' She turned to Jeanie. 'Did you see her garden? Heavens, it was a sight to behold; people came from miles to see it.' She laughed. 'When Imogen let them, of course.'

George sat down, his hands still filthy, his gardening clothes making him look like a tramp, but said nothing, just shot the odd glance at Lorna, a confused look on his face. Lorna didn't seem to notice, however. She just talked on and on, telling them the history of the area, the house, stories of the 'dreadful' Barkworth and the sainted Imogen, sipping happily on her glass of white wine, until George suddenly got up and left the room. He'd barely said one word to her. Lorna pretended not to notice.

'Sorry.' Jeanie was tired of excuses. 'He's not been well recently.'

The old lady nodded in sympathy. 'Retiring some-times has a funny effect on men, don't you think?' she suggested, when Jeanie didn't say what was wrong.

'It's not that. The doctor said it might take a while,' she said, wincing at her own pathetic avoidance of the truth. But she knew the stigma attached to mental illness, and she wanted George to be accepted by the locals without awkwardness. Lorna, she hoped, would spread the word that he was ill at the moment and not just rude.

As the train pulled into Waterloo, Jeanie felt a frisson of excitement. She had spent most of the journey worrying about George. This was the first time she had left him to go to the shop. It was Lorna who provided the solution. She had dropped by to say that 'Sally-from-the-village', who cleaned for her Mondays and Fridays, was looking for more work. Sally was exactly what Jeanie had hoped for: a warm, middle-aged woman who laughed a lot and seemed quite sanguine about George. She would come in on the days Jeanie was away, and call if there were any problems.

As Jeanie made her way up Highgate Hill, she fell

into the old pattern of looking out for Ray. The wilds of Somerset, where the possibility of meeting him was virtually non-existent, had proved something of a relief these past weeks, but as she breathed the air of North London – familiar over a lifetime – the renewed chance of seeing him plunged her straight back into a mood of heightened awareness and thudding heart. She tried to rehearse what she would say if they bumped into each other, but she never got past imagining how it would feel to look into his eyes again.

'That's different.' She checked the new shelving arrangement, and was aware of Jola's anxious wait for her verdict. 'It's much better, less cluttered. What have you done with the maize products?'

Jola grinned in relief. 'I put them here, under tins. No one like them, you know. I throw much away because out of date.'

'You're right, the pasta tastes filthy. I suppose there are more wheat-free options to choose from now, and spelt. No, it looks good.'

'How is country?'

Jeanie sighed. 'It's OK. I'd rather be here.'

'And Mr Lawson? He better now?'

'Sort of. So . . . where's Megan?'

Jeanie liked the new girl. Perhaps a bit of a cliché of

the straightforward, enthusiastic Australian, but she genuinely seemed to enjoy working for Jola.

'She never late, she happy to work weekends, she very good with customer, never get angry,' Jola enthused when Megan went on her lunch break.

'Sounds perfect . . . so you don't really need me any more.' Even though she said it in jest, for a second Jeanie thought she might cry. It was the sudden conviction that indeed she was now redundant, retired, no use to anyone, except to provide George with cheese for his sandwich and whisky for his supper. Highgate seemed to have survived her absence very nicely. Of course Jola protested, but a bleakness settled over her nonetheless.

'I'm going over to see Ellie at lunchtime,' she told her. Despite promises that the family would practically live in Somerset, they hadn't yet visited beyond a rushed Saturday morning the week after the move, when the house was still stuffed with tea chests and bubble wrap and felt more like a furniture warehouse than a home. Chanty said she was too tired, it was too far, and Alex, of course, had his exhibition to finish. She'd missed her granddaughter terribly, and worried the child would have forgotten her.

It was raining as she made her way down the hill to her daughter's house. The autumn had been beautiful till the previous week, more of an Indian summer, but now there was a raw edge to the wind, the promise of things to come. Jeanie tried to shake off her despondency, but even the thought of little Ellie failed to lift her mood. On the opposite side of the road, on the corner of Hornsey Lane, she noticed a couple standing together beneath a large dark-green umbrella. She couldn't see their faces as the umbrella was pulled low, but as she drew level with them, the wind gusted, jerking the umbrella upwards. As the movement caught her eye, she looked and saw Ray. Ray and a girl; Ray with his arms round the girl; Ray laughing into the girl's eyes . . . the beautiful girl . . . the young, beautiful girl.

Jeanie literally thought she would be sick, there and then, on the pavement, in front of the passers-by. Be sick and then die. She found she could not move, as if all the blood had drained from her limbs. The umbrella had been pulled back into place, and moved off slowly down the hill. Ray had not seen her, but still she stood there. Finally the sickness passed into something much worse: absolute despair. She dragged herself left off the main road and managed somehow to get to the house.

'Jean, come in. Are you OK? You look as if you've seen a ghost.' Alex drew her solicitously into the sitting room. 'Ellie'll be awake in a moment, she's so excited you're coming.'

Jeanie managed a smile. 'Could I have some water, please, Alex.'

Her son-in-law didn't move, just stood looking down on her. 'Are you ill?'

'I'll be fine; I just had a bit of a turn,' she assured him, but even to herself her voice sounded strained and weak.

'What sort of a turn?' Alex persisted, and through the fog she wondered if he was remembering his disbelief in the face of his daughter's injury.

'Honestly, I'll be fine. I think I forgot to eat today, what with the train being so early, and then all the stuff I had to deal with in the shop,' she burbled on, finding reassurance in her ability to speak at all.

Alex looked relieved. 'That's daft at your age. You have to eat, especially breakfast. Chant did a programme on it. Apparently schoolchildren who eat breakfast do better than those who don't, because after a night of starvation the brain needs fuel to function.' He laughed. 'Obvious, really. I'd have thought you'd have known it, Jean, with all your health-food experience.'

'I did, but you know how it is.' She laughed as heartily as she could, and saw it was enough to convince Alex.

'I'll make you some toast and tea, then we'll get Ellie up. Marmite or honey?'

'How's the exhibition coming along?' she asked as she munched the honey toast. The fact that she hadn't eaten all day she knew had absolutely nothing to do with her 'turn'. All she wanted now was to process what she had seen, to turn the knife in the wound, but she forced her thoughts back into her daughter's kitchen. 'You seem quite relaxed,' she told her son-in-law.

Alex took a deep breath. 'You've caught me at the eye of the storm. It's a brief window which exists between relief that I've finally finished the work and terror that everyone'll think it's crap.'

'So you'll be nervous on Thursday, then.'

'Um, nervous?' He shivered. '"Nervous" doesn't come close. I'd say more . . . cold sweat arena.'

'I can't imagine,' Jeanie told him.

'You'll be there, won't you? And George.' He hesitated. 'How is George, by the way?'

'I don't know if he's up to it yet, Alex. He never goes anywhere, and I think even the train may be a step too far.'

'That bad . . . Chanty seems to think he's better.'

'He's not miserable like he was, more . . . cut off, lives in his own world,' she explained.

Ellie had not forgotten her. The child wouldn't leave her grandmother's knee, except to drag her up to her room to show Jeanie her toys, burbling on excitedly the while. Jeanie would have liked to have taken her out, but the rain was pouring down now, bouncing off the garden decking in 'dancing dollies' that delighted Ellie as they watched at the window.

'They dancing, Gin . . . dollies dancing in the rain.'

'So how's nursery? Do you like it?'

'I do,' Ellie said solemnly. 'Jack's my friend. I saw a puppet show, Gin.'

'Was it fun?'

'It was,' the child answered, making Jeanie smile at her verbal formalities. Her speech had come on so much in the missing weeks.

'My dolly called Becky, looook, she's toiny and hungry. I got some mork in my bag.' She got out a plastic bottle from the pink zip bag she carried about and began to imitate feeding the doll. 'Now she has to go to sleep,' she said in imperious imitation of an adult, as she laid her in the pink carrycot and covered her tenderly with a blanket. Alex was standing in the doorway.

'I'm hoping this bodes well for the future,' he joked.

'Don't count on it.' Jeanie laughed back. Only her granddaughter was capable of taking her out of herself, but in the moments of lull, the image of Ray and the girl came flooding back, dragging her under like a rip tide.

'Supper's ready, Ell,' Alex said. 'Sausages . . . and ketchup.'

'Ooooooh.' Ellie grinned widely, her eyes sparkling. 'Sodsidges and ketchup. You hungry, Gin? You can share some of mine.'

'I'm afraid I have to go, darling.' Jeanie got up off the bedroom floor.

'You could stay for supper. Chanty'll be back in an hour or so.' Alex grinned sheepishly. 'I don't want you keeling over the moment you leave the house. Chant might think I don't learn from my mistakes.'

'Thanks, Alex, but I ought to get back to the shop. There's so much to catch up on.'

'Are you enjoying Somerset, then?'

He seemed a changed man now his work was finished. The sniping had stopped and there was a real concern in his question. So much so that Jeanie felt her throat tightening. Until today, she realized, she had always fantasized that there was a chance, even if she chose not to take it, that she could be with Ray again. And as a result, Somerset still felt like a staging post, somewhere that did not quite require her commitment.

'I don't know how to answer that,' she said eventually, fighting back the tears.

'Is it George? It must be very hard, with him in such a broken-down state.'

She saw Ellie's little face cloud with worry.

'You sad, Gin?' The little girl came and stood beside her, her arm round Jeanie's leg, the other hand gently stroking her knee.

Jeanie took a deep breath.

'I'm a bit sad, darling, but I'll be OK.' She picked up the small, warm body and gave her a hug.

'I'd better be off,' she said, holding herself together through the goodbyes, down the steps, the wave to her granddaughter and son-in-law, the walk along the road to the corner; but once round the corner she broke down.

The flat above the shop had the dreary chill of an unoccupied space. There had been no one there for nearly two months. Jeanie had had it painted in a neutral white, and replaced the cheap furniture with some from the Highgate house. It was potentially a good space. The sitting room/kitchen was light, with windows at either end, the front on to the high street, the back on to the gardens. The top floor had a good-sized bedroom and a bathroom. She could make it lovely, she told herself, as she turned the heating on and looked for the tea. She hadn't loved the old house so much; there had always been a pervading gloom in the dark, high-ceilinged rooms. But it didn't feel right to be in Highgate and not in the place she'd called home for thirty-five years. All she felt able to do now was wrap herself in the mulberry wool throw from the old kitchen and lie on the sofa in numb disbelief.

Rita looked around the flat inquisitively. 'Hmmm, bit of a comedown from the mansion, but potential as a pied-à-terre, certainly.' She threw herself into the armchair. 'So how's it going, darling? You look dreadful.'

Jeanie had rung her friend and told her about Ray, and Rita had insisted on coming over.

'I feel a fool.'

'Why? You've done nothing foolish . . . unless you count dumping your one true love.'

Jeanie didn't react.

'Sorry, darling, I can see you're not in the mood for my teasing.'

'But how stupid was I, to think that he could really want me when there are so many young, beautiful girls out there? She was lovely, Rita, mixed race, tall and slim with the most stunning smile. I only saw her for a moment but she's gorgeous. Much younger than him, of course, but then his last girlfriend was. He likes them young.' She was thinking out loud, voicing at last the thoughts that had twisted and spun about her head since lunchtime.

'How do you know it was his girlfriend?'

'They were under the same umbrella. He had his arm round her; they were laughing together,' she listed in a dreary monotone.

'Yeah, but they could have been friends who bumped into each other and took shelter from the rain, enjoying a joke together. Were they actually canoodling?'

Jeanie looked at her friend pityingly. 'No, but they looked as if they were just about to.'

'Listen, Jeanie, I've been around long enough to know that assumptions are highly dangerous.' Rita got up. 'Got any wine? You definitely need a drink.'

Jeanie shook her head.

'Well, we're going out then. Come on, you can't just sit here feeling sorry for yourself.'

'But what have I got left now, Rita?'

Rita sighed and sat down again. 'Remember how you weren't actually seeing Ray any more? Remember, in fact, how you were determined not to see him again? Remember how you were hell-bent on dying in Dorset . . . OK, Somerset? I don't quite understand how today changes anything, except to confirm that you're plumb on course.' She paused. 'Unless, of course, you had secret longings you weren't telling me about?' She raised her eyebrows and waited.

'I suppose I thought, selfishly, that he'd be there if I changed my mind,' Jeanie admitted sadly. 'He said, the last time I saw him, "If you change your mind you know where I am." ' She looked up at her friend. 'I mean, obviously he couldn't wait for ever.'

'So you're telling me now that if he was available you'd run off with him?' Rita threw up her hands in exasperation. 'I can't make you out, darling. One breath you can't leave George; the next you're in a lather because Ray, quite reasonably considering you dumped him, has found someone else.'

'I don't expect you to understand. I don't understand either,' Jeanie replied with a rueful smile. 'I told you, I'm a fool.'

20

'George, it's Alex's exhibition tonight. Do you want to come? We can stay at the flat and come back tomorrow. You haven't seen the flat yet.'

George looked at her.

'Of course I'll come. Can't miss Alex's day.'

'It'll mean getting a three o'clock train.'

'Today?'

'Yes.'

'Well, today might be awkward.' He cast a glance outside, where the drizzle dulled the landscape to a grey blur. 'You see, I need to clear the ground for the vegetable patch before we get a frost and it's too hard to dig. I should really . . .'

'Well, it has to be today, George, it's the opening night.'

George pondered this information.

'Of course I'll come,' he repeated uncertainly.

'You don't have to. I can get Sally to pop in. I'm sure Alex will understand if you don't feel up to it.'

'No, I'll come.'

Part of Jeanie desperately wanted him to come, or at least to be in a fit state to come. She so wanted the old George back, the 'solid', 'unflappable' husband and father. The other part dreaded taking him so far from the safety of the house. Supposing he got drunk and behaved as he had at Chanty's that night?

The train was delayed by more than an hour – a signalling failure at Axminster. George had been silent at first, staring morosely out of the train window. But gradually she sensed a curiosity, then an excitement in her husband. His eyes, recently so lifeless, sparked up; he began to talk to her quietly, chatting about things that she'd assumed in his current state of mind he hadn't taken in, as if months of stored-up information had suddenly been let loose. He talked about Lorna and Sally, the house, the family and the garden, of course. By the time they left the train he was, if not animated, at least brighter, as if a cloud had lifted. Jeanie watched in amazement. She didn't question it, but it crossed her mind that his self-imposed solitude in the Old Rectory had done him more harm than good, the lack of stimuli imprisoning him further in his depression. If he could be a husband to her again, she thought, perhaps there would be something to look forward to, something to make her forget.

The gallery was brilliantly lit, the paintings vivid with colour against the stark white walls. Jeanie was delighted by the improvement in her son-in-law's work and sensed a buzz amongst the small number of people self-consciously clutching wine glasses and eyeing the paintings as they socialized.

'Dad, Mum.' Chanty looked relieved to see them, her pregnancy cleverly dressed with an elegant black smock and leggings. Jeanie saw her gaze rest on her father. 'How was the trip up?' she asked, although she seemed not to listen to the answer.

Jeanie could see her daughter was distracted, watching the door, the guests, her husband, gauging each glance directed at his work. Alex looked as he had predicted: terrified, and stood slightly aloof from the group round him, smiling automatically every few seconds, his blue eyes wide with fear like a rabbit pinned in the head-lights.

Gradually the glamorous Spanish girl with a high, swinging ponytail and crimson lips, brandishing her clipboard with details of the paintings, began to place red stickers beside some of the frames.

'I think it's a success! Fingers crossed, they seem to like them,' Chanty hissed into her mother's ear.

'They're good,' Jeanie agreed. 'Particularly that one.' She pointed to one on the wall by the door. 'The colours are amazing.'

'Dad seems to be getting into it.' They both looked at George, who was listening intently to a thin, earnest-looking man dressed entirely in black and sporting a large satchel across his skinny chest.

'If that man's not careful, George will start telling him about the best conditions for bare-root hedging or the wide variety of agapanthus hybrids currently available.'

Chanty looked impressed.

'I saw a catalogue,' Jeanie admitted, laughing. 'He's obsessed.'

'Is that good?'

'Probably not, but that's your father for you. His poor clocks have been entirely thrown over for the agapanthus hybrids. It was odd today, though; he seemed to have some sort of epiphany on the train – he just suddenly opened up and talked almost normally. And look at him now. This is the first time I've seen him really engaging with someone for months.'

'Perhaps he's turned a corner, Mum. I do hope so.' Chanty put her hand on Jeanie's arm. 'Sorry I haven't been there for you these past months; it must have been hell. I hate you being so far away.'

'I miss you too, darling. I think I'll take George off soon; I don't want him to revert. Will you tell the girl I'd like to buy that painting, please?'

'Oh, Mum, you don't need to buy one. Alex will give it to you.'

'Nonsense. Of course I'll buy it. We can afford it, and I want it for the flat.'

'I'm dog-tired, but I enjoyed that,' George declared in the taxi up to North London.

'Me too. I bought one for the flat.'

'Good. Not sure about the paintings myself. As you know, I'm more of a landscape man,' he muttered. 'We should do this more often, old girl,' he added, settling comfortably against her. It was the first time in months he'd called her by the loathsome nickname, but tonight, for some reason, it no longer offended her.

'Drink?' she asked when they got upstairs to the flat, feeling oddly like a host to her own husband.

Later, as they settled to the unfamiliar routine of sharing a bed, she felt a strange tension in George as he lay beside her.

'Are you OK?'

'Jeanie?' George turned to her and suddenly she felt his hand on her breast, tentative, almost apologetic. 'Would you mind if we . . . you know . . .'

She tried not to stiffen, but her whole body rebelled at the thought. This man had become almost a stranger to her. She made an effort to calm her breath and told herself she ought to encourage him. He was her husband; wasn't this what she wanted, for things to get back to normal? He moved closer to her and began to kiss her face, her lips. He smelt old, tasted musty and stale from the wine, and it was all she could do not to push him off. Instead she just lay there, wooden and unresponsive, trying to feel something other than revulsion. He seemed not to notice, but it was over quickly, almost before it had begun. She heard him groan in the darkness and breathed a sigh of relief.

'Thank you . . . that felt so good,' he said breathlessly. 'Sorry it wasn't much of a performance, it's been so long.' He lay back with a sigh. 'Did you enjoy it, though?'

'It was nice.' She spoke lamely into the lengthening silence, almost choking on her lie.

'I think things are going to be OK, Jeanie.'

'What happened on the train, George?'

'I don't know . . . I was looking at the countryside flashing past and I thought how beautiful it was, what an amazing world we live in. I began to see things in colour again; I felt I was seeing them for the first time. Don't know how to explain it, not my forte, but, well, it's been pretty grim recently . . . life . . .'

She listened to his breathing still, then the onset of a gentle snore. George got up, as usual, at five-thirty, and it was only then that Jeanie drifted off to sleep.

21

As autumn wore on, it became clear to Jeanie that she'd preferred the distance George's illness had placed between them. Because as George recovered, he began to demand more of his wife: things that even a year ago she would have been happy to comply with, and nothing more than the normal interchange between a married couple. But Jeanie did not want sex with George, nor to sleep in the same bed as him. She didn't want to give up the shop (which he was now demanding almost daily), she didn't want to socialize with the locals, or accompany him to garden centres far and wide to choose ground-cover plants and stone statuary. She knew she was being unreasonable – was this such a bad life? – and kept hoping her feelings would change.

Meanwhile she gritted her teeth, trying to persuade herself that her life could continue without any hope of Ray. But the persistent image of him with the young girl tormented her still, as if it were lodged in a large frame on the wall of her brain.

'Do you want me to get the bedroom at the front ready for your guests?' Sally wanted to know.

'I think they'd like the back one; it's bigger,' George chimed in.

'But it hasn't got the view,' Jeanie argued, although she couldn't have cared less where Rita and Bill slept. Everything asked of her seemed an imposition; she plodded dully from day to day, living for Wednesday morning and her escape to the shop, despite the fact that her sojourn in London had now been whittled down to one night, not two. George had insisted, and Jeanie, wanting to stave off the pressure to sell for as long as possible, had given in.

'But it's a much nicer room.' He nodded to Sally as if the argument were closed, and Sally accepted his decision without further reference to Jeanie.

They arrived very late on Friday night in the middle of a downpour.

'Bloody hell, darling, this really is the back of beyond,' Rita whispered to her friend as they embraced.

Jeanie had cooked a fish pie, but the Aga was on a go-slow, and it was almost ten before they sat down to eat round the kitchen table, by which time copious amounts of Rioja had been consumed.

'Of course Jeanie loathes it here.' George's tone seemed mild, almost humorous, but Jeanie could detect a sharp underlying anger.

'I don't loathe it,' she countered.

'Of course she loathes it,' Rita, loudly drunk, piped up. 'Who wouldn't. It's the country.' She giggled as Bill shook his head at her.

'It's not the country she loathes, unfortunately.' George ground a generous amount of pepper on to his pie, keeping the mild, informational tone. 'It's me.' He dropped it into the sentence as if he half expected everyone to go, 'Ha, ha, George, good one.' But they took him at his word and there was a deadly silence, everyone shocked out of their drunkenness.

'What do you mean?' Jeanie asked, her heart pounding. Rita shot her a glance, Bill found something fascinating on his plate next to his peas.

'I mean, old girl, that you've well and truly gorn off

me.' He raised his eyebrows at her. 'I can't blame you; I haven't been myself for a while now.'

The silence stretched out, only George still calmly eating as if he'd been talking about the weather.

'You're drunk,' Jeanie muttered.

'I may be drunk, miss, but I'll be sober in the morning and you'll still hate me,' he retorted, parodying Churchill's famous line. No one round the kitchen table laughed.

'Don't be ridiculous. Of course I don't hate you.'

'Stop it, George. Jeanie's right. This is the drink talking.' Bill was always the voice of reason.

George turned to him, seated on his left. 'I can't say these things to her . . . it's too hard.' He'd begun to slur his words.

Jeanie cringed. He seemed so pathetic in that moment, so vulnerable.

'Well, we can either talk about the farmer's market we'll no doubt visit tomorrow, or slope off to bed and hope things improve after a good night's sleep.' It was clear which option Rita favoured. She got up as she spoke and began briskly to clear the plates from the table.

George just sat there at the head of the table and said nothing. It wasn't till Rita and Bill had gone upstairs that he spoke again.

'Sorry I ruined it.'

Jeanie turned from the solid butler's sink, resting her back against it as she removed her yellow rubber gloves.

'Do you really think I hate you?' she asked gently.

He raised his owl-eyes to her. 'Hate's perhaps too strong a word, Jeanie. But you don't seem to take any pleasure in our marriage any more.'

She said nothing.

'It's true, isn't it? You don't want to make love to me. You cling to the shop as if it's your lifeline. I've seen your face on a Wednesday morning; it's like the Great Escape. We hardly talk any more. I just get the feeling you don't want to be here with me.' There was nothing slurred about his speech now.

'I haven't found it easy, no,' she replied slowly, choosing her words carefully. 'I didn't want to move, as you know, and I don't want to give up the shop. You thought I'd come round. Well, I haven't yet.'

Her husband got up and came over to her, putting his hands on her arms.

'But the sex? You lie there as if you're dead. Don't you fancy me any more?'

Jeanie stood tense in his embrace.

'George, it's been a big adjustment. I don't know what I feel, what with all that's gone on. If anything I feel exhausted, just worn out with it all.'

'So you need time? Is that what you're saying?'

Jeanie nodded dumbly, wishing the bloody, bloody tears would hold off, just for once.

'It's not to do with this other fellow, is it? You're not seeing him when you go up to London?'

'Is that what you think? No, of course not. I haven't seen him for months.'

'So it's totally over.'

'Totally and completely over.'

'OK . . . OK.' George stepped back as she angrily brushed him off. 'You seem so keen to go up, that's all, and I thought perhaps it was something more than just the shop.'

'It isn't "just" the shop, George. It's my business, my passion.'

'But couldn't you find a shop to be passionate about down here? It seems so daft, you going all that way each week when you could be doing the same thing in Axminster or Honiton. I could help you look.'

Jeanie held her head in her hands. 'Please, *please* stop nagging me about the shop. I'll sort something out soon, but right now can you just leave it.'

George nodded. 'Just one more thing. The sex . . . you . . .'

Jeanie waited, holding her breath.

'If that man isn't the problem . . . it isn't because of what I told you, is it? The Acland business?'

'Don't call it that, George. Call it by its proper name: abuse,' she snapped, not intending to be mean but hating his ongoing refusal to deal with it. 'Of course it's not. How can you think that?'

He shrugged. 'I don't know. It's such a filthy thing to know about someone. I thought perhaps it'd turned you off me.'

It was Jeanie's turn to offer her embrace. George came into her arms and she felt him relax against her.

'It's nothing whatever to do with that. I'm sorry. I haven't been myself recently, but to be fair, neither of us has.'

'You do still love me though, don't you?'

'Yes,' she reassured him like a child. 'Yes, I do still love you, George.'

Every night was the same now: Jeanie dreaded going to bed because George was there too. She'd allowed him to share her bed when they'd first moved because she was worried about him, he was ill. But since then he'd made it quite clear that he liked it.

'It's cosier,' he told her. 'I hated sleeping alone.'

'But you did it for ten years. You can't have hated it that much,' she'd retorted.

'We're husband and wife, Jeanie. That's what married people do; they sleep together.'

'Telling me it's the norm is a lousy argument.'

'It is because I snore?'

'Partly,' she'd lied. The snoring was annoying, but it wasn't the reason she wanted her own bed. George was famously stubborn, however, and refused to move to another room. Tonight she lay tense, knowing that the embrace she'd given him in the kitchen might prove a green light. George got into bed and she turned away from him.

'Don't worry,' she heard him say, his voice suddenly cold. 'I'm not going to touch you.'

She didn't answer, but that night was a turning point for Jeanie.

'I can't do it any more,' she told Rita as they drove away from the Rectory, en route to buy papers and bread the following morning. Jeanie felt surprisingly clear-headed, despite not having slept a wink.

'What are you talking about, darling? Do drive slower; these roads are terrifying.'

'I can't stay with George. I'm leaving.'

For once her friend was speechless.

'I love him, of course I do. Love him in the way you love someone you've been close to for most of your adult life. But I don't *love* him. Not in the way I should as his wife. And I just can't do this . . . this phoney marriage crap any more.'

'What phoney marriage crap? What are you talking about? Pull over; we can't have this conversation on these roads – we'll die.'

Jeanie laughed, hearing the note of hysteria in her voice. It was such a relief to know at last. She pulled over by a gate to a field, the churned mud frozen solid overnight and crunching beneath the tyres. Winter sun poured through the windscreen. She turned the engine off and just sat there, hands resting on the steering wheel.

'Jeanie, what's happened? This can't be about that stupid conversation last night. He was drunk, darling. We all say stupid things when we're drunk.'

'What he said was true; I have gone off him.' She glanced sideways at her friend. 'I just don't want to be with him.'

'But doesn't everyone go through times like that in a long marriage? I get totally fed up with Billy on a regular basis.'

'I'm not fed up with him, I just don't want to make love to him. In fact, I dread it, don't find him interesting, get sick and tired of him trying to control me. These days I'm only happy when I go up to London.'

Rita's eyes narrowed. 'This isn't about Ray again, is it?'

Jeanie sighed. 'You know that's over. Rita, this is about *me* – I know I sound like a self-obsessed Oprah Winfrey guest, but I have to leave. If I don't I shall surely stab him one day, and he doesn't deserve that.'

'But why so suddenly? I thought you were making a go of it down here?'

'I've tried, believe me I have. But when I realized last night from what George said when you'd gone to bed that he knew exactly how unhappy I was, that I wasn't succeeding in pulling the wool over our eyes, I knew the game was up.'

'Hmm. So what about getting old and lonely and insecure? What about George, left all alone in Somerset?'

'George is a survivor, we've seen that. You've said it: he always gets what he wants.'

Rita shook her head. 'All he wants is you, darling. You know he does.'

'Not as I am now. He's not a masochist.'

'But . . . but so you're really going to do it?'

Jeanie nodded, taking a deep, calm breath in the cold air.

'You've stunned me.' Rita continued to stare at her. 'You seem so sure suddenly.'

'I am,' she said, smiling. A weight had been lifted from her shoulders; a weight, she now understood, which had sat there, dragging her down, for many, many years.

'Poor George. When will you tell him?'

'I suppose when you and Bill have gone.' She did not feel anxious at the prospect, just very sad.

'Woah . . . some weekend this turned out to be. And here's me thinking the country was dull. Darling, I can't sit between you playing happy families . . . that's *so* not going to happen. I better call Bill and get him to invent a drug overdose for his CEO.'

'Coward,' Jeanie smiled sadly.

On the way back from the village shop there was silence in the car.

'Shouldn't you wait till Chanty's had the baby?' Rita asked suddenly.

The euphoria was beginning to wear off. Jeanie had begun to think through what had to be done, what needed to be said, before she could be free. She hadn't forgotten Chanty, the new baby due in a few weeks' time, or how Alex's defection had brought on a dangerously early labour last time. But although she quailed at inflicting pain on her family, the details of how and when did not deter her from her goal.

'You're right, I should . . . I will, of course.'

'Darling, please, think this through really carefully.'

Jeanie shook her head. 'I know it sounds sudden to you, Rita, but it isn't. It's been brewing for months, years perhaps.'

'But you didn't seem unhappy till Ray came along.'

'If he hadn't come along, perhaps I'd have plodded on. But it's a long time since I could say I was really happy with George.'

'Who's happy? Long marriages can't be thrilling all the time . . . or even any of the time.'

'I know all the arguments, but the fact is that you and Bill, for instance, have a real relationship. I can see it. You're stimulated by his company, you're friends as well as lovers, even though you drive each other mad sometimes.'

Rita nodded, 'No, you're right, I suppose we are lucky.'

Jeanie pulled into her drive and stopped the car. For a moment neither of them moved.

'How can I stay with a man I dread making love to?' she asked, almost to herself.

'The best-laid schemes o' mice an' men gang aft awry' had always been one of George's favourite quotes, usually delivered with a knowing sigh and a terrible Scottish accent, and one night, two weeks after Rita and Bill had spent the weekend, Jeanie forgot her duty to her daughter and blurted out the truth to her husband.

She had returned from London just after eight on the Thursday night. George was waiting for her in the kitchen, an unmarked crossword in front of him, a glass of whisky by his side, the only light the dim glow above the cooker. He searched her face as she walked in as if in it he would find the secret of the universe. This monitoring was par for the course on her return home each week, the looks always accompanied by endless tiresome questions about exactly what she had done with every minute of time that she'd been away. Jeanie dreaded it.

'Don't stare at me,' she'd snapped that night.

'I'm not staring.'

'Yes, you are. You do it all the time.'

George had shrugged, but continued to stare. 'Have a good trip, did you?' His tone was heavy with sarcasm.

'Busy, but yes, it was good.' She found she could no longer be honest with him about her work, because if she showed the slightest sign of being tired, or complained about a problem at the shop, he would jump in with yet another needle about giving it all up.

'I spoke to Alan today.' He'd continued to sit there while she began to get supper together. 'He said it was unlikely that you'd sell the business as a going concern in this economic climate, that the money was only in the real estate.'

'Did he?' Alan was George's accountant, a dapper, obsequious man whom Jeanie had never liked.

'He said the best plan for us was just to close the shop down and sell the premises on. The flat above is a big asset, he said, because it can be a separate income or part of the whole.' George doodled on the edge of the crossword with his pencil, big loopy spirals diminishing to a heavy-scored, angry dot.

Jeanie hadn't answered, she'd just poured the watercress soup into a pan and put it on the Aga, unwrapped the Cheddar and set it beside the wholemeal loaf on the breadboard. George had got to his feet slowly and taken the bowls and plates from the dresser.

'Do you want a drink?' He'd waved the remains of a bottle of claret towards his wife. She'd nodded.

'He says he'll deal with it for us.'

Jeanie had been listening to him, her blood pressure gradually rising. She didn't trust herself to speak. Unlike the Highgate house, which had always remained solely George's, the shop was in her name. It had been a gift from her husband when he thought it time she had 'an interest'. At first he had subsidized it heavily, but for the last five years she had begun to make a small profit.

'It isn't yours to sell.' She'd poured the soup into each bowl and slammed the pan in the sink.

George had gone very still, his mouth twisting, the index finger of his left hand tapping threateningly on the wooden table. He had nothing to hold over her, and she could see the lack of control was eating away at him.

'If you persist in playing this game with me, pretending you're going to sell when you're not, then I shall take it as a very hostile act.'

Jeanie almost laughed at his pomposity.

'Hostile act? What on earth do you mean?'

George's face, normally so mild, had coloured a deep pink.

'Don't make fun of me, Jeanie. I'm not the fool you take me for.'

'I have never thought you were a fool, George,' she replied quietly.

'We came down here to retire. You were going to sell the shop, we were going to make a life down here.'

'*You* were. *You* were, George. Why do you insist on pretending this was a joint decision? You completely railroaded me. I . . . never . . . ever . . . wanted to come to the country. Get it? And I am not going to retire. I'm not old.' She was almost shouting with frustration.

Her husband looked at her pityingly. 'You're being ridiculous. Stop yelling at me.'

'Well, why don't you listen to me?'

'So what are you saying? That you're going to keep the stupid shop and wear yourself out travelling the length and breadth of the country every week to prove a point? You're so bloody stubborn.'

'Pot and kettle spring to mind.'

'So are you? Are you going to keep up this ludicrous double life? I've offered to buy you another shop down here. What's so bloody special about that place in Highgate . . . unless you've got another agenda up there, of course?' He was breathing heavily, his eyes boring into her as he delivered this *coup de grâce*.

Jeanie finally understood.

'If you don't trust me – and why should you, of course – there isn't a lot I can do about it.'

'So you're still seeing that man, then.'

She shook her head. 'Did I say that?'

'You didn't have to. I can tell from the way you are with me,' he said sullenly.

'The way I am with you has nothing to do with anyone except ourselves.'

'Yeah, right. That's what they always say,' he sneered.

'Who's "they"? Who are you talking about?'

'Stop playing with me, Jeanie.' Her husband's tone had suddenly changed. Now he was pleading with her. 'Please, this is horrible. I'm jealous, I'll admit it. You always seem so happy on Wednesday morning, and so miserable when you come home.' He'd reached over and put his hand on hers. 'It's twisting me up. I can't sleep when you're away for thinking about what you're doing. It's hell.' She'd seen the tears in his eyes. 'I love you so much, Jeanie. Tell me you're not . . . you're not seeing him again.'

'I'm sorry, George,' she'd finally told him, the hammering of her heart stilled by the truth. 'I can't do this any more.'

George had gone pale.

'Don't, Jeanie, don't be silly.' His voice was feeble and she worried he would have another collapse.

'I promise I am not cheating on you. But I don't . . . I don't want this life. I don't want . . .' She didn't know how to say it, but there was no need.

'You can't leave me,' he said piteously. 'You can't, not after all this time. It's madness.'

She said no more.

'You've been happy with me, I know you have – until that bloody man came and seduced you. We had fun, didn't we? I've always thought we had a better marriage than most of the people we know.' He was talking mostly to himself, trying to make sense of what was happening. He looked up at her. 'If it's the sex, we can stop, I can move to another bedroom. I know you haven't enjoyed all that and I can't blame you. It was me who messed up there.'

Jeanie began to cry. She felt a terrible sadness as, for the first time, she really confronted the prospect of leaving him. Maybe, she thought, she was being stupid, throwing all this away. Maybe she just wasn't over Ray yet. Did it matter that she didn't love George enough, or in the right way? Was she ready to be alone? For a moment she havered.

'You can't do this to me.' George took his glasses off before lowering his head on to his hands and crying with soft, tearing sobs.

That night Jeanie slept alone; he did not come to her bed. But she lay rigid nonetheless, her stomach churning with nausea.

George wanted answers. And when Jeanie's were unsatisfactory, he began to allocate blame: 'That bastard's ruined our marriage'; 'You can't accept you're old'; 'The abuse thing disgusts you and you can't admit it'; 'Rita's been encouraging you to leave me, she never liked me'; 'You're punishing me for wanting to move to the country'; 'My illness wore you out'.

'Blame is pointless,' she told him. 'We're both responsible for our marriage.'

'Oh, please . . . you sound like some smug marriage guidance counsellor. So it's my fault now, is it?' he shot back. Despair had given way to anger, and as the weekend wore on and the wearying battles continued, George became more aggressive.

'I'm not blaming you. I just said, blame is pointless.'

'Well, I feel I'm "responsible" – if that's the word you want to use – for giving you a bloody good marriage. I don't see what I've done wrong to be treated like this.

I've always given you everything you wanted. It was *you* . . . *you*, Jeanie . . .' he stabbed his finger at her, 'who cheated, who let *me* down. Not the other way round. No wonder you don't want to talk about blame.'

Trying to keep calm, Jeanie waited a moment to answer. She realized there was little point in attempting to make George understand – whatever she said only added fuel to the flames – but her frustration was such that she was on the verge of delineating in minute detail his part in their joint unhappiness.

'Well? You don't have anything to say to that, do you?'

Jeanie got up to leave the kitchen, which had become their battleground. As she got to the door, she felt George's hand clutching her arm and dragging her round. He pinioned her in front of him, his eyes flashing with rage.

'Don't walk away from me, damn it. I won't let you go till you give me a satisfactory explanation. You owe it to me, Jeanie; after all this time you bloody owe it to me.' His grip tightened. 'It's that bastard, I know it is. You're still seeing him. All this bullshit about joint responsibility is just a ruse to pull the wool over my eyes. Admit it, damn you! Admit it, will you!' He began to shake her.

'Let go of me!'

'Say it.' His voice was no more than a desperate whisper as he let her go and sank on to the nearest chair.

On Tuesday night she packed the bulk of her clothes.

'I'm going to stay at the flat for a while,' she told him.

'For a while?' he asked.

They were both emotionally exhausted and had resorted to stalking around each other in a charged silence. When George did speak, he nagged her again and again to explain. She couldn't, because she didn't have the stomach to be cruel.

But perhaps she should have told the bald truth: 'I found in Ray what I have never found in you, and although he's no longer available to me, I know the difference now.' Because George must have sensed her deceit and it only made things worse as he became increasingly entrenched in his own innocence. Nothing, he kept repeating, that he'd ever, *ever* done, had contributed to this horrible impasse.

'We're just destroying each other, George.'

'What am I supposed to do without you?' She saw the panic in his eyes. 'I can't live here on my own. I'll get depressed again, you know I will. And what about Chanty? What are you going to tell her? Jeanie, please,' George pleaded. 'You know this'll destroy the family.'

But despite the powerful strings that tied her to this man, she knew she could not give in to his manipulation one more time.

She packed her car with two large suitcases and left the Old Rectory a little after six the following morning. George would normally have been up at that time, pottering around the kitchen making tea. But he stayed in his room and they didn't even say goodbye to each other.

22

From the moment Jeanie drove away from the Somerset house, she felt an overwhelming sense of relief. Her heart was lighter, even her breath came more easily. The guilt sat like a stone in her gut, but she knew she'd have to learn to live with that – it wasn't going anywhere any time soon.

Chanty was her primary concern when she reached London. She knew that the mood he was in, George was quite capable of ringing Chanty and sobbing down the phone. She wanted to tell her daughter herself.

'Hi, Mum, this is early; are you on the train?'

'No, the car, I'm at Archway. Can you meet me on your way to work, darling? Say nine at the shop?'

Chanty sounded puzzled, but Ellie was shouting in the background and she didn't query the request.

'I gave up work yesterday, so any time,' she told her mother.

'Left him? Left Dad? For good?' was Chanty's bemused response.

Jeanie nodded and began her tale with trepidation. But at the end Chanty just sighed, perhaps too wearied by the vicissitudes of late pregnancy to mind as much as she once might have done.

'I can't say I'm surprised, Mum. I thought perhaps it'd be OK, when I saw Dad was more himself again, but Alex and I have both noticed the tension between you for ages now. He warned me this might happen, but I didn't believe him.'

'I don't expect you to like it.'

'I can't really take it in, to be honest . . . you and Dad apart. What will he do?'

'I don't know. He says he won't cope, but he's much better than we give him credit for at finding the help he needs.'

'But that's always been you. He's a damaged man, Mum.'

Jeanie saw the tears and cursed herself for causing them.

'I know, but I can't help him any more – I'm not sure I ever did. I'm so sorry, darling. I don't know what to say.'

'Will you be with that man?' Her daughter refused to call Ray by his name.

'No.' She saw Chanty scrutinizing her face to find out if this were the truth. 'I promise, I'm not seeing him. I haven't seen him for months. George says this is about him too, and I suppose he's right to a degree, but not in the way he thinks.'

'What do you mean?'

'Just that an affair tests a marriage, and ours wasn't strong enough to survive.' She wasn't going to go into details.

'Was it so bad with Dad?'

'Of course not. But we want different things out of life now.'

'Like Somerset?' Chanty shook her head. 'I'd never have supported him if I'd thought it would end like this.'

'I did say,' Jeanie replied gently, regretting that she couldn't tell her daughter the whole truth, but knowing it would not be something she would want to hear.

Chanty sat in silence, holding her huge belly between her hands. She looked so tired.

'I didn't want to tell you till after the baby was born.'

Her daughter shrugged. 'I shan't be in any better a state to hear bad news with a newborn and a fractious two-year-old.' She smiled wryly. 'Still, every cloud . . . at least you'll be round the corner again. Maybe we can persuade Dad to sell that stupid house and come back to town too.'

'Maybe . . . although he seems to love it there.'

'You never know what will happen, Mum.'

Jeanie knew the only reason she had got off so lightly with her daughter was because Chanty and Alex had discussed it and decided this was just another phase, a 'pensioner panic', that Jeanie was going through. They were waiting for her to see sense.

And it was clear that Chanty and her father were of one mind, because George began behaving as if nothing much had happened between him and Jeanie. The only sign of aberrant behaviour was his incessant phone calls. George never normally called her, but now he was phoning sometimes two or three times a day. Not to talk about their separation, however, but just to shoot the breeze, update her on his daily life, even ask about the goings-on at the shop – something in which he'd previously shown absolutely zero interest. She heard he had gone back to his clocks, and had begun to mend clocks for his neighbours. Lorna had started the trend when she found out about his hobby, by asking him to fix her seventeenth-century carriage clock. But at the end of every phone call he would say, 'I miss you,' or 'See you very soon,' as if she were away on a business trip and expected home shortly.

Jeanie had not been home for nearly a month now, and Christmas was looming, hanging over her head like the sword of Damocles.

'So I thought I'd come up a bit before Christmas and stay over till about the twenty-eighth,' George declared in the first of that day's phone calls.

Jeanie had been caught off guard.

'Stay? Where?'

George couldn't have helped hearing the panic in her voice and his tone changed.

'Well, at yours, obviously. Chanty will hardly want guests so close to the birth.'

She took a deep breath, trying hard to control the sense of suffocation at the prospect of George in her space. She had to think of Chanty, she told herself firmly. She couldn't rock the boat right now.

Jeanie cursed Christmas, a festival she had dreaded all her life. Even when she was a small child, her father had become unbearably tense in the run-up, driven as he was to make use of this once-a-year chance to garner new souls to his church. They tiptoed round the house from mid-November, and by the time the Reverend Dickenson stepped up to the pulpit on Christmas morning, the family was in a torpor, caring not a fig for the final version of his sermon – previous attempts read out for their comments almost daily over supper – only that it was over for another year.

'If you stay, one of us will be on the sofa,' she blurted out, immediately hating herself for being so mean-spirited.

There was a hurt silence on the other end of the phone.

'I'm so unacceptable that you can't even share a bed with me for a few nights?' His statement was leaden with shock, but perhaps then he remembered his own behaviour, because his tone became deliberately cheerful.

'OK, fine, we'll toss for it,' he said, attempting a laugh. 'So Christmas is on Friday; I could come up on Thursday and leave the following Monday.'

Four nights, Jeanie calculated. How would she cope?

'Aren't you lonely, holed up in this place on your own

all the time?' Rita paced about, her coat still on, as Jeanie got ready to go with her to the Swiss Cottage Odeon.

'Not lonely as such,' Jeanie replied after a moment's thought. 'I get sad, I cry sometimes, but I don't think it's loneliness. I'm not dying for company.'

She cried not sometimes, but most evenings, not only for what might have been with Ray, but also for what might have been with George. She thought a lot about her own family too, and cried for her brother Will as she never had before, sad that then, as now, the family had been unable to stand together in the face of their trauma.

After Will died, she and her parents slid off into their separate pain. Jeanie tried to talk to them at first, to cry with them, but she never saw either her mother or her father cry, not once. Her mother shrank before her eyes, seemed actually to become smaller, her neurosis vanishing, frightened off in the face of real disaster, and this previously nagging, frenetic woman barely spoke, not even to worry about her daughter. So Jeanie turned to her father. But he seemed to have acquired a permanent and alarmingly beatific smile, certain, he said, that he had been martyred by the Lord, that the Lord had honoured him by handing him Will's precious life to guard. 'Will hasn't been taken untimely, you mustn't think that, Jean,' he insisted, eyes glittering with holy fervour. 'Fifteen years was his allotted lifespan, perfect in itself. God couldn't do without him for any longer. We mustn't grieve, he is with God. Better a life taken in a state of grace than lived without it. We are lucky, we should kneel down and thank the Lord every minute of every day that we were lucky enough to have had Will in the first place.'

Jeanie, days off her fourteenth birthday, stamped and cried with rage at this pious edict.

'You're wrong, God's wrong. You're both stupid, stupid, stupid liars. He shouldn't have died and you know it. Why don't you cry, Dad? Don't you care that he's gone and we'll never, ever, ever see him again? I loved him with all my heart, even if you didn't. Why, why can't you even cry? What's wrong with you?'

She had been brought up to believe in a benign God, a God who cared for children, who blessed the right-eous. And Will, even though a teenage boy, was, by her standards, righteous. He was kind and funny and clever and wise. He never hurt anyone. How could God so deliberately inflict such cruel suffering on a mere child? But more than this, the agony of his death left no room for philosophizing. She just wanted to

howl with the pain of it, and with the ongoing disbelief that this was it, that he was never coming back,
that she would never see him again. Just the smallest
comfort of recognition from either of her parents would
have been enough, she thought. But with her brother's
passing, her parents seemed to forget she existed, forget
each other existed. Three satellites separately orbiting
the memory of her beloved Will, never mentioning
the fact that with his death, they had died also. Now,
as she cried for them all, no longer able to blame them
for reacting in the only way they were able, she cried
too for the repetition of the silent, unspoken pain in
her own marriage.

'I worry for you,' Rita said, as they made their way
down the narrow staircase.

'Don't. I'm fine. At least, not fine, but dealing with
it. This is better than the lie,' she added.

'You'll need your warm coat.' She took the red hooded
parka from the stair newel, and held it out for her
granddaughter to slip her arms in.

'I don't like that coat, want anna-one . . . blue one.'
Ellie backed away stubbornly.

'It's freezing out there, darling. The blue one's much
too thin, and we are going to be outside, by the

Christmas tree, to sing the carols. Come on, put it on
... quick, quick, or we'll miss it.'

She saw Ellie hesitate, weighing up the degree to
which her grandmother would insist, but clearly the
lure of the evening's entertainment won. She grinned
and made no further objection.

'We're off,' she called upstairs, where her daughter
was resting. 'Back about seven.'

'Don't forget the tickets – they're on the side by the
front door,' Chanty called down. 'Have fun.'

'It's dark,' Ellie stated with relish. 'We going to see
big Christmas tree, Gin.'

'And sing. Maybe they'll sing "Away in a Manger".'
Ellie thought about this for a minute.

'Jo at 'ursery put a special scarf on Mina's head and
we stand up and sing for Mummy and Daddy.'

'I know, darling, Mummy told me. Did you enjoy
it?'

'I did,' Ellie replied solemnly.

The gate around Lauderdale House was already
packed with parents and their children, an air of excitement and anticipation in all the pink, frozen faces. Jeanie
stowed the buggy on the stack inside the door, and
held Ellie's hand as they made their way to the back
of the house.

'Wow . . . it's blutiful,' she heard Ellie exclaim as they rounded the corner and saw the tree, huge and glowing with white lights, tinsel and sparkling decorations, a big shimmering star shining on the top. Trays had been laid out on the tables along the wall with mulled wine, and fruit juice for the children, and three girls edged amongst the crowd, offering trays piled high with hot, sticky sausages, mustard and tomato ketchup. The musicians – four girls, possibly students – waited cheerfully wrapped in jeans, boots, many wool scarves and coloured hats. Two of them tuned violins, one had a clarinet and another seated herself at the piano from the house, which they'd set up just inside the open French windows so that the violin strings wouldn't snap in the cold. Ellie was silent, munching her sausage, her brown eyes wide with awe as the music began, everyone holding the carol sheet up to the light from the house. Jeanie wished Chanty could have been there to see her.

'There's Din,' Ellie suddenly announced.

Jeanie spun round, her heart in her mouth. 'Dylan . . . where, darling?'

'Look, over there.' Ellie pointed her finger through the crowd, and sure enough, there was the boy's beautiful face shining in the lights from the tree as he stood staring up at the glittering branches. And behind him, a hand resting gently on his grandson's shoulder, was Ray.

Jeanie tried unsuccessfully to calm her panic. They hadn't seen them yet; there was still time to move, to get away. But Ellie was pulling her hand.

'Come on, Gin . . . see Din.'

Ray looked as shocked as she felt. For a moment their eyes met, both unable to speak.

'Hi, Gin,' Dylan smiled up at her. 'It's a brilliant tree, isn't it?'

'It's wonderful,' Jeanie managed to say through lips frozen not just with the cold.

Ellie reached her arms up to Jeanie. 'Hug,' she said, meaning she wanted to be carried.

Jeanie lifted her up and watched her give Ray a shy smile.

'Hello, gorgeous,' Ray said with a broad grin, briefly stroking Ellie's hand, 'I haven't seen you for such a long time.'

The sound of his voice sent Jeanie straight back to their moments of intimacy, as if the intervening months had never existed.

'It's freezing-meezing.' Ray stamped his feet and clapped his gloved hands to make Ellie smile, but Jeanie didn't yet trust herself to speak. 'Dylan, take Ell to the front so she can see better,' he instructed his grandson. Ellie looked as if she might refuse, eyeing the boy cautiously from the safety of her grandmother's arms, but it was a rare person, even one as small as Ellie, who could resist Dylan's smile. Looking very grown-up, he took the little girl's hand tight in his own and shepherded her solicitously through the crowd to stand plumb in front of the vicar – a young, charismatic man with dark good looks – who held the full attention of the throng.

Jeanie and Ray were a lone island of silence as the cold voices around them struggled to life, wobbly and ragged at first, but gaining confidence by the end of the first verse of 'As Shepherds Watched their Flocks by Night . . .'

Jeanie fixed her eyes on her granddaughter, but her consciousness never wavered from the man beside her.

'How are you?' he eventually asked, not looking at her.

'I'm . . .' she began. 'I don't know how to answer that,' she finished lamely, after a long pause.

She heard Ray chuckle. 'And that was the easy one.'

She couldn't help laughing too, wishing she felt as relaxed as he seemed – his tone like that of a meeting with an old friend, with no hint of the torment she was suffering.

'And you?' she asked, risking a glance at his dear face.

'Nothing to report,' he shrugged, sending her a look which seemed to suggest she had no right to ask.

'I saw you a while back.' She found herself speaking against her will, saying exactly what she had promised herself she would never mention, should ever this situation arise.

Ray raised his eyebrows. 'Where?'

'On the hill . . . it was raining.'

He waited for a moment, perhaps expecting her to explain more.

'Highgate Hill? I didn't see you. I kept thinking I might, but . . .' He looked away, and Jeanie took that as confirmation of what she had seen. 'You should have said hello,' he added, too late.

Ellie was pushing her way back through the bodies. Jeanie lifted her up again.

'Are you having fun?'

The child looked tired but determined. 'Yes . . . that man's singing very loud, like Ray,' she giggled as she gazed at the vicar. 'Kim I have more sausage, Gin? With ketchup?'

Jeanie looked around for the food, but could see only empty plates.

'I'll get her some,' Ray offered, and moved off before Jeanie could stop him, returning after a while with a small paper plate with four sausages and a pool of tomato sauce.

'Sanks,' Ellie said without prompting, her eyes alight at the plateful.

Jeanie held the plate, watching the slow progress of her granddaughter's dipping and munching with increasing desperation, longing suddenly to get away from the stifling presence of this man who clearly no longer cared for her as she did for him. Because she realized with dismay that she did still care, just exactly as much as she had the last time they had met. Time had not diminished her feelings one jot.

The singers had moved on through the carol sheet, voices joyful and determined, taking their lead from the handsome priest. Everything was perfect, picture-perfect, with the shining tree, the stirring music, the frosty air bringing a glow to every cheek, the Christmas spirit palpable in its warmth. All in stark contrast to the pitch of Jeanie's despair, soaring unfettered above the assembled happiness like a heavy black bird. Had she really still hoped, despite the beautiful girl beneath the umbrella?

'We'd better get home,' she told Ellie, praying there would be no tantrum. But the child was too tired to complain, and clung exhausted to Jeanie, her blonde head resting heavy on her grandmother's shoulder.

'Bye.' She gave Ray a last look and saw he was eyeing her with a puzzled frown.

'Nat said you'd moved to Devon,' he said quickly, as she turned to go.

'Somerset. I haven't: at least I did, but George and I have separated. I'm living above the shop now.'

Ray stared at her. 'That must've been hard . . . I'm sorry,' he replied softly.

Flustered, she shook her head. 'It's better this way.'

Ellie began to whimper. 'We must go . . . good to see you.' She heard the almost cold formality of her words, but couldn't help herself, hugging Ellie's small body to her like a shield.

Ray nodded. 'Good to see you too,' he said, but unlike her, he sounded as if he meant it.

The carols were over, the crowd hurrying towards the gate, keen to get home to the warmth. Jeanie gathered the pushchair and tucked in the sleepy child, wrapping her scarf around her knees. Her own feet were nearly numb, the icy wind painful against her cheeks as she strode along the road towards her daughter's house. She would cry later, she told herself, as if she were holding out the promise of a treat. But in truth she could barely contain her grief. Then, to make it worse, she remembered that George would be there in the morning.

George stood in the middle of the sitting room, hands on hips, surveying the space for all the world like a nosey landlord. Jeanie had to remind herself that the flat did not belong to him.

'You've brightened it up – it's cosy. A bit small, but no . . . you've made it very pleasant since I was last here.' He looked at Jeanie. 'You always were good at making a place feel like home.'

She checked his face to see if this remark were loaded, but he seemed relaxed, not ready to pick a fight.

'Tea? Sit down.' She had thought it would be more awkward, seeing George again, but perhaps it was a testimony to their lifetime together that even the recent hostilities couldn't erase decades of familiarity. 'Chanty's expecting us for a drink this evening.'

George rubbed his hands together, grinned at his wife. 'This should be fun, don't you think? I can't wait to see the little one. I've made her a toy box, stencilled things on it. I'd show you, but I've wrapped it already – took some doing. It's in the car.'

'She'll love that, she's so excited. She doesn't really understand what Christmas is about, but she knows it's fun.'

'And the baby? Any sign?'

She handed him his tea – no milk, no sugar, teabag wrung out to its full strength.

'It's due today. Poor girl, she's vast, quite scarily big. Ell was early, of course, but not for the right reasons, so who knows how long this one will be.'

They sat with their tea and chatted, as if there had never been a problem between them. Jeanie wondered if they could keep this up, worrying that George might take it as a sign that they could make a go of it again. She was tired, having barely slept. Chanty and Alex had insisted she stay to supper when she dropped Ellie home from the carol service, and unusually for her she had drunk too much in an effort to stave off her tears. When she got home her despair was so heavy she had felt unable to cry at all. She'd just sat on the sofa in the dark, her thoughts blank and unfocused, until the small hours, when the cold had finally driven her to bed. Now she was light-headed, as if the day were not real and George was not actually there.

'Shall I take my things upstairs, get them out of the way?' he was asking, although he seemed only to have brought his small leather holdall. He saw her looking at it. 'That's not all; the rest's in the car.'

The evening was a triumph of restraint. The elephant sat in the room and no one even gave it the time of day. They all focused on Ellie, on the new baby's imminent arrival, on the sense of family they could still enjoy. Jeanie saw Alex searching her face occasionally, but she was determined to live in the moment and enjoy her granddaughter's infectious excitement.

As they made their way home, George slipped his arm in hers, and she made no attempt to remove it. The sleeping arrangements had been settled the night before, George insisting that the sofa was his and to Jeanie's surprise making no fuss about the arrangement, so she wasn't concerned about sending the wrong message. Both of them were a little drunk, but both, she thought, relieved that the evening had gone off so well.

'Nightcap?' George asked when they got in. Jeanie agreed, feeling suddenly reckless and devil-may-care as she waited for George to fetch the bottle of brandy he'd stowed in his suitcase. I'm in control, I'm brave, I will survive all this, survive both these men, she told herself, ignoring the bubble of hysteria lurking not far beneath the surface.

'So how's it going, Jeanie . . . you up here?'

She could see George was more than a little drunk: his face soft in inebriation; his features, which could be closed and almost prudish at times, now defenceless. He smiled at her.

'Eh? How's it going?' he repeated when she didn't answer.

'It's OK, George . . . strange, of course.'

'Strange for me too. In fact downright odd, you not being there.' He paused. 'I haven't liked it, you know.'

Jeanie said nothing.

'Have you?'

She heard it almost before he spoke, the sudden hardening of tone, but her defences were also down; she was too tired to prevaricate.

'No, George, of course I haven't liked it. You can't *like* separation after such a long marriage.'

He stared at her, obviously trying to work out what she was saying.

'You'll come home, then.' He stated it, rather than

392

asking if it were true, but there was no relief in his voice.

'I didn't say that. I just said it was difficult.'

'But you just said you didn't like us being apart. Well, what could that mean but that you want to come home and be together?'

His frustration drew him up off the cushions and out of his relaxed sprawl to lean towards her across the coffee table.

'Please, don't start. We've had such a good evening.'

He stood up, his long arms tense at his sides.

'You can be a real bitch sometimes,' he snapped, glaring at her impotently. 'I honestly don't believe you know what you want, but you'll keep me on a string till you decide. Is that it?'

Jeanie was shocked. He'd never called her that before, although God knows she'd deserved it. Perhaps for the first time she saw herself and her behaviour as George must see it: selfish, capricious, cruel.

'I'm sorry,' she said.

'That means nothing. Sorry about what? That you don't know what you want? That you've ruined a perfectly good marriage?' He came and stood over her. 'What exactly are you sorry about, Jeanie? I'd love to know.'

Jeanie got up, facing his rage.

'I'm sorry for it all, George.'

George took a deep breath. 'But what does that mean, Jeanie?' Now he was quietly pleading as he reached to take her hands in his. 'Tell me, I need to know.'

Jeanie looked into his intensely familiar face and couldn't speak for the pain she saw there, and the knowledge that she had caused it.

'I *am* a bitch. Don't think I don't know that. And perhaps you're right and I don't know what I want. All I know is that I can't live with you in Somerset, George. I can't do it. We want different things from life now.'

George held tightly to her hands, and she knew he was trying hard to control his tears.

'It's not about geography, though, is it?' he said softly.

She looked at him for a long time, then slowly shook her head.

'No, it's not about geography.'

That night they slept together in Jeanie's bed. Not just for the comfort of being close to each other at the moment they both faced life alone, but also, unconsciously perhaps, as an acknowledgement that this was, finally, the end.

★

Christmas morning dawned. Jeanie and George slept late, battered and saddened by the night's realizations, and said little as they dressed and made coffee. The day stretched ahead of them like a marathon they had no choice but to run, and Jeanie, at least, was daunted by the prospect.

'They're expecting us around eleven,' she said. 'Alex said lunch at one; they don't think Ellie will last otherwise.'

George nodded. 'We'll have to take the car because of the toy box.'

They had bought presents for each other, but neither felt like opening them. The packages, hers a small, neat box-shape, his the soft bulk of a sweater, sat unopened on the coffee table.

'Shall I get something from the shop as a family gift?'

George laughed. 'Not sure they'll want some dodgy wheatgrass juice or three-bean salad on Christmas Day, will they?'

'I meant organic olive oil, or a farm cheese,' Jeanie retorted, then laughed with her husband. 'OK, maybe not.'

'No, that's a good idea, good olive oil never goes amiss.'

So while George packed the presents into a bag, Jeanie ran down to the shop.

'I'll meet you down there.'

It was a beautiful day: bright, bright sunlight; cold, sharp and crystal clear. The fresh air smelt like freedom to Jeanie, cooped up as she had been with all that tension. She felt her spirits lift as she fitted the key in the shop door, almost missing the slim brown-paper package, tied with red ribbon, that sat propped against the step. Curious, she bent to pick it up as she opened the door. There was a small white card slipped under the ribbon. Turning it over she saw no words, just three kisses, written in black ink, in the centre of the card. She knew who it was from immediately, although she had never seen his handwriting before, because the package contained a CD – *Chet Baker in Paris*, the music to which they had made love.

Nothing had prepared her for this. And with her mind still steeped in the shared sorrow of last night's full stop to her marriage, she was unable to take in what it meant. She wasn't sure how long she stood there, the present held carefully in her hand, but suddenly she heard George's voice outside, saw his head peering in at the door.

'What's taking so long? Do you need help choosing?'

She scrabbled Ray's present guiltily behind the counter.

'What's up? Are you OK? You look dreadful.'

Jeanie managed a smile. 'Thanks, just what a girl needs to hear.'

'I didn't mean that, but you've gone so pale.'

'I'm fine, really.' She hastened to the shelf with the olive oil and yanked off a bottle at random. 'Just tired.'

'Hardly surprising,' he commented dryly. As they got in the car, he went on, 'Don't worry, I've decided to go home today, after lunch. I think it's better.'

She nearly said that he didn't have to, that it was fine for him to stay; it was habit and she felt so sad for him, for them. But she resisted, realizing that she was barely holding on till she could be alone again. The silence in the car was solid, dead. They had nothing more to say to each other.

'Will he be OK?' Chanty gazed out into the street after her father's departing car. The meal had been subdued, almost hurried, everyone dying to be able to dispense with Christmas niceties. Chanty looked utterly exhausted, holding her swollen body with both arms as if in an attempt to keep it together. Alex remained largely silent.

'Did you fight?' Alex asked when he came back from putting Ellie down for her nap.

'No. Well, sort of . . . the usual back and forth. I think he's finally realized it's over.' Without warning, Jeanie began to cry and seemed unable to stop, try as she might in front of her daughter and son-in-law. But they did not react with the horror and embarrassment that she expected, as if they had long been waiting for it. She felt her daughter's arm go around her.

'I'm so sorry, this is the last thing you two need to deal with right now. I'll be OK, it's just been so hard. I love your father, but I can't live with him any more, and that makes it harder. That toy box is so beautiful, Ellie loves it. This isn't to do with your dad, he's a good man, but it just doesn't work any more . . . I'm so sorry.' She babbled on, splurging out everything that came into her mind on the subject of George and her marriage, and her listeners just nodded sympathetically.

'Do you think he'll stay down there?' Alex asked eventually.

Chanty nodded. 'He told me he likes it, likes the people. Sally comes in more often. He's got his two obsessions, the clocks and the garden. I don't think he's as lonely as we think.'

Jeanie's tears began to slow. 'It's just so sad,' she said quietly.

'And it's really over? I mean forever? How can you be so sure, Mum, if you still love him?' Chanty queried.

'I'm sure, I really am sure,' Jeanie said firmly.

23

Jeanie lay on the sofa and played Chet Baker over and over again. She let the music sink into her, flow round her, through her, the long, sweet notes taking her back to those unforgettable moments that changed her life. Tonight, for the first time since she had embarked on the separation, she felt free to indulge these memories – because George had finally understood.

Ray's present could mean only one thing, but she hesitated before she got in touch with him. This moment of hope, before the stomach-churning uncertainty of a love affair, seemed so precious to her.

Her Boxing Day text to Ray asked if they should meet. His reply to Jeanie agreed that they should.

Her text to Ray said: *In the park, midday?*
He sent her kisses in reply.

She spent a lot of time that morning in front of the bathroom mirror. Bright sunlight with nowhere to hide, she thought, then chided herself for her vanity. For once she really cared what she wore, tearing clothes from her cupboard she had never worn, trying them on, discarding them in a panic. In the end practical considerations won out – it was cold, it was lunchtime; she would wear jeans, boots and her favourite cream cashmere sweater.

He was there when she rounded the bend that led to the playground, sitting on the bench by the ducks where she had so often found him in the past. Her heart nearly somersaulted at the sight of him.

He stood when he saw her and for a moment they both seemed frozen in time, time past and time present.

'Oh, Jeanie,' Ray whispered, holding out his arms to her. And she went to him, leaning close against his chest, his arms tight round her, and felt an almost insane happiness.

There seemed nothing to say, as if saying anything would break the spell, so they wandered, mostly silent, hand in hand through the park, down the hill and on to the Heath, to the only cafe they thought might be open on a bank holiday.

'You have no idea how much I've missed you,' Ray said, when they were seated in the warmth of the winter sunlight on rickety metal chairs. Dogs swarmed round the area, their owners pulling and nagging at them to rest while they drank their coffee.

'I have,' she said, with feeling. Neither of them could stop smiling.

'But you thought it wouldn't work with me.'

'No, I thought I shouldn't leave George.'

'So what changed your mind?'

'You, I suppose.' She laughed. 'Then I saw you with that beautiful girl and I thought it was all over, that you'd moved on.'

Ray looked puzzled. 'What beautiful girl?'

'You can be honest. I saw you together, under the umbrella. You seemed very close.'

Ray thought for a moment, then suddenly threw his head back in laughter. 'Mica, that was Mica! You thought we were an item?'

'Well, you had your arms round her . . . you looked very close,' Jeanie said, disconcerted by his laughter.

'That's my assistant. She helps manage the centre. That day under the umbrella she'd just told me she was pregnant! Oh, Jeanie, that's hilarious . . . *you* jealous of Mica! You have no idea.'

'OK, OK, don't make a meal of it, it wasn't funny at the time. I didn't just feel jealous, I thought I was going to throw up then and there on the pavement,' she admitted. 'And die,' she added.

Ray nodded. 'I know what you mean, believe me. I was sick and in despair for months thinking of you with your husband.'

'I owed it to him. He still thinks my leaving is partly triggered by the abuse, that I'm disgusted by what happened to him – which I am, of course, but not in the way he thinks. And you. He sensed you, even when we weren't seeing each other.'

'Were you ever honest with him? About us?'

'No. Did he need to know how I really felt?'

Ray shrugged. 'Probably not.'

'You think I should have told him?'

'I don't know, Jeanie. It's not for me to say. I'd like to think honesty is the best policy, but plant an image in a man's head and it can drive him insane.'

'More insane than his imagination?'

'Perhaps not.'

'Let's not talk about George,' she said, reaching for his hand.

'No, let's not.' For a minute they seemed lost in the still surprising reality of being with each other. 'Jeanie . . . do you think we could make something of this? You and me?'

She took a deep breath. 'We could try,' she answered, laughing softly.

Ray shook his head. 'That's the thing. I never need to try with you. I don't think I've felt such absolute ease before with anyone, ever. It's what broke my heart when you left. I knew I'd never find that again.'

'Shall we walk?' Jeanie suggested. 'It's getting cold.'

'I thought . . . I thought maybe we could go back to mine?' Ray smiled.

Suddenly, blissfully, Jeanie realized there was no reason in the world why she shouldn't go.

Their lovemaking was as sensuous, as passionate as before. But this time there was no desperation, only joy. The sadness of impending loss that had overshadowed all their previous moments together no longer tormented them.

Afterwards, Jeanie lay in Ray's arms. His hand played softly along the bare skin of her arm.

'This is heaven,' he murmured.

She lifted her face to his, and kissed him on the mouth. At first softly, then more urgently. Suddenly the sound of her phone interrupted them. She sighed and reached for it. As soon as she saw the number, she knew.

'Alex?'

'I'm taking her in now. I've got Ellie with me. Can you collect her from the hospital?' She could tell his apparent calm was only a veneer. 'The contractions suddenly speeded up or we'd have rung sooner. Where are you? I don't think it's going to be long.'

'I'm on my way. Fifteen minutes.' She snapped the phone shut and threw herself out of bed. 'Chanty's in labour. I've got to get Ellie.'

Ray sat up. 'Wow . . . good luck, hope it all goes well.'

She bent to give him a quick kiss and was gone, running back up the hill to the maternity unit, her heart soaring with happiness.

Little Rebecca Anne was born perfect, weighing nearly eight pounds. Chanty had been too late for an epidural, but the birth was not deemed a difficult one – *easy for everyone else to say*, Chanty had retorted. Ellie thought her little sister a great novelty for about twenty-four hours, then was jealous as hell. But Chanty took it all in her stride, enjoying, perhaps, the contrast with Ellie's first months, when she had been virtually a single mother.

Still Jeanie waited to tell her family about Ray. Still

she dreaded the reaction from them, and the inevitable accusations.

'Just tell them, darling,' Rita nagged her. 'I mean, what can they do? They won't like it, but it's your life.'

'Yes, but if I wait it'll be better; the more time there is since leaving George, the less they'll fuss.'

'If you wait, someone else will tell them for sure. They'll see you and Ray and report back. There's always someone.'

'But what if Chanty won't let me see Ellie and the baby? She hates Ray. I know she thinks he's responsible for me leaving her father.'

'Well, she's right, he is. At least one of the reasons. But Chanty'd never stop you seeing the kids. Of course she hates him now, but she'll come round eventually. She loves you, she'll want you to be happy.' She paused, and the look she gave Jeanie was pure sympathy. 'No one said this was going to be easy, darling.'

'But you don't think there's anything wrong with us being together, do you?'

'Oh, darling, of course I don't. I'm insanely jealous, but that's a separate issue.'

Jeanie laughed. 'More wine?'

'Thanks.' Rita held out her glass. 'I worried you were being impetuous, leaving George. Even though I knew you weren't happy, I thought it was a blip, that you'd settle down, like so many couples do. It felt too dangerous . . .'

'For someone of my age,' Jeanie interrupted her friend.

'Yes, for someone of your age.' She raised her glass. 'But cheers, darling, here's to love.'

'I'll tell Chanty soon. I will.' She made the promise as much to herself as to her friend. And she knew this was the final hurdle, that whatever the outcome, until she'd told her family, she would never be properly free to love Ray.

It was three weeks since she had met Ray on the park bench, three weeks since Rebecca's birth. She talked to Ray every day; they met as often as they could, either Ray staying over at her flat, or Jeanie going to his. Their lovemaking amazed them both, particularly Jeanie. She had never imagined feeling so physically in love.

'Will you take me sailing?' she said sleepily, as they lay in bed together one night. The sheer joy of him being beside her made her dizzy. She felt childish and light-hearted in a way she could not remember. 'A boat in the Adriatic, the sun on our skin, salt on our lips and in our hair, a cool breeze as we lie on the wooden deck, the sails white and still above us. Nat told me you were there last summer. It's what I imagined.'

Ray shifted beside her. 'Come the spring we'll be gone, we'll borrow Phil's boat and take off. We can go wherever you want.'

'What about our work?'

'Even you and me are allowed a holiday, no?' She heard him chuckle in the darkness. 'You'll have to learn aikido, Jeanie, and stop worrying. You think about everything to a standstill – it's not healthy.'

'Do I? Sorry, it's just been very stressful for a long time now. I think it's become a habit.' She turned towards him. 'How has Nat taken it, us being together?'

'She was surprised, I think – she had no idea – but pleased. She likes you and so does Dylan. And I think she's relieved I've fallen for a proper person and not some teenage bimbo.'

There was silence. Both knew that Jeanie was putting off her conversation with her own daughter.

'OK.' Jeanie came to a decision. 'OK. I'm going to tell Chanty tomorrow.'

Ray didn't respond. She had said this before, many times, in the last few weeks. She knew he didn't believe her.

★

Chanty rang the following morning, when Jeanie and Ray were having breakfast in her flat. It was as if she had heard Jeanie's thoughts.

'I'm venturing to Crouch End with Becca this morning, Mum. Ell's at nursery, and I thought we might meet for a coffee at the Italian? Sort of see what the world looks like again.'

'That'd be lovely. What time is good?'

'I should be there about eleven, depending on feeds. Alex is going to pick up Ellie, so I won't need to rush back.'

'See you there, look forward to it.'

She looked guiltily at Ray.

'You can't back out now,' he grinned.

'It's all right for you to say,' she retorted, her stomach already churning at the prospect.

'You make out she's a monster. I mean, how bad can it be? She's probably guessed anyway.'

Jeanie took his empty cup and went to fill it from the coffee machine.

'Why would she, when every time over the past few months that your name's come up I've protested that I'm absolutely not seeing you.'

Ray shrugged, clearly more amused than sympathetic.

'She loves you, trust in that,' he stated simply, taking the cup she offered but retaining her hand in his and planting a light kiss on her palm.

Jeanie took a deep breath. 'Rita said that, and of course I know it's true.'

'But you still feel guilty about me.'

She nodded. 'Yes, well, not about you so much as about breaking up the family.' She paused. 'And I suppose part of me feels there is something a bit indecent, at my age, about being in love.'

'Yeah, brilliant, isn't it? A proper pair of reprobate old bats, you and me. We should celebrate it.' Laughing, he grabbed her and pulled her down on the sofa. 'Take care or I'll make it really hard for you to get to work, or see your daughter, or go out at all today.'

In the end, Ray's refusal to believe there was a problem began to wear off on Jeanie, and she walked down the hill to Crouch End with a confident step.

'Mum, if you promise me you weren't in touch with him till you separated from Dad, then I believe you.'

'You do? Well, your dad won't.'

Chanty sighed, one hand pushing the pram back and forth, the baby fast asleep, wrapped against the cold in a cute white woolly suit and hood with rabbit ears.

'No, obviously Dad won't, but I'm telling you, I trust you, Mum. This bloody man seems intent on causing nothing but trouble for our family,' she added, angrily.

Jeanie fiddled with the sugar packets in the centre of the table, shaking the sugar from end to end of the narrow waxed-paper tubes.

'Everything was just fine between you and Dad before he reared his ugly head. I mean, where does he get off on breaking up thirty-five years of a perfect relationship – and our family?' She glared at her mother. 'I hate seeing you fall for it.'

This was going just as badly as Jeanie had feared, but she felt her hackles rising at the unfair insult to Ray.

'It wasn't a perfect marriage, Chanty.'

'Of course you say that now, and invent all sorts of problems that never existed in order to salve your conscience.' In her anger she was rocking the pram violently back and forth, but Becca slept blissfully on.

Jeanie could no longer control herself.

'The truth is your father refused to have sex with me for ten years before I met Ray, and worse, refused to tell me why. He just moved out one night, saying he couldn't do it any more, and that was that.'

She watched Chanty's face.

'Sorry, I shouldn't have said that.'

'Why? Why then?' Chanty asked, ignoring her

mother's apology.

'It was the day he bumped into Acland. It brought it all back, apparently, the abuse.'

'So you had no idea what his reasons were?'

'Not at the time, no.'

They sat in silence for a moment.

'Listen, darling, I never meant to tell you this, and I don't expect a sympathy vote for my behaviour. It was me who ruined the marriage, not Ray. Me and your father.'

'That must have been very hard, the Dad thing. . . ten years is a long time.' She sighed. 'I suppose he just couldn't bring himself to tell you.'

'No, and I understand that now. But it didn't make it any easier at the time.'

'So when Ray came along . . .'

'I wasn't looking for someone to jump into bed with. If I'd wanted that I'd have done it years ago. I'd just resigned myself to how it was by then. But your dad killed something, a trust I thought we had, when he wouldn't talk about the problem and seemed to have no concern about how it affected me.'

Chanty gazed across the cafe. 'Do you love this man, Mum?' she asked, not looking at her mother.

'Yes, darling,' Jeanie replied, taking a deep breath. 'Yes, I do.'

Epilogue

It took Jeanie a while to remember. She hadn't sailed for over forty years, and never much beyond the Norfolk coast. But Ray was a patient teacher, and in fact took enormous pleasure in helping Jeanie find her way around the sailing boat. *Magda* was beautiful: white and sleek and strong; a dream to sail, Phil's pride and joy. They picked her up in Brindisi, then headed across the Adriatic, pottering up the Dalmatian coast to anchor in tiny coves, swim in the crystal-clear azure water – still cold in April, or what Ray laughingly described as 'refreshing' – or take the dinghy ashore to explore the ports and tiny villages along the way. Ray was nimble and fit about the boat, much more so than Jeanie. But as the days wore on, she began to find her feet.

Now she sat on the deck in the warmth of the early evening sun and looked at the photos Chanty had emailed of Ellie and Becca. Even in the three weeks they'd been away, the baby had changed so much.

Ray's tanned face popped up from below. 'Drink?'

The last three months had been amongst the strangest of her life, but also the most uncomplicated. Being with Ray was like coming home.

Chanty had at first maintained a silence on the subject which, while not exactly hostile, carried no welcome or acceptance of Ray. Then two weeks before their trip – persuaded apparently by Alex that it was not going to get easier with the passing of time – she had asked Jeanie and Ray to supper. And it went well enough. Chanty gradually relaxed under Ray's easy charm and his clear lack of desire to ingratiate himself with Jeanie's family. By the end of the evening Jeanie had witnessed the edges of her daughter's disapproval worn down just a little.

The timing, and Chanty's tentative olive branch, were triggered, Jeanie was certain, by the news from her father.

'Sally is spending more time up at the house,' he'd announced to his daughter one day. And when Chanty failed to comment on what appeared to be merely the unimportant minutiae of his life, and George realized she hadn't picked up on his coded message, he had begun again, this time with emphasis.

'We are spending more time together, Sally-from-the-village and me.'

'You and Sally?' Chanty still didn't cotton on. 'That's nice. What do you mean, Dad?'

George had replied, 'Well, she's . . . staying for supper . . . and things.'

Chanty had repeated this conversation to Jeanie in amazement, but Jeanie wasn't surprised. Sally would care for George, asking no questions, knowing no history. She was a strong, understanding woman with an infectious sense of humour who might offer George the tranquillity that Jeanie had ceased to provide. She was happy for him. Everyone always worried about George's vulnerability, but as Rita had so often said, he knew how to get what he wanted.

'Poor Chanty,' Jeanie had commented to Ray. 'If she thought about it at all, she'd probably have taken it for granted that her parents would enjoy a decorous retirement pottering amongst the garden centres of the West Country.'

★

'Jeanie . . . Jeanie.' Ray was nudging her awake. The cabin was barely light.

'What's the matter?'

'Nothing, nothing at all, don't look so worried.' He smiled down at her. 'But you have to get up, the sun is about to rise and it is so spectacularly beautiful.'

Jeanie was up in a flash, pulling on her shorts and tee shirt and following Ray up the steps on to the deck. They had anchored after dark the night before, in a small cove north of Rogoznica. As she reached the deck, the first rays of sun were coming up over the hills, laying a pale shimmering-gold trail across the water, while leaving the rocks that fell steeply to the sea – bleached white by day – still shadowed purple. It was cool and still on deck, the wood smooth beneath her bare feet, the only sound the gentle lapping of the water against the sides of the boat, and the crying of the seabirds.

Ray put his arm around her, held her close. As the warm sun fell on them, he turned to her, lifting his hand to run his finger gently down the length of her cheek, his gaze clear and intense in the morning light.

'The last time I was here I was in hell. I thought I would never see you again. This paradise seemed to mock me.'

As she watched, his beautiful grey eyes filled with tears.

'But it's never about place, is it?' He spoke softly.

Jeanie said nothing, just reached up and kissed him, tasting the salt on his lips, feeling the strength of his body against her own. And looking up to the sky, she blew an imaginary kiss across the sparkling sea. Thank you, Ellie. Thank you, Dylan, she whispered.

Acknowledgements

This book wouldn't be the book it is without the valuable input I had from the following people: Laura Morris, Jane Wood, Don Boyd, Clare Boyd, Shelley Borkum, Jane Bow, Jenny Ellis, and the whole team at Quercus. Thank you all very much.

Please read on for a short extract from Hilary Boyd's next novel, *Tangled Lives*

PROLOGUE

Kent, 1967

'It's time.'

Nurse Julie stood beside the bed, but she didn't look up at her. She just continued to stare at the baby, asleep, cuddled in the crook of her arms. He was already washed, and dressed in a brushed cotton nightie, knitted blue matinee jacket, matching booties and hat. The clothes seemed to swamp his tiny form and make him seem heartbreakingly separate from her.

'Do you want any help?'

Annie shook her head and eased herself off the bed, turning to place the baby in the waiting wicker carrycot. He stirred as she laid him on the cool sheet and flung his arms outwards in a small spasm. She gently tucked the soft, white, wool blanket close around him, knowing how he hated being put down. Who would understand him now? Who would give him the minute-by-minute attention that she, despite reminding herself there was no future in it, could not resist providing?

The ten difficult days of new motherhood had gone by agonisingly quickly, as if she were careering towards a cliff edge with her baby son. And as each day had brought her closer to this one, the shadow presence of his father grew ever more insistent. She should have told him; she knew it. But every time she thought about the conversation, she imagined the shock, the distaste, the embarrassment on his face. It would be the same expression her mother's had worn since she'd heard the news. She couldn't bear it. If only he'd been in touch after that night. Why . . . ? Why hadn't he called? But it was too late for all that now. She'd made her decision.

The rest of the morning was a blur. Formalities, kindly smiles, pity; she saw the pity. But it was businesslike and left no room for protest, as if she were no longer important in this drama about her baby son's life, played out in front of her by these competent professionals. Which she wasn't, of course.

And then she was in her mother's car, being driven through the glorious spring day towards London.

'I've had your bedroom painted while you've been away,' her mother told her, in a crisp voice which seemed to Annie like a wall, a barrier that protected her mother from knowing – or wanting to know – what her life had been like over the past four months.

'It's still cream, but it looks terribly smart,' her mother was saying.

'Thank you. I can't wait to see it,' she replied, surprised by her own enthusiasm about the fresh paint on her bedroom walls.

I

Annie Delancey stood in the warm, quiet kitchen and slowly peeled apart the last two pieces of streaky bacon. As she fitted them into the large skillet where the other rashers were already buckling and sizzling on the heat, she felt an overwhelming sense of happiness. It was Saturday. Her family was here for the weekend. She would do pancakes.

She glanced round at the neatly laid table, smiling with pleasure at the vibrant golden daffodils lighting up the centre, competing with the glass jug of freshly squeezed orange juice and the square of yellow butter on its white china dish.

Her son Ed, now twenty-six, worked unholy hours as the manager of a restaurant/bar in Islington, and she hardly saw him, so having him home was a treat for her. But this visit, she knew, was not so much to hang out with his dear old mum as to avoid his freezing Stroud Green flat, where the heating was on the blink. When she'd heard he was bringing his girlfriend, Emma, she'd asked Marsha – her second child and barely a year younger than Ed – to come over for a late breakfast.

She took the maple syrup from the cupboard and set it on the table, then moved to the window and gazed out at the well-kept, mature garden with satisfaction. It was beautiful the way the pale spring sun lit up the frosty landscape. She and Richard had planted out the garden, mostly from guesswork, when they'd first moved into the house just before Ed was born. And it had worked, despite the inevitable restrictions of a long, narrow London garden. They had tweaked and improved over the years – mostly Richard's doing – adding the inevitable wooden decking a few months ago. This was now bordered with earthenware pots of various sizes, planted up with herbs, ivy, narcissus, and some dark purple and yellow gold-laced primulas – all slow to bloom because of the late frost.

'Mmm, great smell.'

Annie hadn't heard her husband come in. Richard was leaning his tall frame close to the pan, sniffing appreciatively.

'Shouldn't these go over?' he asked a little anxiously, prodding the rashers with the metal tongs.

Indeed, the bacon was already crisp and on the verge of being burnt. Annie grabbed the tongs from her husband and began to salvage the contents of the pan, decanting the rashers onto a plate lined with kitchen towel before putting them in the warm oven.

'Shall I tell them it's nearly ready?' he asked, pointing to the ceiling.

'Leave them,' she said with a smile. 'They'll smell the bacon if they're even halfway conscious.' She looked at her watch. 'Mash should be here in a moment.'

And sure enough, on cue, the front door banged and she heard footsteps on the stairs leading down to the kitchen.

'Hi, darling . . . you look frozen.' Annie put the oven gloves down and turned to embrace her daughter. Marsha's cheeks were pink from the cold, her blue eyes bright in her oval face, her long pale-blonde hair drawn back into an untidy ponytail. She shivered, slinging the post she'd retrieved from the doormat onto the kitchen table before rubbing her gloved hands together. She eyed the breakfast preparations hungrily.

'Maple syrup . . . I know what that means!' She gave her father a hug and took off her black coat, unwinding her red wool scarf before thinking again and wrapping it back round her neck.

'Shall I wake them now?' Richard asked again. And this time Annie nodded.

Lucy was first down. Annie saw her wince as her bare feet hit the chilly terracotta floor tiles, tugging over her hands the sleeves of a navy jumper that covered her tartan pyjamas. Rounder than her sister, with wavy auburn hair and soft brown eyes, Annie always marvelled that they had produced two such different daughters; different in looks as well as personality.

'It's freezing,' Lucy complained.

Her father smiled. 'My sweater not keeping you warm enough then?'

She glanced down and looked a little sheepish.

'Just borrowing it, Dad. None of mine are big enough.'

'It's only my best cashmere. I don't want syrup down it.'

Annie rubbed buttered paper round a clean pan, and removed the saucer she had put over the jug of pancake batter. She loved the whole process of cooking. The careful preparation, the smells and the warmth and her pleasure in feeding her family. Ladling a small amount of batter out of the jug, she waited till the pan was smoking before pouring the mixture carefully onto the hot surface to form a number of creamy-yellow rounds.

The four of them settled at the large oak table, a steaming pile of pancakes between them. Richard slowly pressed the plunger down on the cafetière. 'We're not waiting for Ed and Emma?'

Marsha shook her head vehemently. 'No way!'

'How was the party?' Annie asked her elder daughter.

Marsha shrugged as she loaded her pancakes with maple syrup.

'OK, the usual media mob. But yeah . . . I met an interesting guy. He had things to say beyond who you know and your latest project. Makes a change – you wouldn't believe the morons out there.'

Annie looked at Richard and raised an eyebrow. This was more information than Marsha usually divulged about her evenings out. A grunt or two, a mind-your-own-business look, a vague 'got smashed', was all they had learnt to expect from the twenty-five-year-old.

'Cute?' Richard ventured, to receive a scornful roll of his daughter's eyes.

'Sorry, who's cute?' Lucy, still half asleep, asked. She had a habit of zoning out of family conversations.

'Nobody,' Marsha muttered, then grinned. 'You should see your faces! Every time I mention a man, you all seem to hold your breath.'

'Tell me about him, Mash, I missed it,' Lucy insisted.

'Nothing to tell. I liked him, but he wasn't my type.'

Lucy groaned. 'Always the case, eh? They're either fascinating but look like a geography teacher, or drop dead gorgeous and brainless pillocks.'

'No way did he look like a geography teacher.'

'So are you going to see him again?'

Marsha shook her head. 'It wasn't like that. We didn't swap numbers or anything, just sat and talked for ages. He's bound to have a girlfriend somewhere.'

Annie noticed a certain wistfulness in her daughter's tone. Marsha hadn't been serious about anyone since Ben, her college boyfriend, who'd gone to Japan to teach English for three months and fallen for a Japanese girl, breaking her daughter's heart.

Richard was checking through the pile of mail. 'All for you.' He pushed it towards his wife. She found a credit card statement, a promotional letter from the gym, next week's copy of *The Economist* in its plastic wrapper. 'You said you'd cancelled this,' she said, waving the magazine at her husband. 'They just pile up and we never read them.'

'I do – occasionally,' he insisted.

The last letter was a brown envelope with a red stamp saying, very indistinctly, Kent Social Services. She turned it over, puzzled. Her name and address were handwritten in blue biro.

'Morning . . . morning, all!' Ed jumped down the last three stairs, coming into the kitchen with a fanfare. Emma trailed sleepily behind him. Despite the chill, he was dressed only in a pair of patterned boxers and an old grey sweatshirt. Emma, luscious and big-breasted with permanently tousled dark hair, huge, soulful brown eyes and a porcelain skin, was almost swamped in the folds of Ed's navy towelling dressing gown.

'Hope you haven't eaten everything.' Ed looked anxiously at the ravaged breakfast table.

'Serve you right if we had,' Marsha retorted.

Annie was surprised at the sharpness in her tone. She had worried from the start about Ed going out with his sister's life-long best friend and now flatmate. But her worry had been for her son – Emma's reputation as a player when it came to men had been established as far back as her teens. She hadn't thought of the toll the relationship might take on Marsha. Her eldest children had been almost like twins growing up – Lucy a bit of an outsider. Was Marsha feeling left out now that the two people closest to her were so wrapped up in each other?

'How was last night?' Emma was asking Marsha.

'She met a cute guy!' Lucy answered for her.

'Shut up! I didn't. He *was* cute, beautiful in fact, but I told you, he wasn't my type.'

Emma shook her head at her friend. 'Nothing new there then! Can't remember the last time you had the hots for someone . . . well, I can, but . . .'

'Just because you fancy everything that moves,' Marsha interrupted.

Emma laughed. 'Yeah, it's easier that way.'

'Thanks, I'm flattered,' Ed said, frowning.

Emma leant forward and planted a sloppy kiss on his cheek. 'And so you should be.'

Annie saw her elder daughter turn away, and knew she had been right.

'I'll make some more pancakes in a sec,' she said as she turned the letter over and pulled at the brown flap.

'Oh, Mummeee . . . you spoil us.' Ed bounced round the table and draped his arms round his mother in a tight hug. She returned his embrace, so happy to have him home. But he wasn't looking well, she thought. He'd never had much colour, inheriting her own blonde hair and the same grey-blue eyes, but now he looked almost pallid. No sunlight with all those ridiculous hours he puts in, she thought, noticing the padding that had recently appeared round his waist. He wasn't tall like herself and his father, more stocky, but he was too young to start putting on weight.

She returned her attention to the letter, drawing a single piece of paper from the envelope.

'What've you got there?' Ed peered over her shoulder. But after a cursory glance, she instinctively closed the letter and pushed it under the pile. What she had glimpsed was almost incomprehensible. Like an automaton she got up and went to the frying pan, stirring the batter, reaching for the ladle, heating the butter. Only when Ed and Emma had their own pile of pancakes, and she had retrieved the remaining bacon from the oven, did she find an excuse to leave the room, knowing that if she didn't have a moment alone, she would explode.